Richard inclined his head mockingly. "So, contrary to what you stated before, you have no aversion in principle to sleeping with a man in order to obtain a good story—as long as his publicity potential is high enough?"

"I meant nothing of the kind," said Rilla through gritted teeth. She might have guessed he would seize on a carelessly phrased remark. She jumped to her feet and faced him squarely. "I'll make myself perfectly clear once more, Mr. Kellerman. You're the last man in the world I would ever consider going to bed with. Is that plain enough for you? Even if we were stranded together for years on a desert island, I just wouldn't be interested."

The taunting smile remained on his face as he drawled, "Why fight it, Rilla?"

He cupped her chin in his two hands and brought his mouth over hers with a thirsty passion.

Rilla was overcome by a drowning sensation and felt her lips soften and respond to the ardent searching warmth of his, as her whole body quickened in a swift spiral of longing....

Dear Reader,

It is our pleasure to bring you romance novels that go beyond category writing. The settings of **Harlequin American Romance** give a sense of place and culture that is uniquely American, and the characters are warm and believable. The stories are of "today" and have been chosen to give variety within the vast scope of romance fiction.

From the Golden Gates of San Francisco, through the tunnels of New York City, to the plush resorts of the French Riviera, the husband-and-wife team of Hilary London unravels an intricate love story of a world-renowned mystery writer and an assertive newspaper reporter. You will agree with us that things are not always what they seem....

From the early days of Harlequin, our primary concern has been to bring you novels of the highest quality. **Harlequin American Romance** is no exception. Enjoy!

Vivian Stephens

Vivian Stephens
Editorial Director
Harlequin American Romance
919 Third Avenue,
New York, N.Y. 10022

Scent of Gold

HILARY LONDON

Harlequin Books

TORONTO • NEW YORK • LONDON
AMSTERDAM • PARIS • SYDNEY • HAMBURG
STOCKHOLM • ATHENS • TOKYO • MILAN

Published October 1983

First printing August 1983

ISBN 0-373-16027-5

Printed in Canada

Chapter One

"There's no justice in this world," grumbled Bill Andersen good-naturedly, shifting his ponderous body in the upholstered chair. "How come you guys all manage to stay so slim and fit-looking? Specially you, Rilla. What's the secret, huh?"

The young woman to whom this remark was addressed responded with a quick warm smile. She was quite attractive, with auburn hair that curled softly around the cheekbones of her oval-shaped face and hung to her slender shoulders. Her complexion was smooth and creamy, with a healthy tanned glow from the California sun, and her large luminous eyes were the gold-green color of sunlight on leaves. Intent on giving a brisk, professional image, she was clad in dark brown slacks and a candy-striped cotton shirt in cinnamon and ivory. A broad brass-studded leather belt encircled her slim waist.

"You could always try eating less, Bill." She laughed, pointedly moving the bowl of salted nuts and tidbits out of his reach. "And an hour's jogging in the morning would work wonders for your figure."

Bill shuddered and promptly signaled the waiter to refill their drinks. Rilla refused a second glass of Chardonnay, but the other two men joined Bill in Scotch on the rocks. Their party of four—the entire editorial and advertising staff of the *Bay Area Arts Reporter*—was gathered for the weekly ritual of celebrating yet another issue of the magazine hitting the newsstands. Their venue varied according to the fluctuating state of Bill's finances, he being sole proprietor and managing editor of *BAAR*. Plus, he was wont to grumble, a slave to the crummy walk-up office suite two floors above a fast-food place on Sutter. That week they were all riding high, literally as well as figuratively. The advertisement revenue from a bumper issue had provided the funds for drinks at the famous Top of the Mark bar in San Francisco's classy Mark Hopkins Hotel.

Enjoying the unaccustomed taste of luxury, Rilla idly twined her slender fingers into the gold chain about her neck and let her eyes drink in the fantastic panoramic view. She wasn't about to complain that life during her twenty-six years hadn't handed out much of that sort of style, but it didn't stop her from having visions of a more glittering future than her present job would ever bring her. Why shouldn't she have the world at her feet? Rilla Yorke, ace journalist, she thought. The job with *BAAR* was merely a stepping-stone into the big time that beckoned her so tantalizingly...seeming as real yet as tenuously distant as the Golden Gate Bridge, which spanned the pewter-blue waters of the bay, constantly vanishing and then reappearing from banks of rolling white mist....

"Will you handle it, Rilla?"

She returned to the present with a guilty start. "Sorry, Bill, what was that?"

Steve Arnott, the advertising manager, who had cast himself in the role of Rilla's boyfriend, gave her a black look. "Why don't you pay attention, honey? I was saying that so far, I've only managed to squeeze a small panel ad out of that new studio theater that's opening on Geary. But if we could promise them a flattering feature, I might talk them up to a full page."

"Oh, yes...sure. Consider it done."

Bill reached out a questing hand for the peanuts, and, absentmindedly, Rilla pushed the bowl back in his direction. "There's something else I want to talk to you guys about," he said. "I had a tip-off this morning that Richard Kellerman is staying in the Bay Area. It seems he's rented some fancy place over at Sausalito."

"Who the heck is Richard Kellerman?" demanded Steve.

"He's a writer, you ignorant young oaf," Bill told him, grinning.

Leaning forward in her chair, Rilla burst out excitedly, "Do you mean *the* Richard Kellerman...the one who wrote that marvelous book on the legends of King Arthur and the Knights of the Round Table?"

"You've got it, Rilla—*Flowers of Chivalry*. Have you read it, by any chance?"

"I'll say! Three times, in fact. The way Richard Kellerman writes, you're totally gripped from page one. I found that I just couldn't put the book down."

"So you're a genuine fan of his," Bill said thoughtfully. "That could be useful."

"How d'you mean...useful, Bill?"

He neatly flipped another couple of peanuts into his mouth before replying. "I've been trying to figure out how we might wangle a personal interview with Kellerman for *BAAR*. From what I've heard, he's a tricky customer to nail."

Hank Meyer, the third member of the editorial team, chipped in confidently, "I'll handle it, Bill. Just give me the address, and I'll get over to see him." As Rilla's senior by a good ten years, Hank took it for granted that all the crack assignments were allocated to him.

"Have you read *Flowers of Chivalry*, Hank?" Bill queried.

"Well..."

"Yes or no."

"Listen, if I tried to read everything..." Hank shrugged. "What the hell? I'll borrow Rilla's copy and get wised up before I see the guy."

Bill shook his head decidedly. "No, Hank. I want Rilla to have a shot at this one. I've a feeling in my bones that she might be just the person to pull it off. From various things I've heard about him, Richard Kellerman is quite a mystery man who's always refused point-blank to talk to the media. So it would be a real scoop for *BAAR* if we landed an interview while he's staying in the Bay Area."

Hank said doggedly, "I reckon you ought to leave it up to me, Bill. I've a high opinion of Rilla, you know that, but she just doesn't have the experience I have."

"In this case, Hank, I think Rilla possesses something more valuable than experience. She's got a plus factor that might just give her the leverage needed. She's an enthusiast about the character, Hank. She genuinely admires the man's work. So what d'you say, Rilla? Are you ready to beard the literary lion in his den?"

"Try and stop me!" said Rilla eagerly. "But, honestly, Bill, people must have the wrong idea about Richard Kellerman. Nobody who can write with such depth of feeling could be a difficult person to get on with. That book of his is pure magic, you know."

Bill grinned. "See what I mean, Hank? How could any man resist such a lost-in-admiration look in those gorgeous green eyes of hers? But you mustn't be too disappointed, Rilla, if he gives you the brush-off. Kellerman is publicity shy. Even when his book was number one on the best-seller lists, he refused to allow the publishers to use any personal promotion whatsoever."

Rilla's heart was thudding with excitement. Fate had thrown her just the sort of challenge she kept dreaming about. She desperately wanted to make a success of the assignment, and aside from work, it would be fascinating to talk to the writer who was something of a hero to her.

"I'll drive over to Sausalito tomorrow morning," she said, busy making plans in her head.

"Hey, tomorrow's Saturday," Steve objected. "We're going to the ball game, remember?"

"Sorry, but duty calls."

"Come on, that's not fair," he said, his dark good looks marred by a sullen expression. "You promised."

"I only said I *might,* Steve. This is important."

"And I'm not?" He turned to the editor. "Bill, you tell her."

Bill Andersen shrugged his massive shoulders. "I leave it to Rilla. As long as she comes up with a good story for our Wednesday night deadline, I'll be happy. I won't inquire when she got it—or how."

"There, you see!" said Steve triumphantly. "Our date can stand."

But Rilla shook her head firmly. "My diary is full for the rest of tomorrow, so the morning's my only chance. You'd better find someone else to go to the game with."

"Honey, be reasonable."

"Reasonable is doing whatever you want me to do? I don't buy that, Steve."

While Bill and Hank discussed another story they

hoped to cover about a gallery up on Washington near the Cable Car Museum that was planning to stage a series of one-man exhibitions for unknown painters, Rilla and Steve continued to argue sotto voce. If she was truthful, Rilla wasn't sorry to have an excuse to duck out of a date with Steve. He seemed to be reading far too much into their relationship, which she wanted to keep on a casual basis, and he had started to show ominous signs of taking her for granted.

Rilla was through with being taken for granted by men. The previous summer she'd had a relationship with a civil engineer from Seattle who'd been in San Francisco to supervise some harbor reconstruction. She'd come around to thinking they might have a shared future together, and it was a bad shock to learn by chance that Theo had a wife and three children back home. On the evening of her discovery she'd made a firm decision that falling in love wasn't going to feature in her schedule anymore . . . at least not for a very long time. Instead she planned to devote herself singlemindedly to her career in journalism. However, that hardheaded, practical life-style hadn't ruled out the occasional date, and Rilla enjoyed quite a full social life. She liked the company of men, and even allowed herself to grow quite fond of some of her escorts, but any heavier commitment was off limits.

Later, as the *BAAR* staff rode down in the elevator, Steve switched tactics and tried to talk Rilla into having dinner with him that evening, but she was adamant.

"I don't think it would be a good idea, Steve. Besides, I'll be busy."

"Busy doing what?" he demanded sulkily.

Busy preparing herself mentally for the following day's big interview, deciding what to wear, and rereading *Flowers of Chivalry*. But she chickened out of telling

Steve that, merely saying, "I've got a house to keep clean, laundry to see to, plus a hundred other things. So forget tonight, Steve."

Bill's car was parked outside and, as often happened after their Friday drink sessions, he offered Rilla a ride home. It meant only a small diversion for the *BAAR* editor on his way to Richmond, where he lived with his wife and two teenage daughters. From behind the wheel he shot Rilla a questioning glance as he made a left onto Jackson.

"It looks to me—or do I read you wrong—that you want out of your involvement with Steve."

"I never wanted in, Bill...not the way Steve seems to think. I have a career to further."

"You'll get there. You've got what it takes," Bill said with a confidence that warmed her. "But don't chase success too hard, or you might lose out in other directions." He turned off Jackson and, after a few blocks, stopped by a green wooden gate that guarded the entrance to a narrow, leafy lane. "Here we are, then. See you Monday. And remember, Rilla, it won't be the end of the world if you fail to connect with Kellerman."

"Okay, Bill. Thanks."

Rilla refused to entertain the possibility of failure the next day as she made her way up the steep pedestrian lane and turned in at the trellised gate of her Queen Anne–style cottage.

The pretty little four-room house with its miniature corner towers and bay windows had been home to her since just before her eighth birthday, when her parents had been tragically killed in an automobile accident on their way to pick her up after school. Her mother's older sister, Elaine Rueger, had promptly swept the bereaved little girl into her protection. Rilla had grown up in an atmosphere that was rich in love, if not in worldly goods. Nurse Elly, as her aunt was affectionately known to the hundreds of grateful patients of the elderly Dr. Steinbeck, whose office she ran, had died three years earlier of kidney malfunction. Rilla had inherited the cottage on Russian Hill, just under two thousand dollars, and a wealth of good advice remembered from over the years.

In her bright modernized kitchen Rilla fixed herself a meal of crayfish salad with crinkly spinach leaves and sliced tomato, plus a liberal handful of walnuts. When she had finished eating, she climbed the narrow staircase to the little bedroom she had decorated in tones of lilac and cranberry to consider what she'd wear the next day.

It took her half an hour of anxious thought to decide on a finely pleated charcoal linen skirt, a cream-colored shirtwaisted blouse, and a scarlet velvet jacket. She approved of the flattering, yet definitely businesslike, look when she surveyed herself in the Victorian cheval glass. In Rilla's mind, Aunt Elly's voice added confirmation.

The next morning, before collecting her car from the parking lot two blocks away, she called in at the neighborhood bookstore. To her great relief she found a copy of the hardcover edition of Richard Kellerman's *Flowers of Chivalry*, which saved her from having to search farther afield. Her own paperback copy was much too dog-eared from constant reading to serve her purpose. In her mustard-yellow Honda she then set off for Sausalito, taking the freeway and heading over the Golden Gate Bridge, which never failed to give her spirits an extra boost. In the company of crowds of San Franciscans out for a Saturday trip, she followed the route that snaked down to the charming one-time fishing village. The way the houses and shops clung to the wooded slopes above the harbor—like a thicket of tall, straight masts—always struck Rilla as being very much like a typical Mediterranean village. It wasn't surprising that such a picturesque spot should be a favorite haunt of artistic types, including a certain eminent author.

The only address that Bill Andersen had been able to provide was Casa del Sol, Sausalito. Rilla stopped on the bustling waterfront to make inquiries and, after several abortive attempts, she was given the directions she needed by a mailman. As her small car climbed the sun-dappled road through the trees there was a heady scent of eucalyptus adrift on the summer breeze. The houses became more widely spaced and grander, and often they couldn't even be glimpsed through the lush shield of foliage. She began to think that she must have somehow taken a wrong turn, then suddenly she spotted it—a carved wooden nameplate screwed to the stone wall beside a pair of ornate wrought-iron gates that stood open: CASA DEL SOL. Her heart thumping with excitement, Rilla swung onto a graveled driveway that was shaded by tall Monterey pines and flanked by azalea bushes in shades of pink and cream and yellow. The garden was a glowing tapestry of color, a lovely blend of perfumes. Not Richard Kellerman's own garden, Rilla reminded herself, but a rented vacation home. It occurred to her for the first time that he might have brought his family with him—a wife and children. How would that affect her chances of talking her way into an interview?

The driveway curved suddenly, and there was the house. It was built in colonial style, with white stonework, green shuttered windows, and a rust-red shingled roof from which rose two chimney stacks and a central tower, which had a weathercock perched on top. Running all along the front of the house was a covered

veranda with pedimented pillars. White ironwork tables
and chairs were set out on its polished woodblock floor.
For anyone sitting there, Rilla realized with a sideways
glance through the car window, the view would be
quite fabulous: a magnificent sweep across the sun-
kissed waters of the bay to Alcatraz Island, the Bay
Bridge and Oakland, and the dramatic high-rise skyline
of San Francisco.

Rilla sighed enviously, imagining what it would be
like to be a best-selling author and to be able to afford
such luxury—and such spacious privacy. Her spirits
took a dive as she realized the enormity of what she
was attempting. As a name, Richard Kellerman was
big, important, famous...yet, the man himself was almost unknown, because that was the way he wanted it.
Top television hosts would compete for the chance of
having him on their shows; the nation's leading journalists would give their eyeteeth to do a profile piece on
him. So what chance did Rilla Yorke—a junior reporter
for a minor San Francisco magazine devoted to the arts—
have?

Gathering together her fast-waning courage, she
climbed out of the car. With her leather tote bag slung
over her shoulder, and the paper-wrapped *Flowers of
Chivalry* in her hand, she made her way up the three
steps of the veranda and crossed to the front door.
There was an old-fashioned iron bellpull, and when
Rilla tugged it, a dull tinkle sounded from somewhere
deep within the house. Slow silent seconds went by,
and she began to think that she was out of luck. Then
she heard rapid footsteps, and a moment later the door
was opened. The middle-aged woman who stood there
had an elfin frame that made Rilla feel enormously tall.
Her gray hair was frizzily permed, and her pale eyes,
behind gold-framed spectacles, were bright and inquir-

ing. Over her dark blue cotton dress she wore a vividly flowered apron.

"Hiya!" she greeted Rilla cheerfully. "Sorry to keep you waiting, but I was upstairs cleaning the bath. How can I help you, miss?"

"I was wondering if Mr. Kellerman was home," Rilla began nervously.

"Well, he is," the woman said, pursing her thin lips, "but he's not available right now."

Rilla sighed, but she wasn't going to be beaten before she'd even reached first base. At least she'd have a shot at getting the refusal from Richard Kellerman in person. It would be too feeble to have to report back to Bill Andersen that she hadn't even made it past the maid.

"I wouldn't keep him for more than just a few minutes," she said, adopting a friendly smile and a pleading voice. "You see, when I heard that Mr. Kellerman had come to stay in this area, I just had to call to ask if he'd be kind enough to autograph this copy of his book for me. I admire his writing so much, and it would be really fantastic if he—"

"No, you got me wrong, miss. Like I said, Mr. Kellerman is home, but he's not in the house right now."

"You mean... he's in the garden somewhere?"

"That's it. He's down at the pool, having his morning swim. I'm not sure how long he'll be, but if you care to sit yourself down, you're welcome to wait."

"Oh, thanks very much."

Gesturing to one of the cushioned ironwork chairs, the maid went on, "So you're a fan of his?"

"Very much so! *Flowers of Chivalry* is a marvelous book."

"I guess you're right—for those with brain power. I

flicked through the copy that's on his desk one morning, but I couldn't begin to make head nor tail of it.''

Rilla recognized an opportunity to extract some useful information, but she had to be careful, in case the maid sensed she was being pumped and clammed up from a sense of loyalty to her employer. As an opener, she tried, "Have you been with Mr. Kellerman for long, Mrs.—''

"Bird. But everyone calls me Birdie. I don't really work for Mr. Kellerman, though, I come with the lease, as you might say. Both my husband and I do. I look after the cleaning and the cooking, and Tom sees to the garden and whatnot. I don't mind telling you it's a nice little number for us at the moment, just having a man on his own staying here. When the schools close for the summer and we get whole families here—sometimes two families at once, with hordes of kids and two mothers—*then* it's not too nice.''

"I can imagine." Rilla laughed, and added artfully, "So I hope you've got Mr. Kellerman for a good long stretch.''

"We should be so lucky! He's been here for just two weeks, and he'll be off again at the end of the month." While speaking, Birdie darted about straightening the chairs and plumping up the sage-green linen cushions. "I wish he were staying longer, that's for sure. He's no trouble at all."

"I've been told that Mr. Kellerman is not an easy man to get to see."

"Well, he does seem to keep to himself, miss. He's given me instructions not to let in any of them reporters or television people. And he won't talk to them on the phone, either. But I guess it's understandable, him not wanting any distractions when he's thinking what to write down for his new book.''

Rilla kept her voice deliberately casual. "What's the book going to be about? Do you happen to know?"

"Something to do with the history of California, I think. Mr. Kellerman spends a lot of time out and about, collecting what he calls local color, and he brings back armfuls of books and sits reading them till all hours. When he's not clacking away on his typewriter, that's to say. Still, you'd best ask him all about it yourself, miss."

"If he'll see me," Rilla said with a rueful grimace.

Birdie chuckled. "I reckon he will. I bet Mr. Kellerman will be quite flattered that you've come here specially to ask him to sign his book."

"For someone so famous, it's amazing how little seems to be known about Richard Kellerman, isn't it? I've never read anything personal about him—what he did before he wrote *Flowers of Chivalry*, where his home is, or even whether he's married or not," Rilla added.

"He's never mentioned a wife or kids or anything to me, and I haven't liked to ask him outright. Mr. Kellerman isn't one to talk much, you see. I'm not saying that as a criticism, miss, he's always pleasant and polite, but... well, he just isn't the chatty type, if you know what I mean."

"Yes, I know what you mean," Rilla said gloomily. Her chances didn't look too good.

"He did mention one day that—" Mrs. Bird broke off, her attention caught by something she'd spotted at a lower level of the garden. "Here comes Mr. Kellerman now, miss. So you haven't had to wait too long, have you?" With a quick smile she scuttled back into the house, leaving Rilla to explain her own presence.

In a whirl of nervous excitement Rilla watched the tall bearded man who was striding leisurely up the path of wide flagstone steps. He wore a thigh-length terry cloth robe that was striped in navy and white, and an olive-green towel was slung around his neck. He appeared deep in thought and was clearly unaware of her presence, so that Rilla had an opportunity to study him in detail.

Richard Kellerman was in no way conventionally handsome, but there was something intriguing about his craggy irregular bone structure and the sculpted sensuous mouth. Rilla felt a sudden knotting of her stomach muscles, a dryness in her throat, that wasn't just from the fact that she was about to meet a hero of hers. Most women would rate this man devastatingly attractive, she decided. She judged him to be around thirty-three or thirty-four.

His height was stressed by the fact that he needed to push aside a low pine branch growing across the path that would otherwise have brushed against his face. The lazy manner in which he lifted his arm to do so was redolent of easy strength, hinting at a tautly muscled body beneath his robe. As the garment parted with each upward step a length of powerful bronze thigh was exposed, and Rilla noted that he was barefoot. His hair and beard, she guessed, then wet and tousled from his swim, were probably much fairer, more like the golden color of wheat, and his skin was smooth and healthily tanned. His deep-set eyes were a vivid shade of blue, and at that moment they seemed to be contemplating some distant, inner world of his imagination until, when he suddenly caught sight of Rilla, they narrowed and focused with compelling directness.

Diffidently Rilla rose to her feet as Richard Kellerman took another few strides, which brought him up the three stone steps to the veranda. There he stood towering above her belligerently, his fists digging into his hips.

"Who the blazes are you?" he demanded, the rich timbre of his voice spiked with anger. "And why the devil are you here?"

"My name is Rilla Yorke," she stammered, wishing to heaven she could have arranged a better opening scenario. "Your maid kindly said that I could wait here for you, Mr. Kellerman."

"Did she indeed?" His tone threatened trouble later for Birdie, and Rilla rushed to her defense.

"Oh, but you mustn't blame her. She only let me stay because I explained that I was a tremendous fan of yours, and how I was hoping that you'd be kind enough to sign this." Rilla slipped the book from its paper wrapping and held it out to show him.

"You want my autograph?" He regarded the book with frowning distaste.

"Yes, please, Mr. Kellerman."

"I wonder if an autograph is *all* you want, Rilla Yorke."

"Meaning?" She cursed the give-away color that was staining her cheeks.

"Meaning precisely what I said— Is that *all* you want from me? But, perhaps, being female, you're incapable of understanding a direct question, so I'll rephrase it. Are you intent on getting something other than an autograph from me, Miss Yorke?" He glared at her, his blue eyes widening in sarcasm. "Have I made myself clear now?"

Rilla swallowed. "I admit that I was rather hoping for a little chat, as well."

"A little chat! With exactly what end in view? Come on, level with me."

"Well, as I explained, Mr. Kellerman, I'm a terrific fan of yours, and—" Oh, what was the use? Those intense blue eyes had turned ominously dark and were drilling into her, laying bare her pitiful attempt at deception. In a little rush of words she went on. "The fact is, I'm a journalist for the *Bay Area Arts Reporter*, and I was wondering—or rather, I was hoping—that you might agree to grant me a short interview, and—"

"So you conned your way in!"

"Conned? That's not fair!"

"Isn't it? What would you call bamboozling your way past the maid—who happens to be under strict orders not to admit any media people—by telling her a lot of guff about being a tremendous fan of mine?"

"But it's true!" Rilla protested. "I really am a fan of yours."

"Flattery might work with some authors, Miss Yorke, but not with me. I'm immune to it."

"I tell you," Rilla reiterated through gritted teeth, "that it's absolutely true. I genuinely admire your *work*." She couldn't resist stressing the word and leaving a distinct implication that she didn't rate him much as a man.

Richard Kellerman leaned sideways against one of the square stone pillars, lifting his arm as a prop. The action caused his robe to gape at the neck, and Rilla glimpsed a triangle of chest where short golden hairs glinted against the deeply tanned skin. It was sickening, she thought wretchedly, that such an attractive man should be such a boor.

"What's your next line going to be?" he inquired sarcastically. "How about this...that you've pored over my words of wisdom, burning the midnight oil and reading on red-eyed far into the night?"

"I can't figure you out," Rilla said in a challenging tone. "You seem to take it as an insult to have your work praised. Are you really so self-contained, so aloof, that you just don't care what people think of you as a writer?"

"Far from it, when the praise is sincere."

"What gives you the idea that mine isn't?"

"The evidence is staring me in the face that you're a scheming little liar," he drawled.

She gasped, outraged. "Hey! You've no right to call me that."

"No?" Richard Kellerman moved from his lazy stance against the pillar so swiftly that Rilla was startled, imagining for a crazy instant that he was going to lay violent hands on her. She stepped back hastily and bumped into the chair she'd just vacated, but his intention, it seemed, was merely to take the copy of *Flowers of Chivalry* from her while his eyes glanced critically at the printed wrapper still in her other hand.

"Bookery Nook!" he read out in a tone of withering contempt. "There's even a faintly pseudo touch to the name. Still, I suppose an author ought to be grateful to any store that sells his books. When exactly did you purchase this, Miss Yorke? Did you drop by at the bookstore on your way here this morning?"

"What's wrong with that?" she demanded. "I had to have a copy for you to autograph, didn't I?"

"Exactly," he said triumphantly. "But you might have had the intelligence to riffle through it a bit and crease a few pages...even invest the odd half–dollar in an unwanted cup of coffee in order to make a few authentic-looking spot marks. This copy," he went on, holding up the book scornfully, "is in pristine condition. It's never even been opened."

"That's because I didn't want to spoil it," Rilla burst out in a flood of indignation. "My own copy, which I bought months and months ago, is a paperback. Only it's so dog-eared by now that I could hardly expect you to autograph it."

"Why not? If you wanted to soften me up with flat-

tery, a book that was dog-eared from constant rereading would be the very thing.''

"I guess you're right, in a way,'' Rilla conceded reluctantly. ''But I didn't think of it like that.''

"And we know why you didn't think of it like that,
don't we?''

"*You* tell *me*,'' she returned, careless then about
creating a good impression. It was obvious that she'd
blown her chance of an interview with him.

"For the very simple reason, Miss Yorke, that the
much-thumbed paperback of *Flowers of Chivalry* you
boast about possessing is nothing more than a figment
of your fertile imagination. Now, come on, admit it.''

"You're wrong,'' Rilla insisted. "I can show you the
book.''

"You mean you have it in your purse?''

"No, but—''

"Can it be,'' he interrupted in a laconic tone, his
glance flicking up and down her shapely figure and
lingering on the swell of her breasts, "that you carry
my book permanently concealed about your person?''

"Very droll! It's at home, of course, but I could get it
to show you if you don't believe me.''

"You're planning to call here again, are you?'' he
queried interestedly. "Next time you'd better let me
know in advance, and I'll arrange to be more suitably
dressed to receive a female visitor.''

Rilla sighed impatiently. "I was just pointing out that
I was speaking the truth. I don't like having my word
questioned.''

Richard Kellerman laid the book on the table beside
him, then folded his arms and looked at her, his eyes
slitted against a shaft of bright sunlight that fell across
his face. There was amusement as well as anger in his
expression...and something else that Rilla couldn't in-

terpret. His next words took her completely by surprise.

"How about tomorrow evening?"

She stared at him in disbelief. "You—you mean that I can—"

"What a problem I seem to have making myself clear to you," he mocked. "Maybe it's because I haven't had the benefit of your journalistic experience. I was merely suggesting that since you seem so anxious to justify yourself in my eyes, you might care to bring along that much-read copy of *Flowers of Chivalry* tomorrow evening, when I'll be happy to autograph it for you."

It was too good to be true. Rilla had to make sure she'd heard him properly. "Does that mean you're going to give me an interview for the *Reporter*?"

"I'm promising nothing beyond my signature in the book. More than that... well, we'll have to see. Come and have dinner with me. Say, eight o'clock."

"Thanks very much."

"It's a bit early to be thanking me," he pointed out dryly, then added, "Don't forget to take your carrot with you, Miss Yorke."

"My carrot?"

He gestured at the book still lying on the table. "The one you bought to lure the donkey."

"You still don't believe me, do you?"

The expression on his lean, bony face gave nothing away. "Let's say that I'm reserving judgment."

Rilla picked up the book and self-consciously returned it to its wrapper. "Well, I guess I'd better be going." She hesitated, then said cajolingly, "You won't be angry with your maid, will you?"

Kellerman's sensuous mouth curved in a disdainful smile. "Isn't it a bit late in the day for you to be having a qualm of conscience?"

"But, I mean—she couldn't possibly have guessed that I'm a journalist."

"True. You don't look the least bit like a journalist."

"Oh?" Rilla's smooth brow creased in a frown. "How do you mean?"

"I'll tell you when we meet tomorrow," he said enigmatically.

Barefoot as he was, he walked with Rilla across the gravel drive to her car, and held open the door for her. "Are you going straight back to the city now?" he queried.

"Sure. I've got work to do. My job is in no way a five-day-a-week one, not any more than I guess yours is."

Grinning, he caught and held her gaze. "I see that I'll have to watch my step with you. If I'm not careful, you'll dig out my every last secret in no time flat."

"Do you have secrets to be dug out, Mr. Kellerman?"

"Don't we all, Miss Yorke?" He stood back and raised a hand. "Ciao! Until tomorrow."

Heading her small car down the steep winding road to the Sausalito waterfront, Rilla felt jubilant. She was near to pulling off the seemingly impossible assignment. Even if Richard Kellerman proved to be as tight as a clam, she could hardly fail to get something to write about the following evening... if only an account of the dinner they'd eaten together.

But she was going to get more than that.... Somehow she knew it by the prickling of her thumbs. It could really be the breakthrough she needed—a scoop interview with a literary celebrity. And he was a most fascinating man, too. A suitable headline was already flashing in her brain: RICHARD KELLERMAN, THE MAN BEHIND THE ENIGMA. By Rilla Yorke!

She felt an urge to call Bill Andersen at home in Richmond to tell him the good news. It wasn't caution that made her think better of it, but a vision of herself triumphantly slapping down the completed article on his desk. She could just imagine his plump face lighting up in admiration as he skimmed through it. "You're a genius, Rilla," he'd say. "That's what you are—a genius."

Chapter Two

Rilla's euphoria carried her through what would other-wise have been a frustrating afternoon. Having driven all the way to San Mateo to interview a man who was setting up a metal sculpture park, she found that he'd forgotten about their appointment and had flown to Los Angeles for the weekend.

Oh, well, you win some, you lose some, she thought philosophically, quoting a favorite saying of Bill Andersen's. And that day the balance was nonetheless weighted heavily in her favor, especially as still to come was a visit to the Berkeley campus, where she was due to cover a one-night stand of a modern dance troupe. She always liked it when her job presented a chance to visit her old university.

With time to spare, Rilla headed out to Berkeley early, driving across the Bay Bridge and along the shore freeway. The rolling folds of mottled clouds that had hidden the sun during the previous few hours were drifting away fast, and only a few ragged skeins ob-scured its golden brightness, giving the sky a softly pearlized glow.

Rilla went first to the University Art Museum, which happened to be showing an Impressionist collection. She'd done a piece on the exhibition in *BAAR* a couple of weeks ago, and was glad to see that it was being well patronized. Maybe, she thought, smiling, her enthusiastic recommendation had actually been responsible for drawing some of the people there that day.

Following her graduation four years ago, Rilla's life had been rather unsettled for a time. Her first job, with a PR firm, ended in disaster when the outfit went up in smoke. There followed a spell with a very minor radio station as a junior roving reporter, a job that paid next to nothing and seemed to be leading nowhere. In any event, it led to a meeting with Theo Strieber, whom she'd interviewed for the nightly *Who's New in Town* spot. It was a few weeks after Aunt Elly's death, and Rilla was still feeling pretty low and suffering from a bleak, empty feeling because she had lost the one person really close to her.

That feeling changed overnight. Theo, who was incredibly handsome and charming, put every other man she'd ever dated in the shade. Rilla had fallen blindly in love with him, and in next to no time they were in the throes of an intense affair. In the dizziness of her newfound joy she had felt committed to Theo body and soul. The shock of discovering that he had no thought of commitment left her reeling with dismay. Theo, she discovered from a chance remark of his, already had a wife and kids back in Seattle.

"So what?" he'd argued with a shrug when she challenged him, on the verge of tears. "How does that affect you and me, sweetheart? I'm here for another four months yet.... That's all the time in the world."

His blithely uncaring attitude made Rilla feel terribly immature, like a foolish, infatuated teenager. How could she confess to him that her whole world had been shattered into a thousand fragments? Concealing her bewildered anger, refusing to let him see how badly hurt she was, she had adopted a cool pose. "I just wish you'd been honest with me, Theo, that's all."

He'd shrugged again, unrepentant. "So now that you know, you can just relax and forget about it. Okay?" he had said.

"No. I've been meaning to tell you...I think it's best that we stop seeing one another."

Theo had stared at her blankly. "Just because you've found out that I'm married?"

Rilla had shrugged, lifting her slender shoulders in a careless gesture. "These things don't last forever, do they, and I reckon that we've been going around together for long enough." Listening to herself, she'd sounded quite calm and unemotional. It was only when she had got home, to the little house on Russian Hill, which Theo had visited so often, that she had dropped her defenses and given way to sobs and scalding tears.

By the next morning, though, her then new philosophy of life was fully formed. She wasn't going to let a man get under her skin again in a hurry. She was going to forge a career for herself in journalism. And the first thing to do was to find a new job that offered real prospects.

Rilla was to find that it was easier said than done. But then a stroke of luck led her to the offices of the *Bay Area Arts Reporter*. Bill Andersen, liking the shrewdly perceptive way she interviewed him for the radio station, promptly offered her a job on his arts magazine. The salary wasn't all that wonderful—only slightly more, in fact, than she was earning at the time. But she never, once regretted making the move. The experience of working for a gifted editor like Bill was worth more than money in the bank, and it looked as if her breakthrough chance had arrived. An interview with someone of Richard Kellerman's caliber would establish her name with editors all over the nation.

"Ten bucks to you, lady."

She stared vacantly at the swarthy, hoarse-voiced vendor. Unaware, she'd wandered over to a crafts display and had been gazing fixedly at his display of embossed leather belts.

"Crocodile skin," he assured her, taking a bite of a hot dog. "The genuine article."

"Huh!" she threw back. "If I believed you, I definitely wouldn't buy one."

He grinned, unabashed. "Genuine leather, anyhow. Make it seven and a half."

"Oh...okay. I'll take this one," she said, selecting a belt that had a shiny heart-shaped buckle.

Glancing at her wristwatch, she saw that there was still more than an hour to go before the dance performance. On a sudden thought she returned to her Honda and drove over to the home of her beloved English literature professor. As she halted the car his florid face, topped by a tangle of white hair, peered at her amiably over a mauve hibiscus bush he was snipping on that fine Saturday.

"Rilla Yorke," he exclaimed in surprise. "My favorite student."

Rilla laughed. "I bet you say that to all the students, Professor."

"Only the ones who graduated Summa Cum Laude. It's very nice to see you, my dear, and you're looking prettier than ever. How's everything in the journalistic world?"

"Fine, just fine. You're looking pretty well yourself, Professor."

"Yes, I manage to keep fit."

They walked together up the garden path to the porch of the Swiss-style chalet, Rilla admiring his display of flowering shrubs. He waved his hand toward a folding canvas chair.

"Sit down, my dear, sit down. I'll go and fetch a bottle of wine. You being here gives me an excuse. I never like to drink alone."

"Where's Isabel today, then?"

"Visiting our eldest daughter at Walnut Creek, helping her to sew curtains or something. I elected to stay home, and I'm glad I did now that you've turned up." He disappeared into the house and returned with a bottle of Chablis and two glasses. "Now, tell me all about yourself, Rilla. I'm always seeing your pieces in the *Bay Area Arts Reporter*. You're enjoying your job, are you?"

"I sure am. It's terrifically stimulating. Every day brings something new and interesting." Then, fully aware that it was the real reason she'd gone to see her old professor, Rilla burst out excitedly, "I've got a fabulous assignment lined up for tomorrow. It could be the thing that gives me a break into the big time."

The professor's shaggy white eyebrows were hoisted. "I'm intrigued."

"I guess you know the name Richard Kellerman?"

"Author of *Flowers of Chivalry*? But, of course, my dear. That book made a big impression in academic circles. His research into the Arthurian legends was most scholarly, and he added a really imaginative interpretation. A most exciting piece of work. The man himself is something of a mystery, though. Nobody seems to know anything about him."

"Well, maybe I'm going to change all that," Rilla declared. "Richard Kellerman is staying in Sausalito at the moment, and he's promised me an interview."

The professor looked gratifyingly impressed. "How did you manage that?"

Rilla thought it prudent to give him an edited version of the facts. "I simply charged over there this morning and tackled him. It—it wasn't convenient at the time, so he suggested I go back tomorrow."

"That's wonderful! You've read the book, I expect? If not, you could borrow my copy."

"Thanks all the same, Professor, but I've read it several times. I think the man's a genius."

Rilla was awarded a shrewdly speculative look. "I can see he's made a hit with you, my dear. Now, how about persuading him to come to Berkeley to give some of my students the benefit of his erudition?"

Rilla scooped back a gleaming tendril of hair and said uneasily, "I'll ask him, if you like, but you mustn't hold out much hope."

"I have every confidence in your powers of persuasion, Rilla. I well remember, when you were here, how you could turn members of the English faculty to your way of thinking."

"I did no such thing," she protested.

He smiled at her indulgently. "Let's put it this way... As a student, you were a very determined young woman, and I've no reason to think you've changed in that respect. I have a feeling that Richard Kellerman might rue the day he agreed to see you. And don't frown at me like that, my dear girl. I was paying you a compliment."

On Sunday morning a cheerful Rilla, clad in a casual denim pants-and-jacket combo, strolled among the crowds at Fisherman's Wharf. All around her was gaiety as the beat of music throbbed on the warm air and vendors hoarsely cried their wares. Rilla loved it all. And, as always, wherever she happened to be and whatever she was doing, she kept a sharp lookout for material for the following week's *BAAR*.

Thinking that she might hit upon a new street performer to write about, she wended her way to Ghirardelli Square, the one-time chocolate factory that had been skillfully converted into a many tiered complex of boutiques, gift shops, and restaurants. She was in luck. On Fountain Plaza she watched a brilliant act by a lugubrious old man who juggled with the most ill-assorted trio of objects: an apple, a black top hat, and a fearsome-looking saber, the razor-sharp edge of which he used to slice off chunks of the apple in midair to catch between his teeth and gobble down. Rilla's chat with him afterward proved rewarding, since he had a fund of anecdotes to tell.

A glance at the tall clock tower reminded her that it was time for her appointment with a woman who sculpted in candle wax. Rilla spent a fascinating hour watching her at work in her little dark cavern, and when she emerged once more into the bright noonday sunshine, she was carrying a fat packet of photographs from which to pick a few suitable illustrations for her article.

"Well, fancy bumping into you," said a familiar, deep-toned voice right behind her. Rilla wheeled around in confusion, her heart beating wildly, and found herself face to face with Richard Kellerman. His eyes, behind amber-tinted sunglasses, were regarding her with keen interest.

He was wearing a short-sleeve, red-and-gray checkered shirt, open at the throat. His long legs were encased in faded blue denims that hugged his hips tightly and were cinched at the waist with a leather belt. His hair and beard, not tousled and wet then, was crisp and springy. Just as she had guessed, it was the rich golden color of wheat, making a perfect foil to the healthy tan of his skin. He really was a compellingly attractive man, she decided with a little shiver of excitement.

"What—what are you doing here?" she stammered, aware even as she said it that the question sounded foolish.

"The same as you, I imagine."

"The—the same as me?"

With a flick of his hand he indicated the package she carried, then patted the bulging back pocket of his jeans. "It looks as if we've both been gathering material for our work."

"Oh, I see. Yes, of course."

"I've been visiting the National Maritime Museum," he explained. "A real treasure house of nautical lore. You know it well, naturally?"

Rilla laughed awkwardly. "I'm ashamed to admit I've never been inside."

"How remiss of you! A San-Franciscan born and bred, I imagine?"

"Yes, I've no excuse."

Richard Kellerman adopted a magisterial tone. "Your time, Miss Yorke, would be far better spent in visiting a place like the Maritime Museum for the enlightenment of your readers, than in delving for personal trivia about a man who happens to have written a book."

"An eminent man, who happens to have written one of the great imaginative literary works of the decade," she amended. "Can I deduce from that, Mr. Kellerman, that you *have* decided to grant me an interview this evening?"

"History," he replied with a lopsided smile, "is littered with people who jumped to the wrong conclusion. I told you to wait and see, Rilla Yorke, and that's pre-

cisely what you'll have to do. Meantime, what are you
doing about lunch?''

Her pulse rate switched to overdrive. "I hadn't
thought about it yet."

"Let's see..." He glanced at the watch that was
strapped to his wrist with a wide gold-link band. "It's a
quarter after twelve. Not too early for you?"

"Oh, no." Rilla could hardly believe her luck. A
friendly, off-the-record chat over the lunch table would
nicely pave the way for a good interview that evening.

"I understand that Neptune's Palace on Pier Thirty-
nine is a good place, if you like fish."

"I like fish."

"Good." He put his hand beneath her elbow, gripping it lightly as he steered her though the crowds
thronging the waterfront. Rilla was vividly conscious of
the pressure of his fingers through her denim jacket
and felt as though she were floating along in a daze of
delight.

"You're sure Mrs. Bird isn't expecting you back for
lunch?" she asked, to cover her nervousness.

"I gave Birdie the morning off, so that she can gird
her loins for this evening's big challenge. She's doing
something special."

"I'm honored," Rilla quipped.

"So you should be!"

They reached the entrance to Pier 39 and went up
the steps to the second level. Strolling at the pace of the
crowd, they paused to look in at a kite shop. "Kite flying is an incredibly ancient pastime," Richard told her.
"Did you know that? Its origins are lost in the mists of
time."

"I'll take your word for it," Rilla said. "I like that big
red one with the dragon's head."

"Shall I buy it for you?"

"Heavens, no!" She laughed. "What would I do with a kite?"

"To fly a kite is to make a pathway to heaven."

"Where did you get that?" she demanded. "Out of a fortune cookie? It sounds corny enough."

"Suppose I were to tell you that it's from one of the great poets."

"Which great poet?"

"Was it Lord Byron?"

"Pure garbage," Rilla declared.

Richard grinned amiably. "Byron might have said it if he'd thought of it. Come on."

As they wandered on along the twisting boardwalk a heavenly aroma of coffee teased their nostrils and mingled with the scents of the ocean. Gulls wheeled tirelessly above their heads, swooping and shrieking. From somewhere unseen came the strident jangle of a banjo.

The seafood restaurant was at the very end of the pier, and the hostess showed them to a table right against the wall of huge windows that offered a dramatic view of the bay sparkling in the sunshine, its rippled, sapphire-blue water dotted with white sails.

"This is a favorite place of mine," Rilla told him. "Not that I've been here more than a couple of times before. But where else can you get such excellent food combined with a fabulous view?"

Richard removed his sunglasses. "I can imagine," he said, looking at her rather than at the view, "that for the rest of my stay here it will be a favorite place of mine, too."

They both chose broiled salmon from the menu, and Richard ordered a bottle of champagne.

"You'll have to drink most of it," she warned as the waiter departed. "I've got to keep a clear head."

"For this evening?" he queried, his vivid blue eyes sparkling with amusement.

"For this evening. And for now, too!" Several times already she'd found her attention straying from her job into realms of fanciful dreaming. She'd agreed to have lunch with Richard Kellerman, she reminded herself sternly, for one purpose only—to help smooth the way to a really first-class, informative, depth-digging interview with him later. But it was difficult to keep that firmly in mind, considering that he was looking at her in a way that seemed to melt her bones. Even if he hadn't been a renowned author, it would be faraway the most exciting interview she'd ever undertaken. There was something about the man, an aura of potent masculinity, that she found intensely attractive. And though it seemed too good to be true, Rilla knew she wasn't imagining that he felt genuinely attracted to her, too. There was a subtle two-way electric current flowing between them that couldn't be ignored.

On the table beside Rilla was the fat packet of candle sculpture photographs. Nodding toward it, Richard commented, "I see you managed to find what you wanted."

"Uh . . . yes," she replied, puzzled by this obscure remark.

"I expect you always do get what you want."

"Usually." She flashed him a cheeky smile. "I'm counting on you not to spoil my success rate, Mr. Kellerman."

"That will depend on you, not me. I have to be sure that giving you an interview isn't something I'll regret later."

"There's no reason why you should, that I can see. Tell me something. Why are you so hostile to the idea of publicity?"

"I'm not—if it's the right kind of publicity. It's personal sensationalism that I object to."

"And is there something sensational among your secrets that I might dig out?" she hazarded.

"That," he remarked tantalizingly, "is one of the questions that you might or might not get answered during dinner tonight."

The champagne arrived, and their two glasses were filled. Richard raised his in salute, smiling. "Here's to you, Rilla."

"To success!" she suggested.

"I'll go along with that, too. Success, you'll discover if you haven't done so already, can come in different guises. So we'll toast success for both of us."

Rilla sipped from her glass, and the delicious prickle of the pinpoint champagne bubbles seemed to diffuse through her whole body, tingling in her veins. Looking at Richard across the table, she found herself wondering how he would look minus the beard. Though it suited him, she had a distinct feeling that he would look even more devastatingly attractive without one.

"Where is your home?" she asked him, trying to make it sound casual.

Richard lifted his broad shoulders in a shrug. "Here, there, and wherever. You could almost say of me that I have no fixed abode. I've spent the past six months in California, starting down on the Mexican border."

"Is this in connection with your next project?" Rilla asked innocently, not wanting to admit that she'd already pumped the maid.

He gave her a lazy smile. "Don't you ever let up on the job, Rilla?"

"Do you?" she parried.

"Oh, yes, often. Like now, for instance. After a busy morning, I reckon I've earned a break—in charming company."

Rilla decided it would be prudent to make her questioning more subtle. "Do you like California?"

"Sure I do. It's not called the Golden State for nothing."

"How would you rate it compared with some of the other places you've been to?"

"Which other places?" he teased.

"The here, there, and wherever you mentioned."

He shook his head, still smiling. "Save it for this evening, Rilla. Just now I want to enjoy my lunch. Here comes our salmon."

They lingered an hour or more over lunch, for the most part talking about San Francisco, which seemed an okay topic with Richard. He was no stranger to the city, Rilla learned, having visited it several times in the past, though he refused to be specific as to when. Rilla found herself enthusing about the many virtues of the Bay Area.

"Your eyes sparkle when you get carried away," he broke in at one point. Rilla stopped in confusion, realizing that he'd been watching her intently. "You really love San Francisco, don't you?"

"I guess I do. But then, it's home. I've never lived anywhere else."

He tilted his wineglass thoughtfully, studying the pale amber liquid. "It must be nice to have roots."

When they finally left the restaurant, Richard strolled back with her to where she'd parked her Honda near The Cannery. He extended his hand to her, and as Rilla offered hers in response he astonished her by lifting it to his lips. The warm pressure of his mouth against her skin sent a flurry of excitement dancing through her.

"*À bientôt,* Rilla," he murmured softly. "Till we meet again."

"Such gallantry," she riposted in an effort to conceal the unnerving effect he was having on her. "Does that mean you have a trace of Latin ancestry?"

Richard grinned, refusing to be drawn in. "I guess most Americans have, from somewhere way back."

Rilla unlocked the door and slid in behind the wheel, and he closed the door for her. "Deadline eight o'clock?"

"I'll be there. And thanks a lot for the lunch."

"A pleasure, Rilla, I assure you."

Rilla remembered a promise she'd made. It seemed to be the right moment. "By the way, I was talking to one of my English professors from Berkeley yesterday. He said to tell you he'd be honored if you'd consent to give an extracurricular lecture to some of his students."

Richard's mouth tautened, and his heavy brows drew together. "You've been discussing me, Rilla?"

"Well, I just mentioned..."

He waited, but when she didn't finish, he said tersely, "You'd better just mention to the professor that the answer is no."

"Won't you even think about it?"

"Not even that, Rilla. It should teach you not to count your chickens prematurely in future."

The sun was westering in a blaze of gilded glory that evening as Rilla headed once more across the Golden Gate Bridge.

Since lunchtime her emotions had see-sawed, from dizzying peaks of excitement—when she recalled the interest in Richard's blue eyes as he'd looked at her across the table—to deep dark chasms of gloom. In her worst moments of insecurity it was painfully obvious to her that Richard Kellerman was merely amusing himself at her expense. After all, an outstandingly attractive man like him would have numerous women he could call on for female company. The fact that the two of them had got on so well together during lunch didn't have to mean anything special. In retrospect, the way he'd carefully avoided being pinned down to any sort of promises suggested that he might try to duck out of an interview when it came to that point.

Would he, Rilla wondered desolately as she reached the Marin County shore, just scribble his name in her copy of *Flowers of Chivalry* and send her away? But he'd definitely invited her to have dinner with him, she reminded herself consolingly. He couldn't go back on that—could he?

The Casa del Sol was bathed in rosy bronze light as she drew up outside, the trees throwing dense splashes of shadow. There was no sign of life, but when she tugged the old-fashioned bellpull, the maid came hurrying to answer its tinkle.

"Mr. Kellerman is on the phone in his study at the moment, miss," Mrs. Bird told Rilla, leading the way to the large living room. "He won't be more'n a minute or two. If you'll pardon me, I must get back to the kitchen."

"Mrs. Bird—Birdie, he really *is* expecting me for dinner, isn't he?" she queried, feeling foolish for having any doubt.

"Bless you, what else? In fact," the little woman confided, "he asked me to fix something extraspecial this evening. So I've done duck with mangoes."

Rilla smiled in relief. "It sounds delicious."

"I did that for Mr. Kellerman once before, and he liked it real fine. I thought it wouldn't spoil, not the way some things would." With that slightly odd remark Birdie bustled off to the kitchen.

Left alone, Rilla wandered around the spacious room, eagerly noting every detail. It was lofty, with an elaborately molded cornice and a chandelier of Venetian glass. A handsome carved wood fireplace graced one wall, surmounted by a fine mirror in an oval gilt frame. The decor was in tones of cream and mushroom and delicate French blue, with easy chairs and a sofa in supple white leather. The total effect was luxurious, but there was something impersonal about the room, as was to be expected of a rented vacation home. She couldn't deduce much about Richard Kellerman from that evidence, except that he found the style congenial enough to have a month-long stay there.

She was standing by the French doors, looking out across the veranda to the steeply sloping garden beyond, when the door behind her was flung open. She swung around to see her host regarding her with a quizzical expression.

"Hi, Rilla," he greeted her, closing the door behind him.

Richard Kellerman was formally dressed in a lightweight vested suit of silver-gray fabric, worn with a cream-colored shirt and a blue silk tie. The sight of him seemed to knock the breath from her body, and her palms suddenly felt damp. He looked even more attractive, more vibrantly masculine, than on the two occasions she'd seen him before—if that was possible. Yet, somehow it made her feel that much more nervous. At lunch they had developed an easygoing relationship, but then Rilla was acutely aware that she was a very junior reporter hoping to interview an eminent author.

"Good evening, Mr. Kellerman," she said rather stiffly.

"Richard!" he corrected. He stood smiling at her, his gaze passing over her slim, curvaceous figure at a leisurely pace. "I like your dress. In fact, it's quite stunning. I can't help wondering if you're all set to entice me into making some indiscreet personal revelations."

"That's a crazy thing to say," Rilla stammered, flushing with embarrassment. "You invited me to dinner, so I dressed accordingly."

She kicked herself for not having chosen something less sexy and revealing than the clinging taffeta sheath with its halter neckline. The sheeny sage-green fabric matched the color of her eyes and highlighted her auburn hair. She'd only worn it once before since buying it for a dinner dance held at the Carnelian Room as a grand finale to an architectural symposium a few weeks earlier. On the occasion the dress had earned her a number of pointedly admiring remarks from the males present.

"Whatever your reason, Rilla, I thoroughly approve." Richard strode across to the liquor cabinet in an alcove, moving with the lithe grace of a panther. "Would a glass of Riesling suit you?"

"Yes, fine."

"I rather expected you to turn up dressed like an eager-beaver newshound," he said chattily as he poured the wine.

"Oh, what made you think that?"

"You were so touchy yesterday when I said you didn't look a bit like a journalist. I thought you'd want to put the image right."

"And how," Rilla asked, taking the tall, fluted glass of white wine from him gingerly to avoid finger contact, "does an eager-beaver newshound look?"

"Not nearly as attractive as you, that's for sure." He tilted his head to one side and again let his glance move over her slender curves appraisingly. "I'd say that tonight you look more like a slinky lady spy who's after the microfilm. And you'd probably succeed, too."

"Am I meant to take that as a compliment?" she inquired coolly.

Richard grinned at her. "What do you think? Do sit down, Rilla...that is, if you *can* sit down in that dress."

How, Rilla wondered wistfully, would a slinky lady spy drop gracefully into the low-slung armchair he'd indicated? She found to her dismay that the skirt needed quite a bit of hitching up—with her one free hand—before she could bend sufficiently. All the while she was conscious of Richard's intent gaze.

"Where's your notebook?" he asked, rubbing one finger along his eyebrow.

"In my purse." She would have preferred to use a tape recorder and then transcribe later at her leisure. But she'd strongly suspected that Richard Kellerman would veto the idea, so it was best not to risk upsetting him.

"And the much-talked-of, much-pored-over paperback. Is that in your purse, too?"

"Sure." Reaching forward to rest her drink on a low glass table, Rilla opened her purse and drew out the book. Richard took it from her, flicking through the pages.

"A truly vintage specimen," he commented dryly. "One of the first paperback printing, I see. You were lucky to find this, Rilla."

"I don't see why. There were stacks of them in the shop."

"Really! What a blow to my vanity."

"I don't get you," she said, puzzled.

"It would be nice to think that once a person has bought and read my book, they'd want to keep it permanently on their shelves at home, not cash it in for the few cents it would fetch at a secondhand bookstore."

"Listen," Rilla said, feeling distinctly annoyed, "how many times do I have to tell you? I bought it *new,* when it first came out in paperback."

His lips curled in a disbelieving smile. "Which, translated, means that you've been running around ever since yesterday, trying to locate a suitably battered copy, and you got lucky this morning at a used bookstore somewhere near Fisherman's Wharf."

She jerked her head, making her auburn waves swing. "What gives you that idea?"

"I saw the package, remember. It was on the table while we were having lunch."

"But that was a stack of photoprints I'd been given by a candle sculptor I'd just interviewed," she protested furiously.

Richard shrugged his broad shoulders. "Don't waste your breath. It makes no difference. The point is that you've managed to secure a sufficiently dog-eared copy to bring along with you this evening. So you've passed my test with flying colors, haven't you?"

"Thank you so much," she replied sarcastically.

Tossing the book aside, he sat down in an armchair beside Rilla.

"Aren't you going to autograph it for me?" she demanded. "You promised you would."

"That's right, I did," he agreed. "And I intend to keep my promise. But I suggest we leave that little matter until later on."

"What's wrong with *now*?" she challenged suspiciously, fishing in her purse. "I can lend you a pen."

Richard smiled and shook his head. "It's not a pen I lack, Rilla, it's inspiration. In a couple of hours time I'll be better able to decide on a suitable inscription to go with my signature."

There was a tap at the door, and Birdie looked in.

"Everything's ready and waiting on the hot plate for when you want to eat, Mr. Kellerman. And the coffee's all set to perk, you only have to switch it on. So will that be all for now? Tom's come for me, and there's a good thriller on television that we don't want to miss."

"That's fine, Birdie, you get on home," Richard said with a friendly, dismissive wave. "And thanks a lot for staying late this evening."

As the door closed behind her, he explained to Rilla, "I normally eat rather earlier than this so Birdie can get away by seven thirty."

"She and her husband don't live in, then?" Rilla felt a curious niggle of unease.

"No, they have a houseboat down at the waterfront," he told her, and went on ironically, "Surprising as it may seem to you, I don't require full-time attendance. I can just about manage to serve myself a meal that's been cooked for me. I've even been known to make coffee and toast for my breakfast without outside help. Actually," he concluded, "I prefer to be alone here in the evenings. It's easier for me to concentrate on work."

"I see," she said, and took the chance to ask, "Do you always find the evenings a good time to work, Richard?"

"Evenings, early morning, anytime—when I'm in full flood, as now."

"Then I'm especially grateful to you for taking time off from work to see me tonight."

"You persuaded me that it would be worthwhile," he said with an easy smile, and added, "What about you, Rilla? I hope that coming here to see me hasn't interfered too drastically with your other plans."

"Other plans?"

"It's Sunday night—a high spot of the week for lovers. Your boyfriend probably didn't like being stood up just because I was inconsiderate enough to nominate this particular time for our interview."

"As it happens, I didn't have a date fixed for tonight."

One thick eyebrow lifted in irony. "I wonder why. Could it be that there's a temporary hiatus in your love life? Or have you so many admirers eager to date you that you can leave it until the last possible minute before deciding which one to favor?"

"You can work it out for yourself," she remarked cuttingly. "Might I remind you, Mr. Kellerman, that it's *you* we're supposed to be discussing, not me."

"We're back to the formal mode of address, I note."

Ignoring that, Rilla took the shorthand notebook and a ball-point pen from her purse. "Perhaps I could ask you a few questions now."

"You look dreadfully severe," he protested. "Rather like a policewoman advising me of my constitutional rights."

"Please be serious," she begged.

"Very well." He adopted a solemn expression. "Now, take down my specifics. Name—Richard Kellerman. Age—thirty-four last February. Height—six feet two inches. Weight—a hundred and seventy pounds, stripped. Have you got all that?"

Rilla nodded, and he continued. "Color of hair you'd better put down as fair, I guess. Men aren't usually called blond, are they?"

Rilla didn't comment, but jotted down a note that his hair was the color of wheat in sunshine. Not that she needed any reminding and neither would she describe him thus in her article.

"Eyes next," he said. "What color would you say my eyes are?"

"I really haven't noticed," she lied and scrutinized

him deliberately. "Eyes... a sort of deep blue, I guess. And next, since you want me to get down to specifics, where were you born?"

"Boston."

"Are there any other writers in your family? Your parents?..."

"They're both dead now, but neither of them were writers. My father was a corporation lawyer, and my mother taught music—the piano."

Rilla put that down. "And have you any brothers or sisters?"

"I wish I had. How about you? Do you come from a large family?"

She shook her head. "As a matter of fact I happen to be in the same position as you. I'm an only child, and both my parents are dead, too."

"So we're two orphans of the storm!" he quipped, his vividly intent blue eyes coming to rest on her face, holding her gaze teasingly. "I think that makes a very promising beginning, don't you, Rilla?"

Shaking herself free of his mesmerizing gaze, she inquired in a brisk voice about his education.

"You won't want me to go back as far as kindergarten, I guess. At school I showed a distinct flair for languages and an inordinate interest in history."

"What about sports?"

"Tennis has always been my favorite game. But I was moderately good at football and slightly better at baseball. And I like to ski."

"Which university did you go to?"

"We won't be *that* specific."

"Why not?" she demanded.

"Because I say not, and I'm the one laying down the ground rules."

Rilla shrugged impatiently. "What did you major in?"

"English. I managed to make the dean's list. I also developed a highly discriminating taste for the female of the species around that time—which just about sums up my salad days."

There was one important question she hadn't yet touched upon. "Am I to take it that you're not married or anything?"

"Or anything! But I won't deny a couple of close shaves when I was within a hairbreadth of getting caught."

"Is that the view you take of marriage—that it's a matter of being caught?"

"Can you come up with a better definition?" he countered.

"I only accept one possible basis for marriage," Rilla said emphatically, "and that's when both partners are in love."

Richard's craggy bearded face took on an expression of incredulous amusement. "What have we here...a hard-boiled media woman who's also highly romantic? A rare combination."

Rilla refused to rise to his sneer but persisted in a level voice, "Can I get this clear, because I'd hate to misquote you, are you saying that you've ruled out the possibility of getting married?"

"Not necessarily. I might decide one day that marriage would suit my life-style. However, any woman I chose as a wife would have to measure up to very exacting standards."

As if suddenly impatient of her questions, Richard rose abruptly to his feet. "Shall we go through to the dining room now? Bring your notebook, if you must. Then you can record a bite-by-bite account of the meal for the edification of your readers."

Chapter Three

The evening sky was like a pastel painting in shades of apricot, crimson, and gold as they went through to the dining room. It had the same look of luxury as the living room but lacked the warmth of a family home. Two places had been set at the long table, one each side of a corner, their closeness lending an air of intimacy. A hostess cart with a hot plate stood nearby, from which rose a savory aroma. A bottle of wine had been set to chill in an ice bucket.

They started the meal with a delicious salad of avocado and prawn with a tangy orange-honey dressing.

"Mmm! It's out of this world!" Rilla exclaimed after tasting the first mouthful.

"Yes," Richard agreed. "It's one of Birdie's specials. I always enjoy it." Then, as Rilla continued eating, he added sardonically, "Hadn't you better jot that down before you forget it? 'Richard Kellerman praised the avocado and prawn salad.' We can't have you missing out on something as vital as that about me to pass on to the great reading public."

Rilla held her fork poised and looked at him, a frown marring the smoothness of her brow. "Why do you object so strongly to the idea of publicity? Surely your readers are entitled to be interested in the man behind the book?''

"My work should stand for itself. Either it's good, or it isn't. Whether or not I happen to like a particular kind of salad, or pineapple chunks, or Boston baked beans is entirely beside the point."

Rilla sighed inwardly, wondering how in the world she was going to produce an interesting article out of the meager tidbits of personal information that Richard was willing to disclose. As he started to serve the duck she covertly watched his lean-featured bearded face through her dark lashes, trying to see through into his mind. To her embarrassment she realized that he was fully aware of her scrutiny.

"You could tell your readers that I'm very much the homey, domesticated type of man," he suggested helpfully.

"But that wouldn't be true," she objected. "I'm not seeing the real you tonight."

Richard put down an oval dinner plate before her and placed the vegetable dishes within her reach. "What brought on that remark?"

While she considered her reply Rilla helped herself to creamed spinach and saffron rice. "Somehow I get the feeling that you're putting on an act for my benefit."

"Why should I do that?"

"I wish I knew."

He gave her an enigmatic glance. "So what do you imagine the real man behind the mask is like?"

"That's what I've come to find out."

"The evening stretches before us," he said lightly. "A far from displeasing prospect, as I hope you agree." He topped up their wineglasses, then raised his in a toast. "Let us drink again, as we did at lunchtime, to success. Success in your endeavor, Rilla."

"If you don't cooperate, there'll be no story."

"And haven't I been cooperating?"

"Only to a limited extent."

"Then I'll have to try to do better." He picked up his fork. "Is the duck to your liking, Rilla?"

"It's delicious. I've never had it cooked with mangoes before." She glanced at him and gave a meaningful sigh. "Am I really going to have to fill my article with descriptions of the meal you served me?"

He laughed. "You're very determined."

"And that's a fault in a journalist?"

"It depends, I guess, on the nature of the motivation." His eyes met hers with a question. "What is it in your case? Were you crossed in love, maybe?"

Rilla swallowed hard and fought to hold back the telltale color from rushing to her cheeks. Damn the man for his shrewdness. She evaded an answer by tossing his question straight back at him. "Am I onto something hot here? Do we owe the flowering of Richard Kellerman's genius to an unhappy love affair?"

He threw back his head with a bark of laughter. "Every one of my love affairs has had a common factor, Rilla...they were all delightful as long as they lasted. And they ended—on my side at least—without regret. Just lots of pleasant memories."

"You talk very much in the plural," she commented sourly, surprised at how much it hurt that he was a self-confessed philanderer.

"Somewhere in your notebook you jotted down my age. I'm thirty-four, remember, and a normal, healthy male."

"Care to give me any details?" she challenged boldly.

Richard smiled at her, maddeningly unperturbed. "I'm not one to kiss and tell. Are you?" His blue eyes,

beneath his thick straight brows, glinted at her danger-
ously.

"I'm merely an unknown journalist, so nobody
would be interested in my love life."

"*I* am."

"Sorry, but I'm not about to satisfy your curiosity."

"Tell me this, then: What brought you to journalism?"

"It's what I always wanted to do, right from when I
was in the first grade. I used to read everything I could
lay my hands on, and I was always scribbling away in
my diary, or writing little poems. Words just fascinated
me somehow," she finished hastily, aware that Richard
was watching her with keen interest.

"Do you plan to stick with journalism," he asked,
"or are you hoping to make it with other types of writing?"

Rilla used her beige linen napkin to dab her lips.
"One day, maybe. But I have a living to earn. After I
graduated from Berkeley, I tried PR for a bit, and then
radio, but I didn't seem to be getting anywhere. Then
this job with the *Bay Area Arts Reporter* came up."

"Do you enjoy it?"

"Oh, yes. It doesn't pay a lot, but it's marvelous experience. The man who runs it, Bill Andersen, is a
really great editor, so I'm happy to stick with the magazine in the hope that it'll lead me to better things."

"And it's led you to me!" Richard's eyes rested on
her for a long moment. "Was it fate, Rilla?"

"I doubt that very much," she faltered, aware of a
pulse beating in her throat. "Just a lucky chance."

"*How* lucky, we are both about to find out," he said
softly, in that richly resonant voice. "You must have
been told countless times that you're a beautiful
woman."

"On such occasions," she parried lightly, "I've always suspected an ulterior motive."

"Ulterior?" He pondered a second, rubbing his beard. "*Webster's Dictionary* would define it something like this, I guess: a motive not frankly stated. How frank do you like a man to be, Rilla?"

"For heaven's sake," she exclaimed with a shaky laugh, "how in the world did we get into all this? I'm the one supposed to be asking the questions. I came here this evening to *interview* you, remember."

"And I *invited* you because I wanted the pleasure of your company. I'm hoping that it will turn out to be a pleasurable evening for both of us."

The tone of his voice made Rilla shoot him a stony glance. "I hope you don't mean what I think you mean."

"I mean," he said levelly, "that any man who wasn't totally out of his mind would leap at the chance of making love to you."

Rilla felt the hot color of anger flaming her cheeks. "If you're suggesting anything like that as a quid pro quo for granting me an interview, you can damn well think again."

"Such an idea didn't enter my head," Richard protested.

"I'm very relieved to hear it."

"I've never in my life, Rilla, found it necessary to *buy* a woman's favors, whether the payment was in cash or kind. For me sex is something that has to be mutual to be enjoyed." He reached for her empty plate and put it aside with his. "Time for dessert. It's caramelized oranges, I see."

Rilla shook her head. "I'm too full, so I'll have to skip dessert." It wasn't really true, she'd eaten very little, but her stomach nerves were jumping.

"I'm afraid I must insist that you have just a taste, so
as not to upset Birdie." Serving her a small helping, he
went on, "I suggest we have our coffee in the living
room."

"Hadn't we better do something about the dishes?"
Rilla asked, glancing at the disordered table.

Richard shook his head firmly. "There's a proper
time for everything, my dear Rilla, and this most definitely is not the time for washing dishes. Besides,
Birdie wouldn't be any too pleased if she thought her
position was being usurped. She told me the other day
that she likes having a man on his own to pamper, as a
change from catering for the families on vacation that
she usually has staying here."

As they walked back to the living room, Richard carrying a tray bearing the coffee things, Rilla made a conscious effort to shake off the curious, and decidedly
unprofessional, mood she seemed to be gripped by.
Once before, she reminded herself, she had let her professional judgment be clouded by her feelings—with
Theo—and what a disaster that had been. But her response to Theo had been something quite different. He
had deliberately set out to charm her from the start of
her interview, of course, and she—perhaps because she
was feeling so bereft and lonely after Aunt Elly's death—
had been only too eager to respond to his smooth line
of conversation. With Richard Kellerman there was no
question of her subject wanting to please her—far from
it. He resented her trying to interview him and had only
agreed grudgingly. And yet, undeniably, there was still
that subtle current between them. She wished that they
could have met in other circumstances, that he wasn't
the famous Richard Kellerman, and then perhaps...

"Do you take cream and sugar?" he asked, pouring
the coffee.

"Neither, thanks." A cup of good strong coffee, the aroma of which was filling the room, might help clear the slight muzziness in her head.

He handed her the cup. "A liqueur to go with it?"

"No, I'd better not. I've got work to do. Now, can we please talk about your new book, Richard? What's the theme this time?"

"I'm writing a history of California, including the Indians, the early explorers like Drake and Dias, the Spanish occupation, the Russian fur trappers, and the period of Mexican rule. There's a lot of colorful stuff... or does it sound deadly dull to you?"

"Nothing you write could be dull," Rilla burst out enthusiastically. She knew that she was gushing but seemed unable to stop herself. "All those characters in *Flowers of Chivalry*—King Arthur himself and Queen Guinevere, and knights like Lancelot and Galahad and Tristan—they were just names to me before, in the same fairy-tale category as Cinderella, Snow White, and Thumbelina. But you managed to breathe life into them for me."

Richard gave her a long, steady look, a curiously thoughtful expression on his lean face. "I'm beginning to believe that you really have read *Flowers of Chivalry*."

So he still wasn't fully convinced, even then. Rilla's feelings of hurt swelled into anger, and she demanded furiously, "Do you honestly imagine that I'd pretend to have read your book just to get an interview with you?"

"Why not? Journalists have sometimes gone to bizarre lengths to try and get an interview with me. Come to think of it, I've known women who were *not* journalists go to extreme lengths to capture my attention."

"Good grief, you have a mighty high opinion of yourself," Rilla retorted before she could bite back the words.

"It's an opinion forced upon me by the attitude of others," he replied evenly.

"Maybe you mistake their admiration of you as a brilliant writer for their admiration of you as a man," she couldn't resist saying.

"*Touché!* But then, I happen to have amassed considerable evidence that as a man too I am, shall we say, *appreciated* by women."

He really was impossibly conceited. Rilla would dearly have liked to say something to cut him down to size, but that wasn't the way to get the in-depth interview she was so desperately anxious to obtain from him, she reminded herself, clinging to her temper.

"How about some music?" Richard crossed to a stereo unit set against one wall, flicked through a pile of cassettes, and clipped one into position. At once the majestic strains of Wagner filled the room, almost unbearably beautiful, with an underlying throb of passion. Ridiculously Rilla felt tears forming against her eyelids and hastily blinked.

"Do you recognize this?" he asked.

"Yes, it's *Tristan and Isolde*. The prelude to Act Two, I think."

"Very good!" He looked impressed. "Are you an opera fan?"

Rilla scooped back a strand of hair with her little finger. "Not really." In her anger with him, she couldn't bring herself to admit that she'd been so fascinated by the link between Wagner's glorious rendition of *Tristan and Isolde* and the story as related in *Flowers of Chivalry* that she'd attended a performance at the War Memorial Opera House by a British touring company. It had turned out to be an intensely moving experience, and in a curious way it had helped her recover from the trauma of Theo's treachery.

As Rilla recalled her feelings on that momentous evening she felt her anger drain away. She was awesomely conscious of being in the presence of the very man whose book had sparked off her interest in the Tristan and Isolde legend. She felt as if she were losing her grip on reality. The visit with Richard Kellerman seemed to be a strange, unworldly experience, in no way related to her job. Unable to sit still, Rilla rose to her feet and went to the open French doors. It was a really beautiful evening—just such an idyllic summer night as was depicted in Wagner's music—the sky a velvety canopy jeweled with stars. The garden was all tones and degrees of darkness, the trees casting long black shadows, the clumps of white flowers standing out like pale ghosts. There was a rustling sound of roosting birds in the creeper on the wall, and the languid fragrance of honeysuckle drifted on the faint breeze.

Presently she became aware that Richard was standing close behind her. As she felt his breath warm upon her hair a little shiver ran through her.

"That genius Richard Wagner certainly knew what he was about," he remarked. "He pruned away the discreet trimmings given to the Arthurian legends by people like Sir Thomas Malory—and later Lord Tennyson—and got right down to basics. His *Tristan and Isolde* is a story of sheer passion. It's all there in the music, one has only to listen. Can you hear it, feel it now, in the love motif... a promise of ecstatic fulfillment?"

Rilla nodded. She had the strangest sensation, as if she were living the music, as if it had reached into her very soul. On it flowed, swelling in volume as the sensuous theme was developed, and Rilla was transported on a great surging wave of emotion. Almost as though she herself were Isolde, she felt the frantic rapture of the lovers' first embrace, the lyric outpourings of their love duet, the crimson thread of passion that bound them.

The touch of Richard's hand on her bare shoulder came almost as the answer to a crying need within herself. Without hesitating she let him turn her to face him, let his arms enfold her. She could feel his heartbeat pounding against hers, the two throbbing in unison with the passionate beat of the music. For long, bliss-filled moments they stood locked together, their bodies swaying in voluptuous contact that was a sort of half-dance. Rilla was acutely conscious of the hard-muscled power of his male strength, and his fingers moving slowly across her back made her senses swirl with delirious excitement.

The music's insistent throb swelled still higher until she lost her last tenuous grasp on reality and knew only a bewildering joy. She felt suffused by a golden glow of pure sensation, drowning in the exultant rapture of the love duet. She was Isolde and he Tristan, overcome by their longing for each other. She made no resistance, nor even thought of it, when Richard tilted back her head and took possession of her mouth with a hard, demanding urgency that forced a response from her. As her lips softened she felt a sweet tension building within her that burst in a swift rush of desire. Her skin, her entire body, seemed on fire, burning with a need that craved fulfillment. Without conscious volition she pressed herself closer against his lean length, sliding up her arms to clasp her hands behind his neck. And still the crescendo of music climbed from one soaring peak to another until everything seemed lost in a pulsating tumult of emotion....

Suddenly the tempo changed as disaster struck. The lovers had been discovered! Rilla was jolted to her senses with a devastating awareness of what she was doing. She wrenched her lips from his and tried to thrust herself away from him.

"What—what do you think you're playing at?" she stammered, her voice husky as she forced out the words through the tightness of her throat.

"I was playing nothing." Richard's voice was also a trifle shaky. "That was for real—and very enjoyable it was, too."

He was holding her in a steel-strong grip from which Rilla struggled in vain to get free. "Please...let me go!"

"Why," he drawled, "after such a promising beginning?"

"Because I haven't the slightest wish to be kissed by you."

His blue eyes as he looked into hers were dark with mockery. "Nobody would ever have guessed that you were engaged in an activity not to your liking."

"That's totally unfair," she mumbled, trying to escape his penetrating gaze. "You took me by surprise."

"Is that so? From where I'm standing you seemed to respond with great enthusiasm."

"I—I was carried away by the music," she muttered foolishly.

"And what's wrong with that?" he inquired with a bland smile. "I'm a great believer in having the right setting for lovemaking. Music...the fragrant darkness of a lovely summer evening...it puts one in a suitably romantic mood."

"That's not what I meant at all." Still trembling

from the emotional impact of his kiss, Rilla felt astonished at herself. She must have been out of her mind to
fall into such an obvious trap.

"So what *did* you mean?"

"Well...the music is so fine and inspiring," she
floundered. "So rich in intricate harmonies, so noble
and—"

"Wagner isn't intended to be intellectually ana-
lyzed," he cut in softly. "His music is meant to be *felt*.
It stirs the very depths of one's soul, which is nothing
to be ashamed of. Just remember this, beautiful Rilla
Yorke: The greatest music in the world cannot release
emotions that don't already exist. You *wanted* me to
kiss you just now, and it's pointless for you to deny it.
All that the Tristan music did was to put you in a mood
to let your emotions take control. Without it we'd have
had to go through the tedious flirtation preliminaries,
two steps forward and one step back, and that's just a
waste of time. But Wagner and his fantastic music
turned a key that allowed you to be honest about your
feelings, as few women can be. It allowed you to admit
that you're as attracted to me as I am to you. That you
want me tonight just as much as I want you."

No way would she let him get away with that. Lifting
her chin, she said haughtily, "I came here this evening
for one purpose and one purpose only: to get an interview with you."

"And solely to that end you put on the sexiest, most
alluring dress you possess?"

"I did nothing of the sort," she denied.

Richard gave a low, intrigued wolf whistle. "Does
that mean you have some even sexier dresses at home?
If so, I'd love to see you in them. But this one is good
enough to be going on with. The designer undoubtedly
knew how to reveal every luscious curve of the female

body and set a man's imagination blazing. Don't pretend, Rilla, that you weren't aware of that fact."

"It—it's just an ordinary party dress," she said defensively.

"Interesting parties *you* must go to!"

Rilla stared at him defiantly. "You seem to think it's a crime for a woman to wear clothes that suit her."

"A crime," he agreed, "for which she must expect to pay the penalty." He laughed softly, deep in his throat. "And the delightful thing is that it's not a penalty at all, because it's exactly what the woman wants to happen."

"If you imagine that I came here this evening wanting you to kiss me, you couldn't be more wrong," she said furiously. Behind them, the cassette ran out and there was silence. But the throbbing rhythm seemed to persist in her head, and Rilla realized that it was the pounding beat of her pulses. She felt quite dizzy and light-headed.

"How about us conducting a little experiment, now that the music has stopped?" Richard suggested lazily. "According to your line of argument, you'll be totally immune to me without the distraction of Wagner's noble music. So let's see."

Before Rilla had time to gauge his intention he had caught her again in the circle of his arms, and his demanding lips found hers once more. In desperation she tried to turn her face away, tried to push herself back from him, but Richard's hold on her tightened, and she couldn't break free. Pressed close against his lean, virile body, she was acutely aware of his quickening desire. Rilla felt a bitter, raging anger, as much against herself as against him, because she couldn't check the treacherous responses of her own body. As his hands slid slowly down her back they left a tingling trail of fire, and she could feel her resistance melting away in the heat of sensual excitement. Against her will, she let out a low moan of delight.

Richard's fingers clenched into the soft flesh of her buttocks, pulling her more intimately against his loins, and Rilla felt hot darts of excitement shoot through her. As the kiss deepened the tip of his tongue thrust in between her lips to taste her sweetness, and she was swamped by a flood of erotic sensation. When he drew back to take breath his hands once more began a roving exploration of her body, shaping the curve of her hips, the slenderness of her waist, rising higher to encompass the soft swell of her breasts while his lips moved with tiny nibbling kisses around the delicate line of her jaw to the petal-soft lobe of her ear, which he nipped teasingly between his teeth.

And then suddenly, startlingly, Richard released her and took a step backward, so that Rilla stumbled and almost fell. She saw his face, as if through a swirling mist, twisted in triumphant mockery.

"You see, my dear Rilla, it wasn't really the music after all."

Her throat felt tight and dry and she could hardly force out the words. "You really are despicable."

"Why should you think that?" he asked, his vivid blue eyes deriding her. "I'm doing you a favor by helping you to understand what a deeply sensuous woman you are. You've proved to be every bit as soft and pliant and eager as any man could possibly wish for."

Rilla took a deep, steadying breath. "It was despicable of you to take advantage of my momentary weakness."

"But it's your strength, not your weakness," he insisted. "You should glory in the possession of such vibrant sensuality."

"Glory in allowing myself to respond to—to cheap seductive trickery? No, I'm ashamed. And so should you be, if you had a grain of decency in your makeup. You assured me while we were having dinner that you didn't expect anything from me in return for granting me an interview."

"So I did," he agreed. "But *expect* is the operative word. I certainly wouldn't expect you to let me make love to you against your will, my dear Rilla. But it's obvious that you enjoyed kissing me just now every bit as much as I enjoyed kissing you." His eyes flashed with contempt. "I was beginning to admire you for being a woman who could be honest and frank about her sexual urges, but I find that I was sadly mistaken. You threw yourself at me, you flaunted your body, and now you dare to pretend that I took advantage of you. But it's a line that doesn't fool either of us. We both know that there's nothing you'd like more than for me to carry you off to my bedroom this very minute and make love to you passionately."

Her face flaming with anger and humiliation, Rilla crossed the room on unsteady legs and snatched up her purse. "I'm not stopping to hear any more of this," she stormed. "I'm leaving right now."

"Aren't you forgetting what you came for?" he asked sarcastically. "I thought you wanted to find out exactly what it is that makes Richard Kellerman tick."

"I already know that," she retorted, regarding him with loathing. "It's become disgustingly clear."

He took a quick step toward her and said in a menacing tone, "If you're foolish enough to put into print what's passing through your head at this moment, that little local rag of yours might find itself faced with an expensive libel suit."

Rilla was about to fling back at him scornfully that he

wasn't worth a single inch of typewriter ribbon when she froze the retort on the tip of her tongue. How would she explain things to her editor if she returned without any usable copy? Bill would wish that he'd assigned the job to Hank, after all, and her glorious dream of overnight fame as a journalist would be wafted away on an off-shore breeze.

In a voice that still trembled, she said defensively, "If you'd been willing to provide me with some straight answers, Mr. Kellerman, and some serious comments about yourself and your work, I could have written the sort of article you'd be pleased with."

"Then hadn't you better sit down again and fire away with your questions? You won't get anywhere standing there like a scared rabbit."

Rilla hesitated. She wanted to storm out of his house, but it was no time for hurt pride. "Will you promise me," she said with cool dignity, "that you— well, that you won't make another pass?"

"You can rest assured," he returned, "that you're totally safe. After that display of shrewish indignation, I'd just as soon try making love to a marble statue."

His tone was so chilling that Rilla felt an icy shiver grip her. "There's no need to be so unpleasant about it."

Richard threw back his head and gave a short, mirthless laugh. "I'll grant you this, Rilla Yorke, you're a true woman in one regard. You expect to have your cake and eat it, too."

"I don't know what you mean."

"So I'll spell it out for you." He came closer, his deep blue eyes turned hard as flints. "You deliberately excite a man into desiring your beautiful, sexy body, then coyly sidestep and demand that he keep his hands to himself. In other words, you offer enticing terms but don't deliver. You're neither being honest with yourself nor with me."

"You're crazy if you imagine for one moment that I'd offer to sleep with a man to get a good story—or even pretend to offer it," she stormed. "That's not the way professional women do their jobs."

"You don't lie and cheat to get what you want?" he inquired in a silky voice.

"I most certainly do not."

"Then it seems that I owe you an apology, Miss Yorke," he said sarcastically. "I had a clear impression that when you called here yesterday morning it was in the guise of a devoted admirer who wanted nothing more from me than my autograph...and a bit of a chat, as you so disarmingly put it."

Rilla flushed deep red. "You only have yourself to blame for that small deception. With the reputation you've gained for being so difficult to interview, it seemed to be the only hope of getting in to see you."

"Which in your eyes excuses everything, I suppose?" He heaved a despairing sigh, shaking his head at her. "You journalists have the strangest ideas about ethics."

"I freely admitted the truth when you challenged me," Rilla persisted. "And, anyway, it was a hundred percent true about me being a fan of yours."

"But this, presumably, no longer applies?"

Rilla drew herself up to her full five feet five and looked back at him coolly. "I thought I'd made it clear already that one doesn't necessarily have to like a man personally to admire him as an author."

"Neither, it seems, do you need to like a man to find him intensely attractive physically."

"I don't find you intensely attractive," she countered furiously.

"No? Would you sooner have me think that you'd

respond in precisely the same way to any man who takes you in his arms?'' he mocked and took a threatening step toward her. As Rilla backed off in alarm he laughed unpleasantly. "You're still like a cat on a hot tin roof, aren't you?''

"Because I don't trust you," she muttered.

"But why in the blazes should I be trusted?'' Richard demanded irritably. "I'm a normal, sexually active male. And when a woman accepts an invitation to dine at my home tête-à-tête and arrives wearing a flagrantly seductive dress—''

"Why do you keep saying that?'' Rilla flared. "I've already told you, it wasn't like that at all.''

He looked deep into her eyes. "Do you seriously expect me to believe that you just grabbed the first dress in your closet to wear tonight, without giving the matter a great deal of careful consideration?''

"I dressed for the evening in a perfectly normal way,'' she averred.

"You mean this is the kind of thing you wear every evening?''

"Of course not. But if I'm going out for dinner, or something...''

"... you take pains to make an impact?'' he suggested lazily.

Rilla tried to meet the challenge of his intent gaze, but she was forced to glance away. "Is there anything so terrible about that?''

She hated the wretched dress then and doubted if she'd ever wear it again. Why hadn't she thought to put on something less revealing and more businesslike? As it was she had given the hateful man the opportunity to make fun of her. What would it have mattered if Richard Kellerman had thought her rather plain and unattractive... even a bit dull? All to the good if he had, for then she might have succeeded better in the job she'd gone there to do.

He was watching her in silence, a strange expression in his vivid blue eyes. She wished she could guess what was going through his mind.

"Hadn't we better get on with it, then?" he said, suddenly becoming abrupt.

"Get—get on with it?" she queried, taken by surprise.

"The interview. That's what you came for. I'll answer your questions to the best of my ability, and then you can scuttle off home out of harm's way."

Richard Kellerman was offering her exactly what she wanted—what many top journalists would wrestle in mud for—yet Rilla felt no sense of triumph. For long moments she looked back at him unhappily, aware that her courage was eroding under his steely gaze. Then giving herself a little shake, she picked up her shorthand notebook once more and said with a gulpy breath, "Perhaps—perhaps we could start by you telling me what first made you interested in the legends of King Arthur and his Knights of the Round Table."

In the next half hour he answered the questions she put to him, seeming to respond readily enough, yet Rilla was uneasily aware that everything he said was on a superficial level. By no means was it the in-depth interview that she had been hoping for. She could form no rounded picture of the distinguished author and what made him function, but only an impression of a cold, remote man with such arrogant self-assurance that he cared nothing for public approval. He repeatedly said that his work had to stand for itself—that it must be judged entirely upon its intrinsic merits. Eventually, with a sigh, Rilla shut her notebook and announced that she was through.

"You have all the information you want?" he asked with a sardonic lift of his eyebrows.

"No way!" she retorted. "But it's plainly all I'm going to get."

Throughout the interview Richard had been pacing the room restlessly. Then he halted beside the carved fireplace and stood with one elbow on the mantelpiece, regarding Rilla with narrowed eyes.

"What more did you imagine you would get from me?" he asked.

"That's precisely what I don't know. It's obvious to me that you've been holding back something of your true self."

He laughed once more without humor. "If so, that's no more than you deserve. Earlier on you were holding back something of your real self. You should have loosened up and let go, Rilla, and then...not only would we have shared a truly memorable evening, but you would have gained a deeper insight into the real Richard Kellerman for your article."

Rilla caught her breath, but she managed to restrain an outburst of anger. "You'd have to be a great deal more important than you are," she said with biting sarcasm, "to make that sort of exercise worth my while."

He inclined his head mockingly. "So, contrary to what you stated so emphatically just now, you have no aversion in principle to sleeping with a man in order to obtain a good story—as long as his publicity potential is high enough?"

"I meant nothing of the kind," said Rilla through gritted teeth. She might have guessed he would seize on a carelessly phrased remark like that.

"In that case, I feel I should point out to you that for someone who professes to be fascinated with words, you fail lamentably to make yourself clear."

She jumped to her feet and faced him squarely. "Then I'll make myself crystal clear now, Mr. Kellerman. You're the last man in the world I would ever consider going to bed with. Is that plain enough for you? Even if we were stranded together for years on a desert island, I just wouldn't be interested."

The taunting smile remained on his face as he drawled, "Why fight it, Rilla?"

"What's that remark supposed to mean?" she demanded, her green-gold eyes flashing.

With an unhurried, negligent movement he slid his elbow off the mantelpiece and took a step in her direction, making Rilla flinch inwardly, though she managed to stand her ground. "If I hadn't received direct evidence to the contrary, I might be fooled by your display of wounded professional pride. But I only have to think back to those moments when I held you in my arms and you were reacting in a totally different way."

As Rilla started to protest he went on. "Do you think it's unchivalrous of me to throw that in your face? But the days of chivalry belong to history, my dear girl. Therefore I haven't the least qualm about reminding you that for a few exciting moments this evening you dropped your guard and let me glimpse your true nature. And a wonderfully warm, passionate nature it is, too. If you want my advice, Rilla, in future you should follow where your instincts lead you. You're making a big mistake acting the narrow-minded prude."

"I can do without social advice from you, thanks. You're just trying to insult me because your nasty little plan has backfired on you. You'd got it all worked out, hadn't you, down to the last detail: tempting me here this evening by promising me an interview, maneuvering things so that we'd be alone in the house, softening me up with an excellent dinner and plenty of wine, and then expecting me to fall swooning into your arms. But I've got news for you, Mr. Richard Kellerman. You're not so almighty attractive to women as you imagine. There might be a few misguided females who would go for your line of charm—"

"A seemingly inexhaustible supply of them," he amended.

Rilla regarded him with icy disfavor. "I've never before met a man as insufferably big-headed as you are."

"I've told you no more than the plain, unexaggerated truth! It may be, as you suggest, Rilla, that such women *are* misguided. It may be that they actually see *themselves* as victor for having briefly ensnared me. The fact that in reality I'm not in the least ensnared hardly matters. It's all part of the eternal game between the sexes."

"So you admit that it's all just a game to you," she cried. "An amusing pastime, without any thought of commitment."

"Commitment!" he scoffed. "Heaven forbid! My commitment is to my writing, and that's quite enough for me."

Rilla knew that it would have been better to terminate the argument right then, just bid him good night and leave the house with dignity, but something held her there. It was a foolish urge to prick the bubble of his massive conceit.

"What an arid future yours will be," she said scornfully, "in which there is no place for—for—" But when she got to it, the word was choked back in her throat.

He waited a moment, then asked with compelling insistence, "No place for what, Rilla?"

"For love!" she threw at him defiantly. "That emotion you write about with such feeling, with such apparent sincerity. No one reading *Flowers of Chivalry* would ever believe that the author could hold such a cold, dispassionate view of the man-and-woman relationship. Your account of the Tristan and Isolde legend is one of the most moving love stories I have ever read."

"It's an account of a *passionate* relationship," he tossed back at her. "As in Wagner's operatic version, I wrote of high passion. But as for wishy-washy romance...neither Richard Wagner nor I had, or have, any time for that." He paused, and the expression in his eyes turned to scorn. "But, of course, for someone who's afraid of passion—"

"I'm not afraid of passion," she denied. "But passion without love and deep commitment...is nothing."

"How can you possibly claim that," he demanded, "when you've never once in your life experienced the heights of passion you're obviously capable of reaching—whether or not you imagined yourself to have fallen in love? I'm right, aren't I, Rilla?"

She couldn't meet his hard challenging gaze and glanced away nervously. Had she felt real love for Theo? Had she experienced true passion with him? At the time of their involvement she would have answered a firm yes to both those questions. But now she no longer felt so sure. It was as if she'd all at once glimpsed a new and wonderful world in which love and passion were elevated to a much higher plane than anything she had ever known with Theo.

"You've no cause to say that," she muttered, still unable to look at Richard. "You hardly even know me."

"Correction!" he drawled. "I know a great deal about you, Rilla Yorke. Far more than you imagine you've told me about yourself."

She threw him a scathing glance. "Maybe you've

been living too long in the world of your imagination. It's given you the idea that you have special insight. I repeat, you hardly know me."

"You think not? Let me tell you what I know about you, Rilla. This dedication you pretend for your work, it's a mask you wear to protect yourself from the fear of being hurt. Perhaps," he added, his blue eyes narrowing shrewdly, "you have been badly hurt, and you're still running away. But you've got to stop running and face up to life. Face up to your own nature. You're a mature woman, with an exquisite body that's crying out to be set alight and brought to magnificent, passionate fulfillment. So grow up! Grow up and start to live."

Rilla took a step backward to put a greater distance between them. She felt curiously afraid—afraid of her own emotions. Despite her utter contempt for Richard Kellerman and his attitude toward life and love, she was overwhelmingly attracted to him. She couldn't prevent herself from wondering what it would be like to surrender to his lovemaking and be swept away on a great tidal wave of sensual excitement.

As a defense against such dangerous thoughts, she sprang to the attack. "I guess you call it living to—to give way to every slightest impulse? To snatch a cheap sexual thrill from a person with whom you have nothing else in common? If that's your idea of growing up, Mr. Kellerman, then I'd rather retain a few of my youthful ideals, thank you very much."

Richard challenged her. "If you had heeded the clamoring demands of your senses this evening, Rilla, if you'd had the courage to follow your instincts, you wouldn't be talking this way now. You'd be on the brink of the most wonderful night of your life."

"My God! You have a mighty big opinion of yourself," she gasped and cursed the thickness in her throat that was making her voice sound husky.

"I can recognize a plain fact when I see it."

"Me, too. I've recognized a couple of plain facts about you this evening."

His eyes flickered with a burning light. "Glad to hear it! That must mean that you've gotten what you came for. And if, in the process, you didn't deliver what I expected... well, the laugh's on me! But it's your life you're wasting, Rilla, not mine. As far as I'm concerned, it's a very temporary disappointment."

"I thought you told me that you expected nothing," Rilla said, unable to resist the opportunity to hit back at him.

"And neither did I—not in the sense of any automatic payment for granting you an interview."

"I guess you thought that once I was here I wouldn't be able to resist you," she flared. When Richard made no reply to that charge, she went on miserably, "I accepted your invitation to dinner, thinking that you wanted to prove to yourself that I really was a fan of yours and that I had read your book, just as I claimed."

He swung back to face her, withering her with scorn. "You imagine that it was important to me? My dear girl, if I'd wanted to get to the truth of the matter, a few shrewd questions would have done it. I could easily have established whether or not you were a fraud within a couple of minutes."

"So why didn't you?" she asked in a tiny voice.

"Because I preferred to leave the matter in doubt. It seemed more amusing that way. But now I no longer care one way or the other. So just go away and write your wretched little article."

"Does that mean that I'm free to write the truth about the sort of man you are?" Rilla demanded, crushing down her pain at having her illusions so badly shattered.

"The truth!" he sneered. "You wouldn't recognize the truth if it came with a sworn affidavit. You prefer to make do with fairy tales. Only, I warn you, don't try turning me into a prince charming."

"There's no fear of that," she said, laughing.

"No, I guess not!" He seemed to find the thought amusing. "Well, don't let me detain you, Miss Yorke."

Rilla felt furious with herself for allowing Richard Kellerman to dismiss her instead of walking out on him while she had had the chance. It was too late to salvage her pride, and saying anything more would only add to his victory. So, with a frosty nod, she picked up her purse and headed for the door.

"Hang on a minute before you go."

Rilla paused with her fingers on the doorknob, not turning her head. Was he about to apologize? She heard a faint scribbling sound, then he was coming toward her.

"You musn't leave without this," he said conversationally. "I'm sure that you'd hate to have to call back for it."

She turned slowly and found that he was holding out to her the tattered paperback copy of *Flowers of Chivalry*.

"I've autographed it for you," he said.

Rilla's hand trembled as she took the book. "You needn't have bothered," she mumbled in a strangely husky voice.

"But I always like to keep my promises. And who knows, the signature of the author might add a few cents to the resale price when you get around to disposing of it."

Rilla bit back a retort, refusing to bandy words with

him anymore. She pulled open the door and left the room on shaky legs. Richard followed her across the hall, reaching the front door first and holding it open for her.

"Good night," he said. "Sleep well. I hope you don't have troubled dreams."

"Good night, Mr. Kellerman," she gritted.

Not until she was well away from the house did Rilla stop to see what he had written. At the Sausalito waterfront she drew the car into a wide parking lot facing the bay, from where she could see the glittering lights of San Francisco across the stretch of dark water. Flicking on the car's interior light, she picked up the book from the seat beside her and opened it nervously.

His handwriting on the flyleaf was bold and black and fluent, and there seemed to be a jibe in every word. "To Rilla Yorke...would-be ace journalist. Perhaps when rereading this book with an acuter eye, she'll discover a few truths about life and love...and about herself. If so, the disappointing evening at Sausalito won't have been altogether wasted."

Rilla sat there, her slender shoulders hunched in misery, unconscious of the passing of time. A man halted on his way past and peered in at her hopefully; then, seeing the grim expression on Rilla's face he shrugged and went on. It was quite a while before she pulled herself together and started the car. Driving back across the Golden Gate Bridge, she kept having to blink away the stinging tears that blurred her vision.

Chapter Four

Rilla's diary was luckily clear of any fixed appointments on Monday, so she called the *BAAR* office to say that she'd be working at home. Sitting at her typewriter, the anger and bitterness that had racked her all the previous night long came spilling out in a flood of words. The first draft was a hopeless mess. Normally, as she'd been taught in her journalism classes, she didn't reckon to do a complete rewrite of her articles. But that one she worked over and over, revising and toning it down until, late in the afternoon, she had produced fifteen hundred crisp and pointed words.

Tuesday morning she laid the typed pages on the editor's desk while he was talking on the phone, then retired to her corner of the outer office, where she nervously awaited his verdict. Ten minutes later Bill Andersen bellowed for her, and she went through to his den with her heart thudding.

He waved Rilla to a chair, beaming with unconcealed delight. "This is hot stuff." He leaned back in his swivel seat, which creaked protestingly under his vast weight. "One gathers that you didn't find your subject a very likable character."

"You can say that again, Bill. The guy is just about the pits. He's a bighead with an oversized ego."

Hank stuck his head around the door. "So what's all the excitement about?"

The editor chuckled. "Rilla's piece about Kellerman. It's juicy! Listen to this, Hank. 'The most striking thing about Richard Kellerman is his genius. A close second, in an almost photo finish, comes his massive conceit. His erudition is impressive, the vocabulary at his command wide-ranging and powerful. How strange, therefore, that it should lack a few of the simpler abstract nouns like modesty and humility.'"

"I like it!" Hank laughed. He went behind Bill's chair to read over his shoulder. "Hey, how about this? 'The world owes a great debt to Richard Kellerman for producing a literary masterpiece in *Flowers of Chivalry,* which will doubtless be matched and possibly even excelled by his forthcoming history of California. He claims that his work must be judged entirely on its own merits, without benefit of personal publicity. An unusual philosophy in a best-selling author, but in his case one wholly to be applauded, since it spares his numerous admirers the need to suffer his overbearing personality.' You've really gone to town with this one, Rilla. I couldn't have done better myself."

She gave both men a doubtful look. "You don't think that perhaps I've laid it on a bit too thick? I could always tone it down somewhat."

"Not on your sweet life," said Bill, slapping his large hand protectively over the typewritten pages. "We don't get nearly enough good, abrasive journalism these days. This piece of yours is going to be printed exactly as it stands. It's sensational."

On Friday, when the *BAAR* came out, Rilla was delighted to see that Bill had given her story prime position on page three, the spot usually reserved for his own main article. Posters had been distributed to the

newsstands, carrying the message EXCLUSIVE INTERVIEW
WITH BEST SELLING AUTHOR. Friday night, although the
week's advertising revenue didn't really justify the expense, the *BAAR* staff celebrated by going to Lord
Jim's on Broadway and sipping generous-size drinks in
an atmosphere of Victorian splendor. When Steve
asked to date her some time during the weekend, Rilla
gave him a curt no, too distracted to wrap her refusal
in soft words.

Saturday morning she was out covering rehearsals of
a Cole Porter revival at a theater on Geary, which
promised to be a big hit, but the afternoon she had free
and she stayed home to catch up on her chores. She
was on edge the whole time, waiting for the phone to
ring, expecting a blast of fury from Richard Kellerman.
He must have read her profile of him by then, and her
number was listed. He might already, she thought with
a sick pang, be venting his anger in the form of an offi-
cial complaint to *BAAR*'s editor. But if so, Bill would
surely call her right away. If only she knew...some-
thing!

Saturday night was overcast and sultry, a thick, dank
mist shrouding the bay. Rilla awoke Sunday morning
feeling depressed. She made coffee and sat over it at
the kitchen counter with the Sunday papers, but she
hardly took anything in. It hit her suddenly that she
simply couldn't endure the prospect of another day
spent in such a state of nervous tension. There was
only one thing to be done. She must drive over to
Sausalito and confront the man—throw down her challenge face to face. "I thought it only fair, Mr. Kellerman," she could say, "to bring you a copy of the
Reporter so you can see what I wrote about you." Yes,
that would be her line of approach.

A drizzly summer rain was falling when she set out,

the windshield wipers making a monotonous, whining background to her anxious thoughts. All the other drivers seemed short-tempered and careless, and entering the tunnel after leaving the Golden Gate Bridge she all but hit the Oldsmobile in front of her when it braked sharply.

When she reached Casa del Sol it looked far less attractive than on her two previous visits, with daggers of rain falling from the veranda roof. For a few nail-biting moments Rilla remained sitting behind the wheel of her Honda, gathering herself together. Then with swift decisiveness she slid out of the car and walked briskly to the front door, the heels of her sandals tapping on the veranda's wood-block floor. From inside she could detect the faint hum of a vacuum cleaner. She tugged the bellpull and waited, her stomach fluttering. After a short delay the door was opened, and Birdie's brightly inquiring face peered out.

"Oh, it's you again, Miss Yorke. I figured it couldn't be the man from Vacation Dream Homes, not on a Sunday."

"Is Mr. Kellerman home?" Rilla asked in a tense voice.

"Why, no. I thought you would've known."

"Known what?"

"That Mr. Kellerman's gone, miss. Something urgent cropped up, he said, and he had to leave in a hurry. Friday, it was. He was packed and away in a couple of hours."

Cold fingers of dismay clawed at Rilla's heart. "He'll be coming back, though?"

"No, he won't. He said it wasn't worth it for the short time left that he'd leased the house. He just upped and went, leaving a message for the rental agency to send the bills on. That's who I thought you were at first, till I remembered that it's Sunday... someone come to do the inventory and check for breakages and so on. I'm more'n sorry to see him go, I don't mind telling you. A real considerate tenant was Mr. Kellerman, and he gave me a nice big tip when he left. Very generous of him!''

This totally unexpected news left Rilla feeling shocked and dazed. Birdie regarded her with concern.

"You've gone quite pale, dear. Now, why don't you come along in and have a cup of coffee? It won't take me a minute to make some, and I could do with a little break myself. My husband's gone to see a basketball game, so I'm on my own."

"Thank you."

Birdie led Rilla through to the large gleaming modern kitchen. "Sit yourself down and get comfortable," she invited, indicating the red padded seats of the breakfast bay.

"Thank you," said Rilla again. "Birdie, where has Mr. Kellerman gone? Do you happen to know?"

"Sorry, he didn't say. Do you want to get in touch with him for something? I expect you could find out his address from Vacation Dream Homes. I'll give you their number, if you like."

"No, it's nothing important," Rilla said with a shrug, desperately trying to hide her disappointment.

A large mug of coffee was set down in front of her, together with a wedge of pecan pie, rich with nuts and syrup, the pastry beautifully short and crumbly.

"My own baking," said Birdie, "along with a load of brownies and blueberry muffins and goodness knows what else. And now he's not here to eat them up. Ah, well, it's lucky my Tom is partial to sweets. Is your coffee okay, Miss Yorke?"

"Yes, it's fine, thanks. And this pecan pie is just

dreamy," she added, picking up the odd crumbs with the moistened tip of her finger.

When Rilla drove off some thirty minutes later, she felt guilty about the way she had accepted Birdie's hospitality and encouraged her to chatter away about Richard, having learned, among other things, that he was fanatic about not having a single item on his desk disturbed, and also that he was especially fond of strawberry shortcake. The little woman had been so friendly and pleasant, and Rilla hoped to heaven that she'd never get around to reading the blistering article in *BAAR*. She'd feel betrayed, thinking that Rilla had bluffed her way into Casa del Sol the previous week on the pretext of being a devoted fan of Richard Kellerman's. No way would Birdie ever believe that it had been for the most part true.

Rilla wasn't sure why she had accepted Birdie's invitation to go in for a cup of coffee. It had just seemed a tenuous sort of link with Richard. But that was crazy, she told herself angrily as she stopped at the toll point on the city side of the Golden Gate Bridge. Richard Kellerman was the last man on earth with whom she wanted any further contact.

During the following few days Rilla was unable to shake off a heavy mood of depression. When Steve renewed his attempts to date her and she again turned him down flat, she wondered if she wasn't being stupid. And yet, somehow, she just couldn't imagine an evening out with Steve—or with any other man—amounting to anything but sheer boredom.

Around noon on Wednesday there was a call for her that finally shook Richard from the forefront of her mind and sent her thoughts spinning in a totally new direction. The caller announced himself as Martin Whitehead, the literary editor of the *New York Globe*.

"I want to talk to you about that piece you did on Richard Kellerman," he said in a brisk voice.

"Oh, yes?" Rilla felt a shiver of apprehension, wondering what was coming.

"I liked it," stated Martin Whitehead to her astonished relief. "You don't pull your punches, Miss Yorke. I was wondering if you'd like to have a stab at something similar for me."

"You mean," she gasped breathlessly, "that you want me to do a piece for the *Globe*?"

"Right! There are several rather prickly authors who might respond to your line of approach. It's worth a try."

"Have you anyone special in mind, Mr. Whitehead?" she asked with a quick bubble of excitement.

"Well...I'm going to suggest a really tough one for starters, just to test you, Miss Yorke. If you can come up with a good profile, then who knows what might develop."

"Great!" said Rilla, injecting confidence into her voice, though she felt a flurry of nerves at the thought of writing for a famous New York newspaper. It was a tremendous challenge. "Who is it you want me to interview?"

"You've heard of Jake Carson?"

"The thriller writer? Yes, of course, though I have to admit that I've not read any of his books."

He chuckled. "I guess you can soon put that right. I'll pay you the usual rate, Miss Yorke, plus any reasonable expenses you incur. But the operative word is *reasonable*."

"That's quite understood." The financial details were the last consideration in Rilla's mind. "Er...can you give me Jake Carson's address?"

"He lives here in New York, in a co-op apartment on Park Avenue. You'll find him in the book. He's already half promised me an interview sometime, so you'll have to hold him to it. One other thing, Miss Yorke. You haven't got too long to do this piece. I want it for my fall books supplement, and I'll need to have your copy by mid-July. Two thousand words.''

Mid-July seemed weeks and weeks away. "No problem,'' she said airily, trying to sound blasé as if it were nothing unusual for her to get commissioned by one of the nation's most influential newspapers.

Her exciting news undoubtedly impressed the others on the *Reporter*. Hank was green with envy, while Bill Andersen beamed his pleasure for her.

"My dear Rilla, I always knew you were destined for the big time," he said. "You must grab this opportunity with both hands.''

Rilla found Jake Carson listed in the Manhattan directory, but when she called, there was no answer. It was the same half an hour later, and again in the evening when she tried a couple of more times from home. She gave up when the zonal difference would have made it nearly midnight in New York. She spent a restless night, too keyed up with excitement to settle down to sleep. In the morning at the office she made two more attempts, still with no luck. It struck her that as Jake Carson lived in a smart co-op apartment building, there was sure to be a superintendent she could talk to. Consulting the directory again, she soon had his number.

"Superintendent's office," answered a gruff male voice.

"I was wondering if you could possibly help me," Rilla began in a brightly coaxing tone. "I've been trying to contact Mr. Carson in Apartment 12D, but I'm getting no reply. Can you suggest the best time for me to catch him at home?''

"You won't do that, miss, not until the fall now. Mr. Carson's at his villa in the South of France for the summer."

Rilla's heart plummeted, all her high hopes dashed to the ground. "You're positive about that, are you? He won't be coming back until fall?"

"Not till September, miss. Or October. Who's this speaking?"

"Oh, you won't know me. My name's Rilla Yorke, and it's in connection with a press interview."

"Why don't you write to him?" the man suggested. "Any letters that arrive here are forwarded on."

It all seemed so hopeless, with a copy date fixed at mid-July, but some inner prompting made Rilla ask, "Could you give me his address in France?"

"I'm not sure I ought to do that," the superintendent responded doubtfully.

"Please!" she wheedled. "It's terribly important, honestly. It'll be perfectly okay—I mean," she elaborated, juggling a little with the truth, "it's to do with an article about Mr. Carson that's going to be published in the *New York Globe*. I just have to get in touch with him at once, you see, to check out a few points. I'm certain he won't mind you telling me, because it's in his own interest to make sure I get my facts straight."

The superintendent hemmed and hawed for a few moments, then gave in. "Well, I reckon it can't do any harm. Just hang on a minute, miss, while I look it up." There was a long wait, then he announced, "His place is called Villa Ambrosia, and the address I've got written here is Chabroux"—he spelled it out—"near Nice, France."

"Thanks a million," Rilla said, scribbling it down triumphantly.

Within minutes she was despondent once more. She

could hardly conduct the sort of interview she needed with Jake Carson either by correspondence or over the transatlantic phone. She would have to report back to the literary editor of the *Globe* and ask if he would nominate some other author she could interview instead. But wouldn't that be too feeble, an admission of failure from the start? What she needed to do was to show Martin Whitehead that she had lots of initiative and get-up-and-go.

A bold thought came darting into her head. Why not fly to the South of France and interview Jake Carson there, at his villa? No, it was a crazy idea! How could she find the time, let alone the money? One thing she was sure of... "reasonable" expenses wouldn't include the air fare from California to the French Riviera.

The answers came into her head inexorably. Getting time off work was no problem. Under the circumstances Bill Andersen would unquestionably agree to her taking her two-week summer vacation at short notice. And as for money, there was a small amount from Aunt Elly stashed in her bank account, awaiting an emergency. And this was it! Rilla could almost hear her aunt's voice encouraging her, prodding her into action. *"Nothing ventured, nothing gained, Rilla. That's what you must remember, honey."*

Within less than an hour all her plans were made. Bill Andersen gave her some fatherly advice on thinking twice before she risked her nest egg on something so chancy, but Rilla could tell that in reality he was almost as excited as she was about her plan, and he shooed her away with his blessing. Steve, unsurprisingly, thought it was a crazy stunt, while Hank couldn't conceal his envy and predicted likely disaster. "Good luck, Rilla," he muttered gloomily. "You'll need it, I reckon."

Rilla called the local travel agent to make a plane reservation for Nice the following day. She checked through her desk diary and passed over essential matters to Hank to deal with, including the feature on the new studio theater due to open on Geary that she'd not yet gotten around to in such a busy week. Then she waved them all good-bye and left.

On her way home she stopped at her favorite boutique on Columbus Avenue to pick up a couple of new things to take with her on the trip. Right next door was a bookstore, and thankfully she was able to purchase Jake Carson's last two titles, *The Gemini Game* and *Exit from Berlin*.

She had a busy evening getting everything ready and tidying up the house, and arranging for her next-door neighbor, Vinny Schofield, to water her indoor plants and generally keep an eye on the place. When she finally went to bed, she took *The Gemini Game* with her. The main character was too tough and macho for Rilla's taste, though the book was redeemed for her by sensitivity in the writing, with a fast and fluent style that was easy to read. It was very understandable that Jake Carson was such a popular author.

The bay glittered silver-blue in the morning sunshine as the plane lifted off the runway at San Francisco International Airport. Rilla had never been to Europe before, so it was a special thrill. But she had work to do, another long Jake Carson novel to be absorbed. She turned back the cover of *Exit from Berlin* and began to read. The drink trolley came and went unheeded. Even the lunch service caught her unprepared.

"Shall I let down the table for you?" a deep voice questioned.

She gazed in surprise at the man who'd moved into the empty seat beside her, unaware that he'd been eye-

ing her interestedly for some while from a few rows
back.

"Oh, yes, er...thanks."

He leaned across to do it. "And where are you heading for?"

"Paris on this plane. Then I'm going on to Nice."

"Very nice, too!" He winked at her, laughing. "Get
it? Nice is very nice!" He was over forty, overfleshy—
and overpushy, by the look of it. Not relishing him as
her companion for the next few hours, Rilla decided to
play it cool and merely gave him a faint smile in response.

The man reached over to turn back the cover of the
paperback in her hand and studied the garish yellow-
and-black illustration. "Jake Carson! Not what I'd
think of as a woman's book. Do you like his stuff?"

Rilla felt tempted to spill out the incredible story of
her upcoming interview with Jake Carson, but a man
like that would probably seize on it as an opening. "He
writes well," she said offhandedly.

"They've filmed several of his books, haven't they?
I saw one on my last transatlantic flight. First-rate en-
tertainment. It sure helped to pass the time along. I'm
in plastics, by the way—the name's Joe Behrman."

The arrival of their lunch trays saved Rilla the need
to give her name. She pointedly kept reading while she
ate her rice, salad, and creamed chicken, and after one
or two abortive attempts to get her talking, Joe Behrman gave up and turned to talk to the man sitting
across the aisle.

There was a wait at Charles de Gaulle Airport in
Paris for the domestic flight to Nice. It was early morning there, and over the Atlantic passengers had been
advised to advance their watches by nine hours to
match Paris time. Rilla stood by a window of the cafete-

ria with a cup of steaming coffee, watching planes taking off and landing against a sky of clear blue. She felt alone and vulnerable, overtaken by creeping doubt. Was she being a prize idiot? What on earth would Jake Carson think of her when he learned that she had impetuously flown thousands of miles just to interview him?

Then she thought with a defiant tilt of her chin, *He damn well ought to feel honored!*

Once through the formalities at Nice airport, Rilla went to a bookstand and bought a folding map of the area. She soon pinpointed Chabroux as a village a few miles inland, and she decided that she'd go there and fix herself up with accommodation before calling the Villa Ambrosia. Without much difficulty she secured a taxi and bargained a price with the driver in a mixture of English and the remnants of her high school French.

In a very short time they were spinning along Nice's world-famous boulevard, the Promenade des Anglais, with its luxury hotels and apartments and the double avenue of palm trees. Leaving the busy city streets behind, they began to mount the Grande Corniche road in an endless chain of hairpin bends. Rilla gazed in awed delight at the superlative views of the rocky coastline that stretched away as far as the eye could see. It made her think of the Scenic Highway One route south of San Francisco, which offered similar breath-robbing vistas across the rugged shoreline to the Pacific Ocean. However, the explosion of vibrant color surpassed anything she'd seen in Big Sur country. Against the glistening cobalt-blue backdrop of the sea the luxuriant vegetation glowed in myriad shades of green, embroidered with bright blossoms of every conceivable hue. The villas were color-washed in white, beige, yellow, pale pink and blue, and eau de nile, with terra-cotta roof tiles and glossy painted window shutters. Over everything the early afternoon sun glittered down with tropic heat.

At one point the taxi driver pointed downward. *"Voilà Monte Carlo."*

Rilla felt a thrill as she looked down at the famous pleasure resort, which rose like a terraced arena around its harbor. Though some distance away, it seemed incredibly close in the wine-clear, sparkling air, looking like something out of a fairy tale.

"Magnifique!" she said, and the taximan nodded and smiled and promptly started talking volubly in French, as if Rilla could follow every word.

A roadside sign told her they were entering Chabroux. Rilla leaned forward, saying, "Can you recommend a hotel here...somewhere fairly cheap?"

He turned his head to stare at her blankly, and she tried again. *"Un hôtel, s'il vous plaît."* Oh, dear, what was the word for inexpensive? Try small. *"Un petit hôtel."* This time she received a brilliant smile.

"Ah oui! L'Hôtel de la Place. C'est très bon."

The village gave an impression of clinging precariously by its fingertips to the steeply rising hillside. The little hotel stood in the market square, a charming old building, its cream walls clad with gracefully drooping pale mauve wisteria. Gaily striped orange-and-white sunblinds graced each window, and the shadowed entry was coolly inviting.

Madame la patronne, severely visaged and encased in rustling black poplin, showed Rilla to a room on the second floor that was neat and clean, with a window looking out across terraced vineyards. To Rilla's relief the woman spoke tolerably good English, so she inquired about the Villa Ambrosia.

"It is quite near, mademoiselle... scarcely more than

a kilometer. But the road is steep. You must make a right turn by the *pâtisserie* on the corner.''

Rilla decided that she'd better call first to fix an appointment with Jake Carson. The little Hôtel de la Place did not aspire to phones in the bedrooms, so after she'd showered and changed into jeans and a cool blue-and-white T-shirt, she descended the stairs and found a phone booth in the lobby. The local directory supplied her with the number, and within a few moments she was connected.

''La résidence de Monsieur Carson,'' announced a placid masculine voice.

''Oh, er ... do you speak English?'' Rilla asked hopefully.

''Mais oui, madame. How can I assist you?''

''I was wondering if Mr. Carson is home.''

The voice sounded guarded. ''Who is this, if you please?''

''Oh, he wouldn't know me—that is, he may just possibly have been told that I might be getting in touch with him.'' She sounded stupidly confused, she realized, and made her tone brisk. ''My name is Rilla Yorke. I'm a journalist ... for the *New York Globe*.''

''One moment, *s'il vous plaît*.''

There was a long pause. In the silence of the hotel lobby a tortoiseshell cat regarded Rilla impassively from its perch on a windowsill. She waited, tense and nervous, dreading a curt brush-off from Jake Carson. To admit defeat at that stage was unthinkable, and her only option would be a frontal attack. She'd have to charge the defenses of his villa, so to speak.

But such a drastic measure was luckily not needed. Coming back on the line, the placid voice inquired as to where she was speaking from.

''The Hôtel de la Place, in Chabroux,'' she told him.

"Have you an automobile?"

"No, I'm afraid not, but—"

"In that case, m'selle, my instructions are that I am to come to meet you. Let us say in twenty minutes, if that is convenient?"

"But it's Mr. Carson personally that I want to—" she began to protest, but was interrupted.

"I shall drive you to the Villa Ambrosia, m'selle."

"Oh, I see. Well, thanks."

Rilla felt jubilant. Until a minute ago she had been wondering if her wild scheme could possibly pay off, and then she was suddenly being given V.I.P. treatment. An optimistic feeling surged through her, a conviction that everything was going to work out splendidly. She slipped upstairs to her room and changed again into something more suited to the auspicious occasion—a shirtwaist dress in pale peach linen, with a plaited sage-green tie belt and open-toe sandals of the same color. Then, thrusting her notebook and a pen into her tote bag, she ran down to await the car on a rustic seat beneath a green-and-white sun umbrella. Deciding that it was best not to appear overeager, she went back into the hotel lobby just in time, for she heard a car purr to a standstill outside. Peeping through the window, she saw a large blue Citroën, its immaculate paintwork and chrome glinting in the sunshine. The driver, a swarthy-faced man in his mid-fifties, dressed in a neat dark gray suit, got out and entered the hotel. He walked straight over to Rilla.

"M'selle Yorke?"

"That's right," she said with a smile. "You were very quick."

He inclined his head. "If you will accompany me, please." He glanced around, frowning in a puzzled way. "Where are your bags, m'selle?"

"My bags? In my room upstairs. Why?"

"You have secured a room here?"

"Yes, I thought this would be most convenient. Being so near the Villa Ambrosia, I mean."

The man shook his head emphatically. "But you are to stay at the villa, m'selle. Those are Monsieur Carson's instructions," he added, speaking in the tone of one who never dreams of questioning his master's orders. "When you telephoned a short while ago, he said that a room was to be prepared for you at once, and that you would be staying for as long as might prove necessary."

Rilla felt bewildered, uncertain what to do. "But I've already checked in here," she explained.

Madame la patronne, who was standing behind the diminutive reception desk, penning some entries in a large black ledger, had clearly overheard every word. She came hastening over to assure Rilla that she need feel under no obligation about the room. Plainly the invitation to stay at the Villa Ambrosia had impressed her. So Rilla returned upstairs and hastily repacked her belongings. Downstairs again a few minutes later, she was bowed out as if she were a royal personage by what appeared to be the hotel's entire staff. Jake Carson, she concluded as they drove off, was a name that rated in those parts!

Within a hundred yards or so they made a right turn onto a narrow side road that appeared to be heading up an almost vertical hillside. The kilometer *Madame la patronne* had mentioned seemed a lot longer, due to the numerous hairpin bends the car was obliged to negotiate. When they eventually came to elaborately carved wooden gates set in an ancient stone wall that was overhung with purple bougainvillaea and other creepers, they turned in and immediately plunged down a snaking driveway bordered by hibiscus bushes in crimson and pink, and the swordlike spikes of aloes. A moment later they drew up beside a white stone villa with a roof of sunbaked red pantiles.

As Rilla got out of the car her gaze was instantly drawn to the view beyond the house, over the terraced gardens. It was a magnificent panorama of coast and sea that stretched for miles in both directions. What a fabulous setting for a house, she thought with a stab of envy.

Rilla's escort led her around the corner of the house and through an archway cut in the tall screening cypress hedge to a flagstone patio. There her escort halted and bowed politely.

"If you will have the goodness to wait for just one moment, m'selle, I will inform Monsieur Carson of your arrival. Please take a seat."

With that he turned and vanished through sliding glass doors into the house, carrying her suitcase and her hand luggage. Rilla stood for a few moments gazing around her, then sat down on one of the padded garden swings, her mind already busily storing up impressions to be recorded later. The villa, a long low building that had been added to and modernized, was in immaculate condition, the olive-green paintwork of the shutters gleaming with newness. Here and there the white walls were trellised to support climbing shrubs unknown to Rilla in California. One had pointed cerise-colored buds and trumpet-shaped blooms in a softer shade of pink; another was smothered with starlike yellow florets. There were climbing geraniums in scarlet and crimson, and a luxuriant rose with golden-yellow petals that gleamed against dark green foliage.

In the somnolent hush of afternoon she could hear a buzzing of honeybees and the warm-throated twitter of birdsong. There was a bright flash of wings, and two small yellowbirds darted out from a buddleia tree, chasing one another flirtatiously. Restless, Rilla rose to her feet again and crossed the patio to a stone balustrade, topped with Grecian urns from which lush greenery trailed, that edged a semicircular viewpoint across the terraced gardens. Beyond the gardens were a rocky coastline and the shimmering blue expanse of the Mediterranean Sea. With her hands resting on the balustrade, feeling the velvety softness of lichen beneath her fingertips, Rilla stood looking at the superb view. The hot sun, dappled into light and shade from the overhanging branch of a beautiful ancient locust tree with fragrant white blossoms and slim silvery leaves, was just pleasantly warm on her face. *What it must be like to have the sort of money that a top-selling author has,* she thought with a sigh, *and to be able to afford to live in a place like this.*

Rilla began to get the feeling that she was being observed. At first she resisted the urge to turn around and tried to dismiss the thought. But it persisted, making her increasingly uneasy. In the end she couldn't prevent herself from glancing over her shoulder. No movement disturbed the stillness. Chiding herself for being overly imaginative, she was about to turn back to the view when her gaze was arrested by a man's figure that was framed in the rectangle of the open glass doors.

Aware that he'd been spotted, the man emerged from inside and came strolling unhurriedly toward her. He was tall, Rilla noted, well-built and lithe, wearing spare-cut fawn slacks and a leisure shirt, open to reveal the bronze column of his neck. His face was shaded against the westering sun, but there was something familiar about the way he walked...a lazy swing of the shoulders that spoke of total self-assurance. He halted directly in front of her and smiled.

"So, Miss Rilla Yorke," he said softly. "We meet again!"

The voice, deep and resonant, added the final, breath-catching certainty. But his face was different. The beard was gone, revealing a strong, jutting jawline that matched the rest of his craggy face.

"Richard Kellerman!" she gasped, feeling her legs go suddenly weak.

"The same!" he said with a mocking bow. "Alas, you don't look at all pleased to see me, Rilla."

"It—it's such a shock," she stammered. "You're the last person I expected to see here." And the last person she *wanted* to see, she could have added. It was the most atrocious piece of bad luck that Richard Kellerman, of all people, should be there at the Villa Ambrosia. Had he somehow contrived the situation just to mortify her? she wondered confusedly. It was the sort of thing the wretched man might be expected to do! "Is—is Jake Carson a friend of yours? Are you staying here with him?"

"I could answer yes to both questions. Or I could equally well say that Jake is staying with *me*." His sculpted mouth curved in a derisive smile, and she noted that there was a small cleft in the center of his square chin. It was obvious to Rilla that he was enjoying her bewilderment.

Pulling her wits together, she said coldly, "I wish you wouldn't talk in riddles. Is this your house, or his?"

"Oh, it's his house, without question. But then again, it's equally *my* house."

"You mean you share it with him?"

"Very much so!" He was grinning widely then,

greatly amused. "Haven't you caught on yet, my dear Miss Yorke? You, a shrewd and hardheaded journalist."

"Caught on to what?" she asked dazedly.

He delivered his coup de grace with an air of triumph. "Why, that I'm Jake Carson, and that Jake Carson is me. We are one and the same man, Rilla."

Chapter Five

For long moments Rilla could only stare at him, stunned. Then she felt a quick upsurge of anger and flung out bitterly, "Just what sort of stupid game do you think you're playing?"

"It's not a game, Rilla." His blue eyes were vividly intent as he watched her face. "Let's call it more in the nature of a test."

"A test? I don't get you."

"It's quite simple. You intrigued me, and I wanted to discover if you really were the determined and dedicated journalist you pretended to be. So I arranged to have a lure dangled in front of you—the chance of an interview with Jake Carson for the *New York Globe*—and I waited with interest to see what happened. I made things that much more difficult for you by being out of the United States. Nevertheless in next to no time you were right on my trail. I won't inquire how you wangled time off from your job, or where you raised the dollars to come flying from California to the South of France. All that matters to me is that you did. You've proved yourself to be one smart lady, Rilla."

She crushed down a ridiculous feeling of pleasure at this compliment and clung to cold anger. "You were taking a mighty big risk, weren't you, just for the sake of having a joke at my expense?"

"How do you figure it was a risk?"

Rilla met his gaze boldly, confident that for once she'd gained the advantage over him. "For some unknown reason you've kept your dual identity a deep dark secret. Yet, now you've let me in on it. I could go off right this minute and spill the beans."

"You could," he agreed in an even tone, "but you're not that kind of crazy."

"Why crazy? It couldn't matter less to me who knows about you."

He tut-tutted reproachfully. "And I thought you were on the ball. Can't you see, Rilla, that you'd ruin a good story by letting it out too prematurely? I'm offering you a journalist's chance in a million, an exclusive, in-depth profile in which you reveal to the world that Jake Carson and Richard Kellerman are one and the same guy. Think what a scoop it would be for you."

Her mind whirling, Rilla stalled by saying, "It seems to me that you've gotten a blown-up idea of your status rating, if you really think your identity matters that much to people."

"Rilla," he chided her with a lazy smile, "don't allow your dislike of me as a man to cloud your professional judgment. It's a big news story, and you damn well know it is."

"If it's such a big story, why are you offering it to me?"

"That," he said reflectively, stroking his eyebrow with a forefinger in a gesture that Rilla remembered noticing at Sausalito, "is a question I've been asking myself."

"And what answer have you come up with?"

"Does it matter? Why look a gift horse in the mouth?"

"It might be a Trojan horse, that's why, full of tricks."

He sighed in exasperation. "Must you be so suspicious?"

"I'd have thought that Rilla Yorke would be the very last journalist you'd want to have reveal the secret of your two identities."

"Why should you say that?"

"I mean, after the piece I wrote about you—about Richard Kellerman—for the *Bay Area Arts Reporter,*" she said provokingly. "Or didn't you get around to reading it?"

"Oh, I read it, Rilla. With considerable interest."

"Weren't you mad at me?"

"Was it your intention to make me mad?"

"I didn't care whether you were or not," she retorted defiantly. "I just tried to tell the truth about Richard Kellerman as I saw it."

"The plain truth and nothing but the truth?" he mocked. "Or could it be said, perhaps, that a small degree of malice crept in here and there?"

"If it did, then you've got no one but yourself to blame. And you still haven't answered my question about why you chose me. You must have set this whole thing up with the connivance of Martin Whitehead of the *Globe.*"

"Martin is an old friend of mine," he explained, "and one of the very few people who knows my little secret. We have an agreement that when I decide it's the right moment to reveal my dual identity, he'll get the story as an exclusive for the *Globe.* I'm standing by that, but I told him the other day that I wanted you to be the journalist to write it up."

"But why me?" she asked yet again.

His keen blue eyes gleamed in a challenge. "Don't you feel capable of handling the assignment, Rilla?"

"Of course I can handle it," she replied with haughty confidence.

"Well, then, there's your answer."

Rilla pondered on that for a few moments before saying embarrassedly, "You must realize that I can't stay here at your villa."

"Why not? Would such close proximity to me put too great a strain on your powers of resistance?" His lips curved in a smile of sardonic amusement. "Dare I congratulate myself that in Sausalito I actually started to thaw out the ice maiden?"

"I'm not an—" Rilla broke off, refusing to rise to his bait. "It's obvious that I can't stay under your roof. It wouldn't be...appropriate."

"On the contrary, I'd say it was highly appropriate. Staying here for as long as it takes and joining in my everyday life, you'll get a fair idea of how I function. You'll be in a position to present the *New York Globe*'s readers with a well-detailed picture of your subject."

"Warts and all?"

He met her gaze. "Warts and all."

"It's agreed that I don't pull any punches?" she persisted.

"I wouldn't want you to, Rilla."

She still felt suspicious and uneasy, but, grudgingly, she had to admit that however she viewed the situation, he was undoubtedly offering her quite a scoop. She'd be insane not to grab at the chance with both hands. How often was a journalist lucky enough to observe her subject at such close quarters, for as lengthy a period as she thought necessary?

"So long as it's firmly understood," she stated, "that this is strictly a business arrangement."

"Strictly business," he confirmed. "Scout's honor! While you're a guest in my house you'll remain as untouched as you choose to be."

That was an ambiguous reply to say the least, but Rilla judged it prudent to press him no more. "There's something I still don't understand. If you're so keen on having your two identities kept separate, why have you suddenly decided to reveal the truth now?"

"Because I couldn't hope to keep it under wraps for very much longer. Besides which, it's no longer important."

"I don't follow you."

"The point is this, Rilla. If it had been revealed when *Flowers of Chivalry* first came out that its author, Richard Kellerman, was none other than Jake Carson, the best-selling thriller writer, I would never have known for sure whether the book succeeded on its own merits, or only because of the media attention it would inevitably have received."

"So what? Does it matter either way?"

"I think it does."

"But the more media attention an author gets, the more of his books get sold. And pushing up sales is the name of the game. Or am I wrong?"

His mouth tightened. "It was a question of vanity. I'm proud of what I've achieved with my Jake Carson novels. They're well-written, exciting stories in their own particular genre, and they give a lot of pleasure to a lot of people. But I wanted to show the world that I could equally well succeed with an entirely serious work. Now, with the colossal sales of *Flowers of Chivalry,* the point is proved beyond all doubt."

"The way I see it," Rilla said coolly, "that attitude is just another indication of how bigheaded you are."

He bowed in mocking acknowledgment. "'The Arrogance of a Best-Selling Author'... How about that as a title for your article?'' Giving Rilla no time to make a comeback, he went on smoothly, ''I'll show you to your room now. When you're ready, come downstairs and we'll have a cocktail out here on the patio.''

Rilla nodded. ''Very well, Mr.—er, what do I call you?''

''Jake,'' he said firmly. ''Not Mr. anything. Jake Carson is my real name, given to me at birth. Richard I borrowed from my father, and Kellerman was my mother's family name.''

He put his hand lightly beneath her elbow to lead her inside the villa, and Rilla shivered at the touch of his fingertips on her bare flesh. It swept her back instantly to the momentous evening she'd spent with him at the house at Sausalito. The devastating effect he'd had on her then had remained with her like a high-tension charge, however hard she tried to believe that she'd succeeded in thrusting him out of her thoughts.

They entered through the sliding glass doors to a large living room with cream-colored walls, furnished in a comfortable style and zinging with color. The polished parquet floor was strewn with vividly patterned Spanish rugs, and bright cushions were ranged along the two large L-shaped sofas that were covered in a pale apricot rough-textured fabric. A stone carved fireplace centered one wall, and beside it was a basket of cut logs. Another wall had cream-colored bookshelves running its entire length, with several modern abstract paintings hanging above them. Rilla noticed a handsome rolltop bureau in a grained reddish wood, which appeared to be a genuine antique.

They passed through an arched doorway to a hallway tiled in black-and-white hexagons, and Jake led the way up a staircase of open treads to the upper hall. Walking beside him, Rilla was acutely aware of his sheer virile masculinity. She could almost feel the warmth of his body emanating from him, and she detected the evocative, tangy fragrance of his after-shave. There was a magnetism about him that was deeply disturbing, bringing sensual images into her mind that threatened to override her judgment and common sense. Rilla hadn't believed that any man—especially a man she didn't even like—could have such a potent effect on her senses. She must be crazy, she thought with a rising sense of panic, ever to have agreed to stay under his roof.

Jake threw open a door and stepped aside to allow her to enter. "Let Pierre know if there's anything you need, Rilla. He and Jeanne-Marie take pride in making houseguests comfortable."

"Jeanne-Marie?"

"Pierre's wife," he explained. "Alas, though, her English is minimal, so unless you have fluent French, you'd better confine your requests to Pierre."

"He seems very pleasant," Rilla commented. "Very willing and helpful."

"Pierre and Jeanne-Marie are perfect housekeepers...efficient and discreet." With a quick smile Jake was gone, leaving Rilla to debate uneasily the wisdom of what she was doing. But, good grief, she could take care of herself, couldn't she? She studied the room she'd been allotted. It was attractive in a simple, unfussy manner that fitted a guest room in a bachelor's house. In contrast to the ivory flock wallpaper and pale silk bed quilt, the carpets and window drapes were in strong, cool-looking shades of green and turquoise. Rilla crossed eagerly to the padded window seat to take a look at the view, but her attention was at once caught by the tall, athletically built man who stood by the bal-

ustrade, gazing out across the silver-blue waters of the
Mediterranean. Jake Carson—she must school herself
to think of him by that name—looked somewhat lost in
thought. After a moment or two he seemed to become
aware of her gaze upon his back, for he spun around
and looked directly up at her window. Rilla stepped
back quickly in confusion, unsure whether or not he
had seen her.

Her luggage had been brought up ahead of her, and
she spent several minutes unpacking and arranging her
clothes in the dresser and ample closets. Then, after
freshening up, she made her way downstairs and went
through the living room and out to the patio.

There was no sign of Jake Carson, though, and Rilla
experienced a curious sense of letdown. She went to
where she had seen him standing, by the stone balustrade, and drank in the superb view. From that point
the town of Nice lay down to her right, its white buildings glittering in the sunlight against the shimmering
aquamarine of the sea.

After a few moments Rilla heard approaching voices,
one of them unmistakably feminine. She turned to see
Jake walking with a man and a woman through the
arched gap in the cypress hedge, the woman's arm possessively linked through his. In her early thirties, she
was extremely elegant, with a slender sylphlike figure.
She had a pale creamy complexion, with gleaming
raven-black hair wound in a high coif that came to a
widow's peak on her forehead. A magnificent diamond
bracelet sparkled at her wrist, and her long tapered
fingers were heavy with rings, one of them a gold wedding band. More diamonds glittered at the plunging
neckline of her haute couture moiré silk dress, which
was in a vivid shade of flamingo-pink. The whole effect
was quite stunning.

Eyes that were as black and hard as jet stones surveyed Rilla coolly as Jake performed the introductions. "May I present Miss Rilla Yorke, from California. Rilla, this is Princess Antoinette von Hohenzollern, and her brother, Prince Ferdinand."

Taken aback, Rilla murmured a few polite words of greeting. She realized then why the couple had seemed vaguely familiar to her. Not long ago their photographs had appeared in *Town & Country* in a feature on exiled royalty.

It was the first time Rilla had actually met anyone with a title, and she felt a little intimidated, which was precisely what this woman intended her to feel, she guessed.

Rilla drew herself up to her full height and met the princess's critical scrutiny with what she hoped was a look of calm reassurance.

The brother, Prince Ferdinand, was three or four years younger than his sister and every bit as elegant— too elegant for a man, Rilla decided. Likewise tall and slimly built, he wore white slacks that had knife-edge creases, and his dark blue silk shirt was so immaculate that it looked brand new. There was a certain weakness detectable in his classically handsome features, a lack of determination in the set of his chin. His manner, though, was a great deal friendlier than his sister's. His long-lashed, dark brown eyes were regarding Rilla with the frankest admiration.

"I am most charmed and honored to meet you, mademoiselle," he said, taking her hand and sweeping it to his lips. "I trust—ah, but truly!—I trust that you are here for an extended visit?"

"Well, Rilla?" Jake's blue eyes drilled into her remorselessly. "How do you answer that? In the affirmative, I hope."

"I'm not sure how long I'll be here for," she said warily. "Just as long as it takes to get what I came for..."

"And what, if I may inquire, is that?" the princess demanded. Her voice had a velvety huskiness that might have been attractive if her manner hadn't been so imperious.

"I'm a journalist," Rilla informed her, "and I'm here to do a profile of Mr. Carson for the *New York Globe*."

"And for that purpose you are staying at Villa Ambrosia?" The question was rapped out.

Rilla expected Jake to fill in with an explanation, but he just stood there with an affable smile on his leanly carved face. She had an uneasy suspicion that he was enjoying himself.

"That's right," she agreed. "I'm staying here."

"Surely this is not necessary, just for the task of preparing a newspaper article."

Though still dubious herself about the need to stay there Rilla wasn't about to admit that! She wondered whether Princess Antoinette was one of the select few who knew of Jake's alter ego as Richard Kellerman. To be on the safe side, she decided that she'd better not mention it.

"As a matter of fact," she replied with a casual shrug of her shoulders, "I did check in at a hotel in the village. But Jake suggested that it would be far better if I moved in here temporarily and, of course, he's quite right. If I'm to produce an in-depth profile of someone, I need to see a good deal of my subject to appreciate what makes him tick."

She glanced at Jake and found that he was regarding her with a devilish smile of amusement.

"I can assure you, Antoinette, that Rilla will sooner

or later dig out every single thing that's worth knowing about me. She's a very determined lady, and she's prepared to go to almost any lengths to get her story." The stress he put on the word *almost* was so slight that only Rilla noticed it.

Or maybe the princess *had* noticed, for her dark eyes shrank to sharp, angry pinpoints. But her husky voice was sugary sweet as she addressed her brother.

"Ferdie, *chéri*, do you not want Jake to show you his new photographic equipment?" When the prince looked confused, she added on a note of irritability, "You told me that you would like to own such magnificent equipment yourself."

"But, yesterday, Antoinette, you said that you thought it was a ridiculous idea."

She glared at him blackly for daring to argue with her. "Perhaps I will change my mind, who knows? Go and look at the camera now, Ferdie, while you have the opportunity."

The princess appeared to be totally blind to the fact that in effect she was ordering Jake to show his camera to her brother, whether or not he wanted to. But Jake gave no sign of resentment.

"Come on, Ferdie," he said pleasantly. "And afterward we'll all have drinks."

As the two men disappeared into the house the princess sank gracefully onto one of the white-fringed swing hammocks and touched the cushion beside her to indicate that Rilla had her gracious permission to be seated also. But Rilla chose to remain on her feet. Strolling across to a large Grecian urn filled with red and pink geraniums, she stood fingering a trailing frond of leaves, releasing the sweet, spicy scent.

From behind her the princess's voice came floating on the warm air. Apparently casual, it was charged with an underlying threat. "I think, Miss American Girl, that you are playing with fire. Do you not realize this?"

Rilla threw a glance over her shoulder. "For some reason you seem to resent my being here, Princess. I wonder why?"

"Resent!" The casual pose slipped. "You fool, I speak in your own best interest. Have you no conception of the kind of man you are dealing with?"

"I've a fair idea, I guess." Rilla was amazed at her own calmness. "And, of course, to learn *more* about Jake Carson is precisely why I'm here."

She heard the princess's sharp intake of breath. "This article you are supposed to be writing for the New York newspaper... it is all an elaborate fiction, *n'est-ce pas*? It is nothing but a pretext you have invented as a means of getting close to Jake. And how clever of you to persuade him to invite you to stay here in his home! But let me tell you this. Jake will take whatever he wants from you on *his* terms, not yours. He is far too wily to be caught in your pathetic little spider's web."

Seething with anger, Rilla opened her mouth to proclaim hotly that she wanted *nothing* from Jake Carson, except enough information for her profile of him. But no way would she allow the autocratic woman to see that she'd gotten under her skin. Swinging around and facing the princess squarely, Rilla inquired in a tone of light amusement, "Am I to presume that your advice is the result of your own personal experience?"

She received an icy stare that was meant to freeze her dead. "How dare you speak to me in such an impertinent way!"

"How dare I?" Rilla echoed incredulously. "Just because you happen to have a handle to your name, Princess Antoinette, it doesn't give you special privileges in the courtesy stakes. I wouldn't have said what I did to you if you hadn't first been damn rude to me.''

Fortunately any further exchange was prevented by the arrival of Pierre, bearing a large silver tray with bottles and glasses that tinkled invitingly.

''Monsieur Carson instructed me to say that he will be out directly, Your Highness,'' he said, placing the tray on a low white table.

The information was received with a curt nod. ''I do not care to wait. You will fix me a Campari and soda at once.''

''But, of course, Your Highness. Most certainly.''

Rilla remained standing, accepting a glass of white wine from Pierre, but she waved away the platter of interesting-looking canapés he offered her, afraid she might choke on food in her present mood. When Pierre withdrew into the villa, she and the princess maintained a frosty silence until the prince and Jake rejoined them.

Ferdinand was most enthusiastic about Jake's new camera, but when he launched into details concerning shutter speeds and electronic flash equipment, he was brought to a stumbling halt by a single sharp glance from his sister. Jake, pouring drinks for himself and Ferdinand, inquired amiably, ''To what do I owe the pleasure of your visit this afternoon, Antoinette?''

The princess fluttered her long black eyelashes at him. ''Ferdie and I were motoring home from Monte Carlo, where we'd been lunching with our great-aunt Sophie. The old girl is so deaf now that it's a terrible bore trying to make conversation with her, but one has these tedious family obligations, *n'est-ce pas?* I decided, on the spur of the moment, that we should take the Grande Corniche road back and drop by on you, Jake *chéri.* You see, I happen to be unexpectedly free this evening. The

Duhamels have had to cancel their reception at the last moment—Lucille has contrived to fall and break her ankle in some idiotic way—so I thought it would be nice for you and me to dine together.''

"That would have been delightful, Antoinette. Unfortunately, though, I can hardly desert my houseguest on her first evening here. Unless," Jake added as an afterthought, "we make it a foursome, with Ferdie and Rilla?"

Before the princess had a chance to dismiss the plainly unwelcome suggestion, Rilla said quickly, "Count me out, please. I'm not really in the mood for—for socializing.''

Jake nodded understandingly. "That's okay. You must be feeling jet-lagged after that long flight.''

"I guess I am.''

"We can spend the evening quietly at home, Rilla, and it might be a good idea for you to get to bed early.''

Antoinette didn't trouble to conceal her anger at being thwarted. "If Miss Yorke is so tired, Jake, she will hardly welcome your company. In any case, she's made her choice, and you're under no obligation to spoil your evening.''

What would you say, Princess, wondered Rilla impishly, *if I suddenly announced that I'd changed my mind and would be happy to join you and the men for dinner?* She felt half tempted to do just that, but why should she spend a miserable evening merely for the sake of a moment's vindictive pleasure?

"You have to remember, Antoinette," said Jake with a rueful laugh, "that Rilla is here for a serious purpose. If I'm to think of my image, I must endeavor to present myself to her as a dedicated writer, not a habitué of the Riviera nightspots. So, all things considered, I guess I'd better remain home this evening.

Still, I might persuade Rilla to make up a foursome for dinner some other night. I'll call you about it in a day or two."

The princess rose to her feet, gathering up her silver leather clutch purse and matching gloves. Ferdinand at once leaped up also, though he hadn't finished his drink. "You may telephone if you wish, Jake, but I'm not at all sure whether I shall have any evening free in the near future. One has so many social engagements." Nodding coolly to Rilla, the princess walked off with languidly graceful strides, followed by the two men. Presently Rilla heard a car start up and drive off.

"And what did you think of our émigré royalty?" Jake inquired when he returned.

Dodging the need to give an opinion, Rilla posed a question herself. "Where is it they come from? I read something about them recently in a magazine, but I don't remember the exact details."

"Their grandparents came from Transylvania, but Antoinette herself was born in France. She has a magnificent villa on the coast near Saint-Jean-Cap-Ferrat, and she's renowned all along the Riviera for the grand balls she gives."

"What about her husband? I noticed that she wears a wedding ring...among all her other jewelry."

Jake's blue eyes gleamed with amusement. "Other women never fail to spot a wedding ring, do they? Antoinette is a widow, Rilla. Her husband was a well-known French industrialist who died four years ago, leaving her an extremely wealthy woman. Ferdinand, though, has no money of his own and he's obliged to look to his sister for every franc he spends."

"He has no career?"

"His career is dancing attendance upon Antoinette." Jake gave her a challenging look. "You haven't yet answered my question, Rilla. What did you think of them?"

"I thought Prince Ferdinand was extremely pleasant," she said evasively. "Very charming."

"He's the type of man you go for, is he?"

"I didn't say that."

"No, you didn't," Jake agreed. "And you didn't express any opinion of Antoinette, either."

"She—she's an extremely beautiful woman," Rilla said through tight lips.

"That's undeniable! Antoinette in a swimsuit is a truly sensational sight. On the beach she's the focus of every man's eyes."

"Including yours?"

"It figures! I'm a healthy virile male, Rilla, as you've got reason to know. Or do you need another demonstration?"

She felt a flurry of sensual excitement at the very thought of it, and a pulse began to beat in her throat. "I'll remind you," she said stonily, "that you gave me your promise that I could stay under your roof in perfect safety."

Jake smiled lazily. "As the proverb says, my dear Rilla, promises are like piecrust—lightly made and easily broken."

She rose quickly from the swing feeling too vulnerable there. Giving him a hard stare, she said, "I expect you to keep your hands off me while I'm in your house."

"But not away from the house, is that what you mean?" He gave a soft laugh. "Then let us instantly repair to some sylvan spot beyond the boundaries of my domain, and you can throw your inhibitions to the wind."

"Cut that out!"

The teasing smile vanished from Jake's lean face,

and he moved quickly to close the gap between them. With despair in her heart, Rilla felt the contact of his hands on her bare arms, sliding upward over her slender shoulders until they reached the soft skin of her neck, where his sensitive fingertips made tiny stroking movements. There was a long minute of silence between them as she felt his eyes burning into hers.

"Rilla...you just don't know what you do to me." With a groan he cupped her chin in his two hands and moved his mouth to cover hers with thirsty passion.

Rilla was overcome by a drowning sensation of helplessness. Unwillingly she felt her lips soften and respond to the ardent searching warmth of his, felt her whole body quicken in a swift spiral of longing. Jake drew her closer against his lean frame and let his hands roam sensuously, exploring her feminine curves through the thin fabric of her dress.

"Can you wonder that I want you like crazy," he murmured into the silken softness of her auburn hair, "when you make yourself so incredibly seductive and desirable?"

Sudden anger flared in her, and she thrust herself forcibly back from him. "So it's all my fault, once again! But this time it's utterly ridiculous to suggest that I'm dressed with the deliberate intention of enticing you. What I'm wearing is an ordinary summer dress."

Jake's chest rose and fell as he took a shaky breath. "You can't really be so naive, Rilla. Don't you realize what an entrancing picture you make? No man could be blamed for wanting to snatch you into his arms and make passionate love to you."

Rilla gasped in outrage. "My God, you have a nerve! What it amounts to is that whatever I decide to wear—

even if it's a scruffy old pair of jeans and a floppy T-shirt—you'd still accuse me of deliberately trying to attract men."

"What else?" he agreed blandly. "It's a woman's natural instinct to attract men. But few of them succeed as well as you do."

"Princess Antoinette is one who does, apparently," she threw back. "So why don't you concentrate your sensuous thoughts on her, Jake, and let me alone?"

"Is that what you'd really like me to do, Rilla?" he asked challengingly.

"Definitely."

"Suppose that I'd arranged to have dinner with Antoinette this evening, leaving you here on your own?"

"It wouldn't have bothered me any," she insisted, trying to steady the betraying tremble in her voice. "In fact, I'd have preferred it that way."

Jake ran a hand through his fair hair, his face stiffening to a mask of coldness. "I see! Right, then, Rilla. Far be it from me to go against the wishes of a lady." With that remark he swung on his heels and strode purposefully toward the house.

Rilla watched him go with a sense of dismay and felt tempted to call him back. If she did, though, Jake would read it as an invitation. No way would she let him get the impression that she was willing to go to bed with him in return for the favor of granting her an exclusive interview.

Feeling sick at heart, she resumed her place on the swing, tucking up her long slender legs beneath her and leaning back against the cushions. Shadows were lengthening across the sun-baked landscape, and the trees and the prickly pear hugging the steep hillsides were brushed with gilt by the setting sun. The sea, no longer silver-blue, was a shining sheet of hammered bronze that dazzled the eyes. Rilla put her fingertips to her temples, massaging gently to try and soothe the throbbing pain in her head. Somehow the golden beauty of her surroundings had all at once lost its enchantment, and she found it curiously depressing. She felt a stranger there on the fabulous Côte d'Azur—an interloper. It was not her world, and she had no part of it.

On the far side of the villa she heard a car start up. Its exhaust booming, it swept up the drive to the zigzag mountain road, and the throaty sound echoed in the hills until at last the evening silence returned.

So, Jake was going to dine with Antoinette after all! And Ferdinand? No, the princess's younger brother would be told to make himself scarce, and he would meekly obey.

Chapter Six

At a sound behind her, Rilla turned swiftly to see Pierre arriving to collect the drink tray. He looked at her oddly, no doubt speculating about Jake's abrupt departure.

"Pardon, m'selle, about dinner... What is your preference?"

"Er... I'm not really hungry."

"Then might I suggest perhaps a *pissaladiera*?"

"*Pissaladiera*? What's that?"

"It is a *spécialité* of this region, m'selle, a flan of onion, with anchovies and black olives to flavor it. *Très bon!*"

"It sounds delicious, thank you."

It wasn't worth changing her clothes to eat, Rilla decided. Feeling wretchedly at loose ends, she stood up and began to wander around the garden. It was larger than she'd originally supposed, falling in a series of informal terraces down the steeply sloping hillside and offering enchanting new vistas of the sea at every turn. There were a number of exotic trees—feathery tamarisks and delicate-leafed acacias, pencil-slim cypresses and shady umbrella palms, and in one secluded corner near the swimming pool she came unexpectedly upon a very ancient olive tree with the most beautifully sculpted branches that thrust up like gnarled old fingers against the swiftly darkening sky. A heavenly scented white rambler rose scrambled luxuriantly over a rustic pergola, and there was a golden mass of Spanish broom that intoxicated her with its heady fragrance. All the scents of the garden seemed to be even stronger at that time of day, drenching the silk-soft air with their sweetness. Under any other circumstances Rilla would have reveled in having such beauty surround her, but she couldn't shake off her melancholy mood.

The stars were beginning to shine, and only the faintest glow remained in the western sky when Rilla heard Pierre calling from the house.

"M'selle! Le dîner est servé!"

In the simple country-style dining room a single place had been laid for her at one end of the polished pinewood table, seeming to accentuate her solitude. Though she had little appetite, the *pissaladiera* was indeed delicious, with beautifully light pastry. It was served with a crisp green salad. For dessert there was a dish of sharp-sweet alpine strawberries and a silver jug of cream. Coffee was brought in by a smiling woman in a plain gray dress trimmed with white—Pierre's wife, of course. Recalling what Jake had said about the woman's lack of English, Rilla tried the French she remembered from high school.

"Bon soir . . . Jeanne-Marie, n'est-ce pas?"

"Ah oui, m'selle!" She added something incomprehensible, but Rilla nodded and smiled, and it hardly seemed to matter that she didn't understand. She had a feeling that Pierre's wife had taken the opportunity to inspect the houseguest and that, luckily, she approved.

After dinner Rilla felt even more at a loss. The villa was very silent, apart from a faint murmur of voices that she assumed to be emanating from a television in the servants' quarters. She could have switched on a television herself, but what was the point when it would all be in French? She couldn't settle down to read, not even to finish off the last few pages of Jake's book *Exit from Berlin*.

Restlessly she wandered out through the sliding doors to the patio. The shimmering lights of Nice, far below, drew her to the balustrade. Such incredible beauty! The great curving sweep of the Promenade des Anglais glittered like a necklace of diamonds against the dark bosom of the sea. Somewhere down there—in a smart hotel or restaurant, or even more intimately in Princess von Hohenzollern's luxury villa—Jake was dining tête-à-tête with the glamorous woman who was undoubtedly his mistress.

Rilla gripped the cool smooth stone of the balustrade with tense fingers to try and stifle her pain. Why did it hurt so much to think of them together? Jake Carson was an insufferable man, overwhelmingly arrogant about his magnetic appeal to women. Nothing could prevent her admiration for him as a writer—under both his names—but as a man she despised him utterly.

And yet—Rilla closed her eyes, holding back the tears that pressed against her lids. What was happening to her? From the time of her disillusionment with Theo she had thrown herself single-mindedly into building her career, not allowing herself to be diverted by emotional entanglements, not even conscious of feeling the lack of an emotional life. But, even though she knew Jake Carson to be shallow and ruthless in his relationships with women, she felt irresistibly drawn to him. The effect he had on her was devastating; it had rocked her completely, and she would never be the same person again. The days she spent at the Villa Ambrosia would be sheer torture, and when she finally departed with all her data gathered for the profile of him, she would leave behind a large segment of her heart.

It was going to be a long while, if ever, before she forgot Jake Carson. Her only defense against the constant yearning for him would be to drown herself in work. It was undeniably true, as Jake claimed, that the exclusive story about his dual personality would be a tremendous feather in her cap, certain to lead to bigger things careerwise. But the idea didn't excite her anymore. Whatever success she might achieve as a journalist would be a hollow shell without Jake himself playing a major role in her life.

In a sudden, breathless, heart-stopping rush Rilla thought, *Suppose I was to yield to him and let him make love to me?* Her whole body quivered and was thrilled at the prospect. It would be a glorious fulfillment for her; a taste of ecstasy, just as Jake had promised. She didn't doubt that for an instant. So why fight against her feelings...why not allow the hot flames of desire to flare up within her until she was utterly consumed in a blissful sharing of passion? How easy it would be to arrange; a single enticing glance from her would be enough, and Jake would take the hint. Then afterward, when she had returned to California, she would have something indelibly precious to carry in her memory.

Who was she kidding? The memory of her submission to Jake would remain forever a raw, open wound, a torment for the rest of her days.

Should she leave there immediately, then? Should she abandon the once-in-a-lifetime story and just turn tail and run? Rilla tried telling herself it was professional pride that made her reject such a solution. But basic honesty caused her to face the truth—the mortifying truth that she couldn't bear to leave the Villa Ambrosia a single minute before she was obliged to.

Whatever it cost in pain and humiliation, she would remain there as long as possible just to be near to the man she loved....

It was madness, she scolded herself, but there was no fighting the new knowledge that left her gasping with dismay. She was in love with Jake!

It could only be love—the swamping, overwhelming emotion that took no account of good or bad, of practicalities and common sense. What she'd felt for Theo paled before it into trivial insignificance, seeming hardly more than a mild sensual attraction that had been instantly destroyed by the discovery that Theo had been two-timing her. The bitter realization that Jake would never be able to return the love she felt for him did nothing to diminish her feelings. Love, she was beginning to understand, could represent a one-way ticket to a hell of suffering.

The glittering lights of the town far below merged into a misty glow as tears filled Rilla's eyes. She pressed her palms against the cool stone of the balustrade and let out a long, despairing sigh. Jake's resonant voice, from close behind her, startled her and sent her senses reeling.

"How I envy the man," he said with a soft chuckle, "for whom the beautiful maiden sighs so soulfully."

Rilla spun around to face him. "What—what are you doing here? I thought you were—"

He took a step nearer and his eyes glinted in the starlight. "You thought I was...where, Rilla?"

"I—I didn't expect to see you back so early," she stammered.

"Were you waiting for me?" he jibed. "Am I to understand that the heavy sigh you heaved was from impatience at my absence?"

"Oh, do me a favor!" Rilla wanted to stride past him

and go straight up to her bedroom, but her legs felt so shaky that she was afraid to abandon the support of the balustrade. Trying desperately to control the tremor in her voice, she remarked acidly, "I wonder how you managed to tear yourself away from Princess Antoinette so early. She couldn't have liked it."

"What makes you think I've been with Antoinette?"

"Well, haven't you?"

Jake perched himself leisurely on the balustrade beside her. A riffle of evening breeze blew a lock of his hair across his brow.

"As a matter of fact, no."

He remained quite still, watching her, making no attempt to explain. In the end Rilla was driven to ask in an edgy voice, "Where were you, then?"

"What do you care? You made it very plain that you preferred to do without my company."

"Maybe. But I didn't expect you to feel driven out of your own home just because of something I happened to say."

Jake laughed, and with the lightest touch of his fingertips he traced a line down her bare arm, from elbow to wrist. Rilla tensed into stillness, stunned by the wave of erotic pleasure that flooded through her. Even after Jake's hand had dropped away her skin seemed to burn from his touch and her whole body trembled.

"The dull truth is, Rilla, that I took the opportunity to do some research. Part of the action of my current thriller takes place in this area, and I wanted to tune my ear to some genuine village bar talk to authenticate my dialogue. So I drove down to Chabroux and spent a couple of hours in the bistro."

"You missed your dinner."

"Not to worry, I had a bowl of steaming hot bouillabaisse—a delicious fish stew they make hereabouts that's rather like cioppino. You must try it, Rilla. I'll take you down to the bistro one evening.''

"Oh, I don't know about that...." The thought of being escorted anywhere by Jake filled her with panic. The thought of just being in his company filled her with panic... as now, when she was so intensely aware of his nearness. He seemed to emit vibrant sensory signals to which she was acutely attuned, almost as if speech were a clumsy and unnecessary means of communication between the two of them. She wished that she could summon up the strength of will to move away from him, because she was terrified that he might touch her again. And yet she longed for it to happen....

"Do I need to teach a journalist like you how to do research, my dear Rilla? If you're ever to get a true picture of Jake Carson at both work and play, you'll have to go around with him. Won't you?''

"Er, yes... I guess so."

As silence fell between them there seemed to be a breathless hush all around, broken only by the chirping of cicadas and the sad, sweet song of a nightingale in one of the cypress trees. Rilla felt like a trapped bird herself, her heart thudding so violently that it threatened to break free of her suddenly fragile body.

"Rilla... about Antoinette," he began at last.

"I don't want to talk about her," she cut in sharply. "The sort of profile I plan to write won't include the sordid details of your sex life."

There was another lengthy silence, then Jake said quietly, "Maybe that's exactly the sort of information the *Globe*'s readers will be avid to know about me."

"And you'll be happy to provide them with frank revelations," she retorted. "I suppose you enjoy boasting about how you make out with women, so as to prove what a tremendously virile guy you are."

"How did we get into this?" He sighed, then added, "I don't see anything to apologize for in my life-style."

"No, you're proud of it, aren't you? Proud of your ability to charm any woman you happen to fancy into bed."

He slid off the balustrade and stood looking down at her from his commanding height. "Would I be able to charm you into bed, Rilla?"

"Oh, get lost!" She went to push past him, but his hard fingers clamped around her wrist, jerking her to a halt.

"I asked you a question, Rilla, and I'd like an answer, please."

"I'd have thought the answer was glaringly obvious."

"It's far from obvious to me. The fascinating speculation is to what extent your stubborn puritanism can override and suppress the needs of your sensuous body. As far as your body alone is concerned, the answer is a very definite affirmative. I've felt you quiver at my slightest touch, remember. I've felt your heart beating wildly when I've held you in my arms."

Rilla tugged in vain to free her wrist from his viselike grip. "You're making far too much out of a totally trivial situation." She faltered. "It—it meant nothing at all."

"If it was so totally trivial and meant nothing," he suggested, "there's no reason why we shouldn't have a rerun now."

"Except that I don't want to."

"What you mean is that you don't want to give in to me too easily."

"I mean that I won't give in to you at all! And if you don't let go of me this instant, I—I'll—"

"Scream for assistance?"

"What would be the use?" she threw back at him bitterly. "I've no doubt that you have Pierre and his wife well trained to turn a deaf ear."

"So, with screaming ruled out, what are you going to do if I refuse to let you go? Give a highly colored account of my brutal assault on you in your profile of me?"

"I wish you'd cut out the jokes."

"I'm serious. Isn't it your aim to give the *Globe*'s readers the unvarnished truth about Jake Carson? Just as you did about his other half, known as Richard Kellerman. You didn't pull your punches that time, Rilla."

"You told me before that you didn't object to that article of mine," she reminded him scornfully.

"Nor did I. Your piece in the *Bay Area Arts Reporter* will have sold a few extra copies of *Flowers of Chivalry*."

"And I suppose you imagine that a titillating piece about you in the *New York Globe,* with fully annotated details of your freewheeling life-style, will be equally good publicity for Jake Carson."

"It would be superfluous, Rilla. The Jake Carson books sell themselves nowadays. They always make number one on the best-seller lists. The least I've ever had is six printings."

Despite her fury Rilla felt tingles of excitement running through her veins from the pressure of his hand. She could smell the faint, lingering odor of his aftershave and she was headily conscious of his masculinity. Why did her treacherous heart prompt her to throw pride and discretion to the wind and twine her arms about Jake's neck, seductively inviting him to kiss her? She resisted the temptation by storming at him angrily, "I don't think I've ever in my life met a man who's so arrogant and—and—"

"Opinionated?" he suggested. "Is that the word you wanted? Actually, though, you're mistaken. What you choose to call my arrogance, Rilla, is merely the lack of false modesty. It happens to be a certified fact that my books sell in vast numbers, so why should I pretend otherwise?"

Again Rilla made an effort to free herself from his grip, but Jake held her wrist captive in the iron clasp of his fingers. "Please," she muttered, "you're hurting me."

"Correction, Rilla. It's you who's doing the hurting by trying to escape. If you like, though, we'll change to a more comfortable position."

"For pity's sake," she began as she found herself jerked into Jake's arms and pinioned against his lean, hard-muscled frame. But her instinctive cry of protest became a gasp of arousal as she felt a surge of sweet tension flood through her from the sensuous contact of his warm flesh. His kiss sent Rilla rocketing to the stars, and when at long last he withdrew his lips from hers, she breathed out a soft sigh.

Dear heaven, how could she find the strength to resist this man, whose caressing hands were stirring flames of longing deep within her body? She could feel his heart beating in time with her own, a primeval pulsing of desire that swept aside all reason and common sense.

Without conscious thought Rilla's own hands slid up across the molded wall of his chest to clasp around his neck, drawing herself closer to him. Jake caught his breath, holding her even more tightly, and she couldn't avoid being aware of the thrusting pressure of his loins, the throb of his urgent need.

"Oh, Rilla...exciting, enticing Rilla," he murmured, his voice sounding thick and husky as it rose

Scent of Gold

from the deep recesses of his throat. He bent his head to bury his face in the fragrant cloud of her silky hair, then in sudden hungry possession he found her lips once more, and her last shreds of reserve dissolved in another great upsurge of exploding emotion. There was nothing anymore beyond the two of them, clinging together passionately, his insistent kisses forcing a response from her, his tongue probing thrillingly into her warm and willing mouth.

Jake freed one hand to slide up and close over the soft curve of her breast, his thumb teasing the pointed bud through the thin linen fabric of her dress until Rilla shivered in ecstasy and arched herself even more intimately against him. As if in a daze she felt Jake lift her and carry her to the padded softness of a swing. There was no past, no future—only that glorious present moment, that lost world of passion. She rejoiced in the erotic demands of his lips and lay back under the persuasive pressure of his hands until she was reclining full-length, with his weight crushing her into the billowy cushions. She felt his fingers at the buttons of her dress, sliding in warmly to capture her breast, caressing the tingling nipple through the gossamer shield of her lacy bra, and she let out a long, low moan of delight. But when Jake impatiently tugged the bra aside, she was conscious of a faint warning voice within her. She struggled to pull back from his kiss.

"Jake, it isn't fair," she protested weakly. "I don't want this to happen."

"Why fight it, sweetheart? It'll be wonderful, I promise you."

He began to kiss her again, but very gently, his lips blazing a trail of delicious sensations across her brow and down her cheek. He kissed the two corners of her small curved mouth, and moved downward to the warm, sensuous softness of her throat. Rilla moaned again in delight, his tenderness stifling her will to resist. Clinging to him anew, she tangled her fingers into the crispness of his hair and let herself float on a wave of happiness. Then she felt her dress slipping from her shoulders, and in a swift movement he had captured her naked breast, nipping its hard, swollen peak between his lips until she almost screamed aloud in ecstasy.

"You're so beautiful," he murmured, his voice vibrant with desire. "It's nothing less than a crime to hide such loveliness with clothes. I just can't wait to see your magnificent body revealed in all its exquisite perfection. Tonight, Rilla my sweet, I'm going to show you such lovemaking as you've never even dreamed of before."

Jake drew off her sandals, and they dropped to the flagstones with a soft thud. Then, in a swirling fog of excitement and happiness that bemused her senses, she felt him undo the braided waist tie and pull her dress away, felt him remove the wispy barriers of bra and panties with eager sensitive fingers. The cool touch of the evening air was like a silken caress to her fevered skin as she sank back onto the swing cushions, waiting while Jake threw off his own clothes, his smooth naked skin gleaming in the faint light. After only moments he was with her again, spreading his long length on top of her, and Rilla gasped as she became unmistakably aware of the hard, throbbing heat of his desire.

"I want you, Rilla," he breathed in a husky voice. "Oh, God, how I want you!"

She writhed beneath him joyously as his seeking hands roamed her slender body, stroking and kneading its soft curves, finding places that brought her to a quivering pitch of delight—the insides of her elbows, the warm hollows of her armpits, the tiny secret cave of her navel, the responsive channel of her spine, and the velvet smoothness of her thighs—while his mouth wove patterns of tiny nibbling kisses around her cheeks and ears, along the delicate line of her jaw, and down her throat until he once again captured a taut nipple between his lips and rasped it with the tip of his tongue.

"Jake!" she moaned softly, her voice quivering away into the star-studded canopy of the night sky. Just the sobbing out of his name was her complete acquiescence, the candid admission of her need, an entreaty for fulfillment. As if in response he moved a roaming hand slowly, purposefully upward across her quivering thighs toward the center of her being. Such sensual pleasure as Rilla had never known before began to build within her, mounting wave upon wave of rapturous torment until she shuddered in a crescendoing passion of desire, thrashing wildly and arching her soft body against the hard virility of Jake's, her fingers frenziedly clawing his back, gliding over his contoured muscles and raking his hot moist skin. And at last, when she felt she could bear the torment of wanting him not a moment longer, he joined their two bodies in the act of love, and they moved in unison toward their ultimate goal. She sobbed his name lovingly through lips that lay pressed against the pulse-throbbing curve of his neck. She felt Jake pause, felt his body tremble on the brink, then the heavens seemed to erupt, and the stars cascaded down in a silver fountain of pure delight.

They became still, the swing moving gently beneath them. Slowly sounds from beyond their own small cocoon of bliss returned: the call of a night bird, the rustling sigh of the evening breeze through leafy branches,

the faint drone of an aircraft high in the starlit heavens.
Jake eased his weight from Rilla, then drew her against
him, his movements languid, his caresses gentle in the
warm afterglow of their passion. He touched her face
with his lips in a hundred tiny kisses.

Jake shifted a little and began to trail his fingertips
slowly and sensitively up Rilla's side, from her knee
and thigh up over the swell of her hip and into the
molded slimness of her waist, diverting from its direct
course to encircle the ripe mound of her breast before
rising again to her shoulder, her neck, up the smooth
curve of her throat, and over her chin, tracing out the
shape of her lips. Playfully Rilla nipped a roving finger
between her teeth.

"Ouch!" he said fondly, not pulling away. "I knew
how it would be with you, sweet Rilla. You've turned
lovemaking into a whole new experience for me. It's
never been this good before with any other woman."

The chill of doubt reached through to Rilla only
slowly, penetrating the cushiony layers of her happiness. With a little shudder she drew back from him.
"I'm going to get dressed."

"Hey, what's the hurry? We're quite private here,
sweetheart. Nobody's going to come and disturb us."

"I'm sure they won't," she said bitterly. "This is a
situation that Pierre and Jeanne-Marie must be well accustomed to, and you've told me how very discreet
they are."

"So? Why should that thought make you angry?"

Without answering, Rilla sat up and swung her feet
to the ground, reaching for her clothes and sandals,
which lay on the flagstones in a heap. Hastily she
slipped on her bra and panties, then the peach-colored
linen dress, pulling its braided cord tightly about her
slim waist. Jake, unabashed by the nakedness of his tall

bronze body, stood and watched her. Then, shrugging, he bent and retrieved his slacks, drawing them on and zipping them up. But he left his torso bare, and Rilla averted her eyes, ashamed that even then she felt a tug of longing to be held in his arms again.

"I asked you a question, Rilla," he said quietly. "Why are you angry?"

"You ought to know the answer."

"If I did, I wouldn't have asked it."

She gestured toward the swing with loathing. "How many other women have you—"

"Does that matter?"

"Not to you, obviously. In your eyes I'm just one of a long string of conquests."

"You are very special, Rilla," he murmured.

"Am I supposed to be flattered because you award me a high rating?" she hurled at him in a bitter voice.

"You enjoyed it as much as I did," he stated brutally. "Don't try to deny it now, it's too late for that."

"I'm not denying anything. I'm a normal woman with normal instincts, and I can be tempted just like everyone else...especially when a man deliberately uses every seductive trick he knows to win me over."

Jake chuckled softly. "I didn't have to work all that hard. Anyway, what are you complaining about? You were being seductive with every move and gesture you made."

She gasped in outrage. "According to you, I'm being seductive merely by existing."

"No doubt the instinct is so deep-rooted in you that you lead men on without even thinking about it."

"You make it sound as if I'm utterly promiscuous," she blazed.

"I hardly imagine," he drawled, "that I'm the only man with whom you've become sexually involved."

"I've not become involved with you," she protested, choking. "What happened just now was a mistake."

Jake caught hold of her by the shoulders and his eyes glittered with fury. "Don't trivialize what happened between us, Rilla."

"*Me* trivialize!" she gasped in anger. "You're the one who makes sex casual and meaningless."

"That's garbage and you know it. Haven't I just told you how wonderful it was for me?"

"I guess that's the sort of smooth flattery you give to every woman," Rilla stormed. "You're patterning yourself on the macho heroes of the Jake Carson thrillers. Some role models! They're always 'scoring' with one woman after another, regarding themselves as experts at lovemaking. *Lovemaking,*" she repeated scornfully. "It's sacrilege to use the word as you did, reducing something that should be beautiful and wonderful to just a crude act of lust."

"If that's the way you see it," he ground out savagely, "then you'd better stop giving me the come-on all the time. It's clear that, mentally, you and I are on totally different wavelengths. For a few magical moments I really believed that you were being your true self, Rilla, and the memory of those moments will be difficult to erase...a tantalizing mirage of what things could be like between us."

"Never again!" she moaned in an agony of remorse.

"You're dead right about that," he returned cruelly. "I'm only interested in women who can express their emotions honestly and freely, who aren't ashamed of revealing the passionate side of their nature."

"And that's all you want from life? Fleeting moments of cheap passion without any kind of commitment? Without love?"

"Oh, *love!*" His scathing voice was like the lash of a thong-tailed whip. "I suppose by that you mean an insipid romantic conception that reduces passion to a pale ghost of what it can be."

Shivering with a strange sense of sadness, Rilla drew herself up to her full height and regarded him defiantly. "I feel sorry for you, Jake Carson, I really do. How pathetically empty your life must be, if all you have to look forward to is the barren pursuit of sexual gratification. If that's what circulating in your supersophisticated world means, then I'll be thankful to stick to my naive romantic dreams."

Jake's eyes were two smoldering fires of anger as he glared back at her. "You may happen to possess the body of a goddess, Rilla, but you have a hellcat's tongue. So I'll leave you to your cozy little fantasies. I don't reckon that you'll get much rest tonight, though. For once in your life you've had your senses aroused by a man who isn't afraid of true passion, and I'll give you ten bucks for one that the memory of this time we've spent together will haunt you during plenty of sleepless nights in the future."

With that Jake strode off briskly into the house, leaving Rilla alone in her misery. The warm scent-filled Mediterranean night suddenly felt bleak and chilly.

Chapter Seven

The hours of darkness were indeed a long torment for Rilla. Tossing and turning in a state of fevered misery, she wondered how she could possibly remain another night under Jake's roof.

But to leave at once would be to abandon the story she had flown all those thousands of miles to get. Although it no longer seemed to matter, what else was left in her life except her career as a journalist? Whatever the future might hold, she knew that she'd never be able to love another man as she loved Jake Carson. It would be better, then, to focus all her emotional energy on her job, to immerse herself in whatever assignments came her way, and to try to block out tormenting thoughts of how wonderful her life could have been, if only Jake had been cast in a different mold. To love a man who was incapable of loving seemed the cruelest possible fate for any woman.

A distant cockcrow marked the dawn. Exhaustion claimed Rilla at last, and she slept. Even then Jake remained with her, in her dreams...a different Jake, whose passion for her was expressed in tender, loving words. She awoke with a heavy feeling of listlessness. The chink of crockery outside drew her to the window. Below, on the patio, Pierre was setting one of the white tables with breakfast things. She caught a tantalizing aroma drifting up from downstairs and suddenly felt a craving need for a cup of strong hot coffee.

It took her scarcely fifteen minutes to shower and pull on beige slacks and a sleeveless silky lemon-colored sweater with a small turtleneck. When she walked out into the sunshine, she found Jake seated at the table, reading a newspaper. He was wearing jeans and an olive-green T-shirt, and his bronze forearms, sinewy with muscle, glinted with tiny golden hairs. Seeing Rilla, he got to his feet and drew out a chair for her to sit on.

His glance was outwardly polite and friendly, but she could tell there was mockery lurking somewhere. "Good morning, Rilla! I hope you slept well on your first night here."

"Excellently, thank you," she lied.

A curve of his lips showed that Jake was not deceived. After pouring from the pitcher of iced orange juice, he put a glassful beside the place set for her. "When I'm in France I usually have a simple European breakfast. Will croissants and cherry conserve suit you? Or shall I ask Jeanne-Marie to cook you ham and eggs or something?"

"No, thanks, I never have more than cereal or toast," Rilla told him as she took her seat. "This morning, though, I'll just stick with coffee."

Jake lifted the glazed earthenware pot and poured her a steaming cup, handing it across to her. "Cream?"

"Yes, please...a little."

"I'll leave you to help yourself," he said, pushing the small jug toward her. "Do try a croissant, Rilla. They're very good. Home made."

It seemed easier to accept one than to argue about it.

The flaky crescent, light as a feather, was delicious, but she just had no appetite and crumbled most of it on her plate. The coffee was welcome, though, and helped to revive her spirits a little.

"I thought some sight-seeing would be a good idea today," Jake said pleasantly.

"Sight-seeing? But I'm here to work, not have a vacation."

He lifted his straight thick brows in derision. "You are here, as I understand it, Rilla to talk to me and observe me and altogether discover how I function. We can't live in a vacuum while you're doing that, and sadly the most interesting activity I can think of seems to be vetoed. Going around sight-seeing is a poor second best, of course, but under the circumstances..."

She ignored his innuendo and said, "I trust that I won't take too much of your time, when you should be writing."

"The way I see it, it's in my best interest to make a good impression on you, so that you'll go home and write nice things about me."

"I thought you said that you didn't care what I wrote about you."

Jake's smile was enigmatic. "It's settled, then. We go sight-seeing. Be ready in half an hour, okay? No need to change," he added, forestalling her question. "You look terrific just as you are. But, as I've mentioned before, you look terrific whatever you wear—or don't wear!"

Rilla flushed from both embarrassment and irritation. Having accepted the fact that what had happened between them on the previous night was not to be repeated, why couldn't he avoid making those snide remarks to remind her of it? Frowning, she asked, "Where do you plan to take me, Jake?"

His smile then was teasing, but in a friendlier way. "I thought that I'd make it something of a mystery tour."

"Oh?" It was strange that she suddenly felt excited and happy at the prospect of the day ahead.

The morning was quite glorious, the few fleecy puffs of white clouds only intensifying the serene blue of the sky. The air was like warm silk, and as they drove off in Jake's dark blue convertible the breeze fanned Rilla's auburn hair, whipping little tendrils against her cheeks. The narrow twisting road alternately climbed steeply and plunged suddenly, but all the while they were mounting ever higher into the wooded foothills of the mountains. Now and then, where the road turned back on itself, they gained a dramatic glimpse across fruit orchards and groves of silver-leafed olive trees to the bright sun-gilded Mediterranean.

Rilla was fascinated to spot a short distance ahead of them a tight cluster of dwellings built right on the pinnacle of a hill. Each structure seemed to be clinging to its neighbor with a life-and-death desperation.

"It looks a bit like a giant eagle's nest," she commented to Jake.

He flashed her a sideways glance. "Not a bad simile! Are you an authority on the subject of eagles?"

"Hardly." She laughed. "But one summer when I was at high school I worked on a golden eagle count in Oregon as part of a science project. They're magnificent birds . . . sadly just another of the many endangered species."

Jake nodded. "Well, that village up there on the hilltop was put where it is to try and make it safe from attack, just like your eagles' nests. It's one of the renowned *villages perchés*."

"Perched villages?"

"Exactly that. Long ago, back in the dark ages, the

local peasants always built their homes in such a way, as a protection against the Saracens and various marauding bands of robbers and other attackers.''

When they eventually reached the village, Jake parked the car in a cobbled square opposite a pretty little bell-towered church. Side by side, they strolled through picturesque alleyways where market stalls were piled high with a colorful abundance of vegetables: fat cabbages like green footballs, mountains of pink-gilled mushrooms, radishes as large as apples, great pyramids of glossy red tomatoes, and long, ridgy cucumbers.

They paused to look into a little courtyard where a group of elderly women in aprons and head scarfs were gathered around a stone fountain, doing their household laundry, gossiping happily as they worked. A loud braying noise made Jake and Rilla turn. On the dusty cobbled lane behind them a thin donkey, led by an old man wearing a black beret, was laboring under a load of building stones in two huge pannier baskets.

"The twentieth century hasn't quite arrived in some of these villages," Jake said with a smile. "They still do things the way they've always been done for centuries past, as if the internal combustion engine and electricity had never even been thought of. It's a hard life."

"But a contented one, I should imagine," Rilla said thoughtfully. "I guess these people feel that they really have a stake in the world. I think it's good that some of the simple ways of living are still being preserved."

Jake made no comment, but she felt curiously in tune with him. They wandered on, pausing again to watch a black-eyed urchin wobbling on an ancient bicycle several sizes too large for him, and they laughed together at the self-important gait of a little brindled dog with a frisky tail and a knowing eye.

After a cup of coffee at a tiny sidewalk café under

a trellis of vine leaves, Jake suggested driving on. Presently they arrived at a fair-size town, and Rilla was entranced by the seductive charm of its medieval stonework and narrow, stepped streets.

"This is Grasse," he told her. "The center of the French perfume industry. Before we set out this morning I called a friend of mine who runs a *parfumerie* on the outskirts of town, and he promised to give us a conducted tour."

"Oh, how marvelous!" she exclaimed eagerly.

Jake gave her a thoughtful look that seemed to hold a hint of tenderness. "It was worth thinking up something to please you, Rilla, just to see the pleasure written all over your face."

"Well," she parried, suddenly embarrassed, "what woman wouldn't be interested in exotic perfumes?"

The *parfumerie* consisted of a series of long, low whitewashed buildings surrounded by dark green cypresses standing like sentries on guard. The air was drenched with the fragrance of flowers, and all around them were acres and acres of the most gorgeous roses in every imaginable color, from deepest reds to palest blush pinks and virgin white; from vivid sunset orange to the fresh bright yellow of lemon skin.

"What a heavenly scent!" said Rilla. "It's quite out of this world."

"For some reason that nobody understands, the scent of the oriental tea rose is finer when grown around the Mediterranean than in any other climate," Jake told her.

"I've never seen so many rose bushes. There must be millions of them. However can they need all these?"

Jake laughed. "It takes a ton weight of rose petals—can you imagine how many thousands of handfuls that is?—to make just a couple of pints of rose essence. Which explains why the finest perfumes of Grasse are so wickedly expensive."

They were shown into the office of the owner of the *parfumerie,* Monsieur Henri Rigaillaud, who proved to be an aristocratic-looking man of about sixty, with a twirled mustache, gold-rimmed pince-nez, and the most courtly manners. He bowed over Rilla's hand, touching it to his lips.

"You are most welcome to my small establishment, M'selle Yorke," he said in a delightful Maurice Chevalier–style accent. "I was greatly pleased when my friend Jake telephoned this morning to say that he wished to bring you here."

"Believe me, Monsieur Rigaillaud, it's a great pleasure for me to visit with you," she responded sincerely.

Jake explained how the two men had become friends. "I first met Henri when I was researching for my book *Scent of Gold.* If you remember, Rilla, there was a murder committed in the laboratory of a *parfumerie.* The plot hinged on stealing the secret formula of their latest creation."

"I'm afraid I haven't gotten around to reading that one yet," she murmured apologetically.

"Then you must make a point of it, *ma chère m'selle,*" advised Henri Rigaillaud. "*Scent of Gold* is a very exciting book, and in its honor I have named the most exciting creation of my own laboratory Parfum d'Or."

Monsieur Rigaillaud led the way from his office across a paved courtyard overhung with long pink-mauve racemes of wisteria and into the largest of the buildings. As they walked he told Rilla that the organization of his *parfumerie* was on a small scale.

"I have altogether less than forty men and women in

my employ," he said. "Small, as I think you say in America, is good, *n'est-ce pas*? And everything here is from nature, you comprehend? We use no synthetics, no mass production. Just the pure natural fragrance of our wonderful Provençal flowers, skillfully blended into masterpieces of artistry."

Inside the building were huge copper vats in which, Monsieur Rigaillaud explained, the fragrances of the flower petals were absorbed into a specially prepared fatty substance during the flowering season. "Then later on," he said, "we use a steam process to liberate this collected essence, and the fat itself is used for making soap. So, you see, nothing here is wasted."

They passed on through the blending room, where white-coated men and women were working at benches, and then through to the packaging department, where the end result of all the painstaking skill was measured into tiny fluted glass vials of very distinctive design. Rilla remembered having seen Rigaillaud perfumes on display at Macy's on Union Square—at prices, she also remembered, that had made her eyes widen.

"Come," said Monsieur Rigaillaud, "I will now introduce you to our supreme *artiste*. The gentleman whom we call the nose."

"Nose?" queried Rilla as they set off across the courtyard once more, heading for a small white building that stood by itself.

"He's the man who blends the various flower essences together until an entirely new perfume is created," Jake explained. "Some perfumes consist of more than a hundred individual flower essences. Isn't that so, Henri?"

"*Ah oui, mon ami,* on occasion even more. As many as two hundred."

"So you can see the vital importance of Marcel Fabri's unique nasal organ." Jake laughed. "The poor man may neither smoke nor touch alcohol. And if he should catch the tiniest chill—"

"Mon Dieu!" exclaimed Monsieur Rigaillaud, paling at the mere thought.

"It sounds rather like a wine taster," Rilla suggested.

"There is a resemblance, m'selle. Just as wine possesses many subtle nuances, so perfume has different notes."

"Did you say notes?"

Before Monsieur Rigaillaud could answer, Jake interposed again. "Let me dazzle her with my knowledge, Henri, and you will see how much I remember from my research for *Scent of Gold*. He means notes as in music, Rilla. The top note of a perfume is that which strikes one immediately, but it quickly fades. Then comes the middle note, which is the heart of the fragrance. But this too mellows as time passes until we reach the base note, which lends a special character to the perfume, a sense of completeness. How was that, Henri?"

"Bravo, my friend."

"And of course every perfume yields a different aroma, depending on the woman who wears it," Jake continued. "On one woman it may be just a pleasant scent, but on another it may be a heady intoxication that robs a man of his senses."

Rilla flushed, because he was looking deeply into her eyes as he said that. Henri Rigaillaud chuckled. "And such a woman, I think, is M'selle Rilla Yorke. But it would need the very finest of perfumes to enhance the rare beauty that she possesses."

"You're very kind, Monsieur Rigaillaud," Rilla murmured awkwardly, "but I'm afraid that's a wild exaggeration."

"It is the truth," he protested gallantly. "Eh, Jake?"

"Every word of it!"

They entered the laboratory building and, after crossing a tiled vestibule, they passed through a door into a white-painted room that was lined with shelves holding row upon row of small stoppered glass bottles, all neatly labeled. A man who was seated at a bench rose to his feet and bowed a welcome. He was about the same age as Monsieur Rigaillaud, and a grave and aesthetic-looking person.

"Marcel, I have brought an American lady, M'selle Yorke, to see you at your wizardry. She is a special friend of Monsieur Carson here."

"*Bonjour, m'selle...monsieur.* It is a privilege that you call on me."

They spent a fascinating half hour in the laboratory. Monsieur Fabri spoke reverently of the many flower fragrances they used—not only rose but jasmine, blue hyacinth, narcissus, violet, rosemary, lavender, and orange blossom, all grown locally in their respective seasons. The journalist in Rilla spotted that it could all be written up into a most interesting article. A vision floated through her mind of a by-lined feature in the *New York Globe*'s Sunday supplement. Spurred by the exciting thought, she asked numerous questions to clarify points she didn't completely understand. Each was answered with the greatest patience and courtesy.

Before Rilla and Jake left, Monsieur Rigaillaud insisted that they adjourn to his office and take a farewell glass of wine with him.

"Your good health, *mes amis,*" he toasted, raising his stemmed glass.

Jake and Rilla murmured a response before sipping the ruby-red wine, which proved to be deliciously smooth and fruity. Rilla remarked on how well she liked it.

"You are most kind to say so, m'selle. But for how much longer, I wonder, will we French be able to claim preeminence for our wines? Your Californian growers are producing vintages that equal anything produced on this side of the Atlantic ocean."

"You know California, Monsieur Rigaillaud?"

"*Mais oui!* I was there three years ago, visiting a friend of mine who has set up a small *parfumerie* close to Los Angeles. I remember seeing the superb camellias of the Descanso gardens.... Ah, a truly beautiful flower that, alas, so rarely has a scent. And such roses you have in California... almost the equal of our roses of Provence. You come from San Francisco I believe, M'selle Yorke? A magnificent city."

"Thank you, Monsieur Rigaillaud. I'm so glad you like it."

"Is that where you and Jake met one another?" he inquired with an interested smile.

Rilla hesitated, wondering how to answer that. Jake intervened smoothly. "We did, Henri. I was paying a short visit, and Rilla came to interview me for an article in a local arts magazine."

"And now she is staying here with you?" Monsieur Rigaillaud touched the points of his mustache and adjusted his pince-nez, giving them an arch look. "Ah, but it does the heart good, *n'est-ce pas*, that romance can still blossom so quickly." He raised his glass once more. "I drink to you, *mes enfants*. I wish you every joy."

Rilla flushed in embarrassment, but Jake merely smiled amiably. A few minutes later, having said goodbye to the *parfumeur* at the door of his office, they walked back to the car. Jake held the door open for her.

"What's this?" Rilla exclaimed in surprise as she spotted a small white package lying on the passenger seat, neatly tied with gold ribbon.

"You'd better get in and take a look," Jake said dryly.

Slipping off the satin ribbon and outer wrapping, Rilla discovered a cardboard packet that was richly printed in gold and royal blue, similar to ones she'd seen in the packaging department.

"It's a bottle of Parfum d'Or!" she said delightedly, then read the inscription on the deckle-edged white card, which had fallen to her lap. "This masterpiece of the *parfumeur*'s art is offered in homage to a very beautiful woman."

She looked at Jake uncertainly. "Oh, dear, I don't know that I ought to accept this."

"Why not?" he asked, his brow ridged in a frown.

"Well, Monsieur Rigaillaud is obviously under a misapprehension about us—"

"Henri is a Frenchman," Jake cut in dismissively, "which is equivalent to saying that he's an unashamed romantic. What's that got to do with whether or not you accept the perfume?"

Rilla tilted her head to one side and scooped back her auburn hair while she considered. "I suppose it's okay," she said finally. "I mean, he manufactures Parfum d'Or wholesale, so to speak, so one small bottle isn't going to break the bank. It was a sweet thought, wasn't it? I'll write him a little note when we get back to say thank you for the gift."

Jake shot her a quick look, then shrugged. "No, don't do that."

"But I must."

"You can leave it to me," he said tersely, "to decide

what's the right thing to do. Next time I talk to Henri, I'll mention how pleased you were with the perfume."

"If you're sure . . ."

Jake gave an exasperated sigh. "I'm sure. Now, drop the subject, for God's sake."

As they started off, driving between the lush fields of flowers, Jake remained silent and his craggy features were set hard. Presently the road dipped down, and they entered another village. Without a word he stopped the car beside a simple little church that had a square belfry.

Gradually Jake's mood of sullen hostility seemed to leave him as they wandered together through the cobbled streets, admiring the picturesque narrow-fronted houses, each with a balcony of bright flowers and trailing greenery. After a few minutes they came to a small square with a level sandy surface. There, in the leafy shade of plane trees, a group of men were engaged in a ball game that looked rather like a rough-and-ready version of lawn bowling.

"It's called *boules*," Jake explained, "and it's a great favorite in Provence. As you can see, it's played by both old and young men."

They stood watching for a few moments till Rilla became uncomfortably aware that the men were casting interested glances in her direction and murmuring ribald comments to one another.

"Let's move on," she whispered, embarrassed.

Jake seemed amused. "As I said, young and old alike enjoy playing *boules*. Equally, young men and old men enjoy looking at a beautiful woman. You surely don't begrudge them, Rilla. It's a harmless enough occupation."

"Harmless! From all the nudging and winking that's going on, it's quite obvious what sort of remarks they're making about me."

Jake grinned. "You should thank your lucky stars that I'm here with you, Rilla. If you were alone, you'd be exposed to a lot more than the men nudging and winking among themselves. So look upon me as your protector." He darted her a challenging glance. "Or would you prefer me to make myself scarce and leave the field free for one of those lusty dark-eyed young guys to proposition you? I've been told that American women find Frenchmen irresistible."

"Can't you give it a rest?" she grated.

"I'll not utter another word on the subject. Let's clinch matters for our audience, shall we, with a little demonstration of our relationship."

Before she realized what he intended, Jake laid an arm lightly across her shoulders and bent and nuzzled his face into the fragrant cloud of her hair in an affectionate gesture. Rilla froze, horrified by the intense stab of longing that shafted through her. All that morning, through incredible self-control, she had steeled herself not to respond to his nearness, not to give a betraying shiver when every now and then he happened to brush against her, or he took her elbow to steer her somewhere. But that...it was too much to bear.

"Cut it out!" she said sharply. "I don't want any of it."

Jake laughed, unrepentant. "You're in no danger. I'm not about to throw you to the ground and make passionate love to you with people looking on. Let's go and eat now. I'm ravenous even if you aren't. There's a bistro just across the way, and if I'm not mistaken, they do a very good bouillabaisse there...remember, the savory fish stew I told you about?"

The café had tables set outside, shaded from the hot noonday sun by a red-striped awning. A cheerful girl in a blue print dress came out to take their orders. While they waited for the meal they sipped the local rosé wine Jake had chosen, which was cool and deliciously refreshing.

"You'll have an opportunity to try out your perfume this evening," said Jake. "I'm taking you to a party."

"A party?" she echoed, pleased. Then more cautiously she added, "Where? What sort of party?"

He looked into her eyes and laughed. "You don't need to worry, it'll all be very proper. The sort of party that has formal printed invitations. I phoned Zelie Lamont this morning to explain that you were staying with me, and she insisted that I take you along."

"You mean you twisted her arm?"

"I don't mean I twisted her arm. Zelie and I know one another intimately." He caught Rilla's swift glance and laughed again. "And I don't mean intimately the way you're thinking. I'm extremely fond of Zelie Lamont, but she happens to be a rather short, dumpy lady of about fifty. Moreover, she's very happily married to one of France's top portrait painters. Victoire Lamont is the sort of artist who gets commissioned by the world's rich and elite. You'll like them both, Rilla."

"It sounds as if it'll be rather a swank affair," she said anxiously, thinking of what she could wear.

"Nothing that you can't take in your stride. Good, here comes the food."

As the steaming, aromatic tureen was placed in front of them, with a basket of crisp melba toast, Rilla said apologetically, "I still feel a bit guilty about keeping you from work. You don't need to spend the whole day with me, Jake."

"It's all in a good cause. In any case, I managed a couple of hours of productive work while you were still in bed, besides having a swim."

Rilla took a spoonful of the stew and nodded her head appreciatively. "This is really good. What's in it exactly, do you know?"

"I imagine that every individual chef adds his own special touch of mystery. Basically, though, bouillabaisse is a fish called rascacio stewed together with red gurnard and conger eel. And probably some crab and crayfish, too. Then it's all dolled up with onion and tomato, and herbs like thyme and sage and fennel, and bay leaves." He grinned, taking a breath. "Plus a touch of orange peel and garlic and seasoning. And perhaps a spoonful of good French Cognac to add that final something."

"What a memory." She laughed. "I wouldn't have expected you to be interested in cooking, Jake."

"That's something else for your profile. I'll have you know, Rilla Yorke, that I could whip up an *omelette aux fines herbes* as good as anything you could do."

"Better, probably," she said with a rueful grin. "Making omelets is not one of my major accomplishments."

"You have plenty of plus factors already, without needing to add cordon bleu cooking to the list."

Rilla kept silent, not knowing how to answer that. Jake had spoken lightly, yet there was something in his tone that made the remark more significant than a flip retort. A loud cheer from the direction of the *boules* players, marking some sort of victory, gave her an excuse to turn her head and look away from him. She watched a peasant woman dressed in dusty black shuffle across the square toward them with a laden market basket, mumbling to herself. After a moment Rilla glanced at Jake covertly from behind her lashes and found to her dismay that he was studying her face intently. Feeling color creeping to her cheeks, she quickly looked down at her soup bowl and tried to continue spooning with a steady hand.

"Rilla..." He said her name so quietly that she was able to pretend not to have heard. When he repeated it, she looked up at him nervily, a dry feeling in her mouth.

"About last night..." he began, and his rugged face had a strangely serious expression that she couldn't identify.

"I don't want to talk about last night," she said flatly. All at once she was ridiculously flustered, on the edge of hysteria. She had to put down her spoon and rest her hands in her lap to keep them from trembling. Her throat felt tight, knotted, but somehow she forced out a flow of chatter to head Jake off from a dangerous subject. "I—I don't know what I ought to wear this evening. Will it be very formal, or what? I—I mean, I do have one long dress with me, an uncrushable pleated one in a sort of lime-green color, and maybe that would do—"

It was Jake's turn to interrupt, brusquely, with sharp impatience. "You'll look fantastic whatever you put on, Rilla, and you know it damn well."

"I'll wear that one, then, if you think that it'll be suitable."

"Suitable for what?" he said, a note of anger in his voice.

"Suitable for the occasion, like I said."

"If it's as sexy as that dress you wore when you dined with me at Casa del Sol," he said gratingly, "the effect you'll have is easy to predict. The other women present will mostly detest you on sight, while the men will drool over you. A number of them will undoubtedly make a pass, too. Only they won't get anywhere, I'll make sure of that."

"I don't need your protection," she flashed back. "I can look after myself." Rilla then caught her breath, containing her fury. "I won't go to the party. There's no point."

"And you're supposed to be smart!"

"Meaning?"

"Meaning, Rilla, that if you want to make it as a top journalist, you mustn't pass up on the opportunities that come your way. You'd have to wait a long time for another chance to meet such a collection of in people in a relaxed and friendly atmosphere. So are you coming or not?" he demanded impatiently.

She hesitated. Showing independence by saying no would feed her ego. But Jake was right, and he knew it. She looked at him with bitter resentment.

"I guess I might as well."

He showed no emotion, one way or the other, and merely nodded his head briskly. "So that's settled."

The road to Nice that evening took them through more exotic flower fields, and the soft air passing through the open windows of the big Citroën was drenched with the scent of roses and carnations. Those blooms, Jake explained to Rilla, weren't grown for making perfume but for the cut-flower trade, which had markets extending all over Western Europe.

The hostility that had sprung up between them over lunch still remained, and the only conversation was when Jake tossed her such snippets of information in a terse voice. Rilla felt far from enthusiastic about the party they were going to. Thank heaven that as an afterthought when packing her suitcase she'd slipped in the long dress of silky crepe. The subtle, gleaming shade of green that was somewhere between lime and turquoise suited her coloring, and she knew that the softly flowing pleated style flattered her slender figure, which would at least help bolster her confidence. Jake was looking immaculate in a white tuxedo and dark trousers, in utter contrast to the casual jeans and T-shirt and espadrilles he'd been wearing all day.

They reached the outskirts of Nice and within a short time were heading along the curving seafront boulevard, with its double avenues of palm trees and magnificent pink-and-white palaces. Trying to ease the tense atmosphere, Rilla asked Jake why it had been named the Promenade des Anglais.

"It was the English, back in the last century, who were responsible for making this whole Riviera coast so popular," he explained. "Those who could afford it built homes here to get away from the British climate. Now, though, those lavish private residences have either been torn down and replaced by modern hotels, or converted into luxury apartments. Our hosts tonight, the Lamonts, are among the elite few who still occupy an entire house on the Promenade des Anglais."

"They must be filthy rich."

"They're not short of the odd franc. Victoire can command an astronomical fee for a portrait these days, while Zelie has a private fortune. Her father owned a banking house in Paris."

Jake made a right turn into a forecourt that was bordered with exotic flowering plants in sculpted stone urns, and parked the Citroën among twenty or thirty other cars. Together he and Rilla mounted a flight of pink marble steps to the imposing entrance doors. A butler bowed them in, and they advanced into the splendidly ornate salon, which was lit by three glittering crystal chandeliers. It was already crowded with people, some of whom were dancing to the music of a five-piece band on a raised dais. Almost at once she and Jake were pounced upon by a short stoutish gray-haired woman in an expensive-looking gown of crimson taffeta with batwing sleeves. Though she was not classically beautiful, breeding and character showed in every wrinkled line of her face, and she had an attractive vivacity.

"Jake, *mon cher,* I am so happy that you bring your charming young lady to my little reception. Introduce me instantly!"

He took both her hands in his and bent to kiss the proffered cheek. "This is Rilla Yorke, Zelie... the journalist from San Francisco. As I explained on the phone, she is staying at Villa Ambrosia for a while. Rilla, this is Zelie Lamont, an old friend of mine and one of the Riviera's most fascinating ladies."

"What outrageous flattery! Jake is a dreadful tease, as I expect you know already. But I am most delighted to meet you, *ma chère.* Ah, how like Jake to find himself such a beauty! And with such chic. You American women stole that word from our language, you know."

"Maybe," Rilla answered with a smile. "But I don't think we can match French women when it comes to chic."

"But then you are not standing where we are standing. Eh, Jake, my friend?"

To change the conversation Rilla said hastily, "It was kind of you to invite me to your party, Madame Lamont. I only hope that I wasn't foisted on you."

"Foisted? What is this word?"

"I mean that Jake could easily have come this evening without me."

Zelie Lamont laughed merrily. "*Mais non!* He made it very apparent to me that he would not be parted from you for an instant of time. But, my dear child, you are most, most welcome. We have far too many aging matrons here and far too few pretty young women. Come, you must meet my husband, Victoire. And I am Zelie, remember, not Madame Lamont. I will not be put in the grave by one foot until it is necessary."

As the three of them approached a group in a corner of the large salon, one of the men broke off an earnest conversation to stare intently at Rilla. He was of medium height, with shoulder-length dark hair and a Vandyck that were turning to gray. His features were sharply chiseled and he possessed the most penetrating black eyes that Rilla had ever seen.

"Victoire, *chéri*," called Zelie, "I wish to introduce you to—"

He held up his hands to silence his wife, the palms thrust forward dramatically. "No, no, my angel...do not reveal her name yet. I perceive such an intriguing mystery here, such a complexity of emotion. I see great passion...but passion that has not been permitted to come to its full flowering. It is not true, m'selle, that you tremble on the brink of life and love? It frightens you, yet you are irresistibly drawn to taste its nectar."

"Victoire!" his wife admonished. "Can you not see that you embarrass our guest?"

But he paid Zelie no heed. Coming forward, he clasped a hand to each of Rilla's shoulders and studied her face assessingly. "You will allow me to paint your portrait, my unknown beauty?"

Rilla demurred, smiling apologetically. "I'm afraid, Monsieur Lamont, that I couldn't possibly afford your fee for a portrait."

"Pfff!" he exclaimed scornfully. "I am obliged to paint for money...yes! One must have bread and wine and a roof over one's head. But I am an *artiste,* and sometimes I have a need to paint from the heart. You will sit for me, beautiful creature, and I shall capture you on canvas not as you outwardly appear, but with the essential inner truth laid bare for all to see."

"Rilla will be honored to sit for you, Victoire," said Jake, meeting her glance in a long admiring look that made her heart skip a couple of beats.

"Rilla? This is her name? It is fitting. But I shall call you *La Belle Énigme*. It is agreed, then, that you come tomorrow in the morning? I cannot wait to commence."

"I—I can't possibly—" Rilla began to protest, but Jake interrupted her.

"She'll be here, Victoire. You can count on it."

As the host and hostess left them to greet newly arriving guests, Rilla demanded in an angry hiss, "Why on earth did you tell Monsieur Lamont that I'd sit for him, Jake?"

"Do you have any reason why you shouldn't?" he returned blandly as he took two glasses of champagne from the tray of a passing waiter.

"Well...for one thing, I won't be here long enough for him to finish a portrait of me."

"Victoire works very fast when he's enthusiastic about a model. You'll be here long enough, Rilla, believe me."

She felt excited, there was no denying that. To be painted by a world-famous artist! "What was that he called me?" she asked.

"*La Belle Énigme*. The Beautiful Enigma. Victoire is very shrewd, with that perceptive artist's eye of his. He summed you up in a single instant," Jake added, leaving Rilla deeply thoughtful.

Jake seemed to know just about everyone present and he took her around the room, introducing her to a confusing number of people of various nationalities. As Rilla made polite social noises—fortunately most of the guests spoke excellent English—Victoire Lamont's words were ringing in her mind: *". . . you tremble on the brink of life and love. It frightens you, yet you are irresistibly drawn to taste its nectar."*

An attractive slender girl of Rilla's own age whose name was Hélène sniffed the air as they said hello. "Do I detect a waft of Rigaillaud's Parfum d'Or?"

"How clever of you to guess!" Rilla explained how Jake had taken her earlier that day to see the *parfumerie*. She added, "It was such a surprise to find the bottle of perfume on the seat of the car when we came out. Wasn't it nice of Monsieur Rigaillaud to give it to me?"

"Nice? A miracle, I'd call it. Henri Rigaillaud is a charming old boy, but he's also a shrewd businessman." Hélène laughed. "He must have taken a real fancy to you, Rilla, to present you with some of his most expensive perfume. Aren't I right, Jake? Parfum d'Or is almost worth its weight in gold, you know."

At that moment the band struck up again, and Jake suggested that they dance. As he drew Rilla forward to the cleared space in the center of the room, she said anxiously, "I still feel that maybe I shouldn't have accepted such a pricey gift from Monsieur Rigaillaud."

"The perfume," he replied curtly, "was given in homage to your beauty."

Rilla left it there, aware that for some reason the subject displeased him. Jake was a superb dancer, as she might have guessed. In one way it was sheer bliss to move in unison with him to the dreamy, romantic beat of the music. Yet the close contact, being held in his arms and pressed intimately against the warmth of Jake's strong, muscular body, was having such a shattering effect on her emotions that she was almost thankful when the number came to an end.

Leaving the floor, they found themselves face to face with Princess Antoinette von Hohenzollern and her brother, who had just arrived. Rilla received a cool, brief nod from Antoinette, but Ferdinand greeted her warmly and was extravagantly complimentary about her appearance.

"May I be permitted the honor this time, Rilla?" he inquired with a dazzling smile as the music started once more.

"I guess so, Prince Ferdinand. Thank you."

"Please, I beg you...I am simply Ferdie to my friends. And you and I are already good friends, is that not so?"

He danced well, though much less fluidly than Jake. Away from his sister's overwhelming presence, Ferdie was quite chatty. But Rilla paid little attention to what he said. Her mind was focused on another couple on the crowded floor—Jake and Antoinette. The princess, wearing a fabulous bare-shouldered, sheathlike gown of white satin, and glittering with diamonds at her throat and ears and wrists, was pressed close against Jake's body as they moved in smooth unison—just as she had been a few moments earlier. Rilla was overcome with such stabbing jealousy that she felt sick to her stomach.

"It was a great pleasure," Ferdinand was saying, "to find you here tonight, Rilla. I had not anticipated this."

With effort she dragged her mind away from that other pair of dancers. "I didn't know myself that I was coming until this afternoon. Apparently when Madame Lamont heard that I was staying at Villa Ambrosia, she insisted that Jake bring me along."

"Already, from two different people," Ferdinand

continued, "I have heard that Victoire has insisted on painting the beautiful American. You must be very pleased."

"Well...naturally. I mean, I feel terribly flattered that such a renowned artist should want to paint me. I'm not sure that I can accept, though."

"But you must!" Ferdinand sounded quite shocked. "It is a great honor, you understand. The people who commission a portrait from Lamont are required to wait a long time for their turn to come. I happen to know this very well, Rilla. My sister made her request to him before last Christmas, and it will still be many months before he can commence to paint Antoinette."

Rilla felt a shameful little bubble of triumph. The fact that Victoire Lamont was so keen to do a portrait of her, starting the very next day, would make bitter hearing for the haughty émigré princess.

At the end of her dance with Ferdinand, Rilla was instantly claimed by a distinguished-looking man with silver-gray hair who wore the insignia of the *Légion d'honneur*. Gallantly, with the expertise of much practice, he steered her through the Viennese waltz that followed. From their conversation Rilla gathered that he held a post of some importance in the government.

"*Merci, m'selle,* that was most delightful," he said, bowing, as the music stopped. "And now permit me to find you some refreshment."

He led Rilla through to the dining room, where a sumptuous-looking buffet had been set out on a long table, including dressed lobsters and succulent hams, whole sides of smoked salmon, platters of deviled drumsticks and stuffed eggs, cold meats and pâtés of all descriptions, and mountains of colorful salads. There were crystal bowls of strawberries and brandied peaches, and the most gorgeous gooey *gâteaux* and cheesecakes. Picking up one of the delicate porcelain plates that was edged with gold leaf around a design of vine leaves, the gentleman inquired attentively as to which of the many delectable dishes she would care to sample.

Rilla suddenly became aware that Jake was standing right beside her, and with him was Princess Antoinette, who clung to his arm possessively. When Rilla's elderly companion had placed a spoonful of caviar and some rice and mushroom salad on her plate, he too noticed Jake and exclaimed with a chuckle, "Ah, *mon ami...* what a lucky fellow you are! This charming young lady has been telling me that she has come to the Riviera to write about you for one of the American newspapers. What a delightful surprise it must have been to discover that the journalist sent to interview you was *une belle dame.*"

Jake laughed. "But it was no surprise to me, *Monsieur le Député.* You see, I already knew Rilla in California... knew her, in fact, very well."

"Ah, you sly dog! So you cunningly arranged matters so that your interviewer would only write complimentary things about you, eh?"

"Complimentary things? I seriously doubt that. Despite what appearances may suggest, I assure you that Rilla is ruthless in her dedication to hard fact. She's also a very perceptive woman. She'll write nothing but the truth about me—warts and all! Her very phrase."

Antoinette gave a low, throaty laugh. "But, Jake, *mon cher,* how can she write the truth about you? Rilla doesn't really know you, not as I do."

Whatever Jake might have replied was interrupted by their hostess, who bore down upon Rilla with an apologetic smile.

"Oh, my dear, I've been wanting to have a little

word with you. I beg you, do not be upset by my husband's lack of tact. Victoire is such an enthusiast about his painting that he cannot bear to be thwarted when he sees an ideal subject for a portrait. I do hope that you will indulge the poor man, Rilla, and agree to sit for him tomorrow."

"With the greatest of pleasure, Zelie. I feel most honored that he should be so keen to paint me."

There was a look of sheer outrage on Antoinette's face. Her eyes blazed and her lovely features were contorted with fury. Disengaging herself from Jake's arm, she picked up a plate and started helping herself to some wafer-thin smoked salmon.

Zelie Lamont was saying "How many days, *ma chère,* do you plan to stay at Villa Ambrosia? Will your assignment take very long? I do hope that you will not be rushing away from us."

Before Rilla could answer, Jake interposed. With his lips twisted in a rueful little smile, he said, "It's no use, Rilla darling, we can't hope to keep our secret for very long. They'll all have to know."

"Know what?" demanded Zelie, excitement dancing in her vivacious sherry-colored eyes. "No, do not say it, because I can guess. You two are affianced, *n'est-ce pas?* Engaged to be married? Don't tell me that I am wrong."

Jake slipped his arm around Rilla's slender waist and drew her close against his side, giving her no chance to resist. "You see, darling"—he laughed, bending his head to kiss her on the brow—"it's impossible to keep such things from Zelie."

Their hostess gurgled with happy laughter. "I am so overjoyed for you both." She kissed Rilla warmly on each cheek, then did the same to Jake.

Rilla, still in a daze of disbelief, tried to make her

brain function. Jake's arm around her waist, to all appearances fondly casual, was in reality a circle of steel. In desperation she said to Zelie, "Please...listen to me. You've got it all wrong."

But Zelie didn't hear. Already she was clambering onto one of the little gilt chairs. Balanced somewhat precariously, she clapped her hands to command attention.

"*Écoutez*...everyone. I have something very exciting to announce."

Fighting against Jake's restraining arm, Rilla said frantically, "Stop her before she says any more."

"It's too late," he replied with a shrug, not seeming to care.

"Too late? For pity's sake, you should have contradicted her at once. What in the world are people going to think?"

Zelie was then in full flow. With a sinking heart Rilla realized that it was unthinkable to interrupt at that stage and make Zelie look foolish before her assembled guests. The story of their "engagement" would have to be explained away later as a regrettable misunderstanding.

"I can reveal to you now, *mes amis,* that these past months when we imagined that our good friend Jake was at his home in New York City, working on his new novel, he was in reality spending the winter in California. And the reason is not hard to grasp. He was, it emerges, cultivating his romance with this delightful newcomer to our midst, Mademoiselle Rilla Yorke. When Jake returned to the Riviera a few days ago, he said not one word of explanation to any of us, and when Rilla herself arrived, he announced that she was a journalist come to write about him for a New York newspaper. This is the truth, perhaps, but it is only a tiny piece of the truth. You see, *mes amis,* these two sweet people are engaged to be married. So let us raise our glasses and drink to their good health and happiness.''

There was a general cheer, and congratulations came showering from every side. Rilla, her cheeks crimson with embarrassment, could only stare at the floor. If ever an earthquake would have been welcome, that was the moment.

Jake, still keeping his arm firmly about her waist, made a speech of response in rapid fluent French. Rilla couldn't even begin to follow what he was saying, his words seeming to boom hollowly in her brain. Forcing herself to look up, she saw a confused sea of smiling faces and raised glasses, and from among them, springing suddenly into sharp focus, one face that was not smiling. Antoinette von Hohenzollern's jet-stone eyes were narrowed in jealous fury, and her beautiful face had become a hideous mask. But even as Rilla watched, the princess won the upper hand over her emotions, and her features smoothed to an expression that was distantly related to a smile. Rilla gave her credit for iron self-discipline.

In the throng of people who were all pressing forward to offer their good wishes, Rilla and Antoinette became thrust against one another.

''So!'' the princess hissed into her ear while Jake's attention was diverted by friends wanting to shake his hand. ''You have managed to capture him with your cute American ways. But how long will you keep him, ask yourself that!'' Then Antoinette was gone, carried away by the eddying crowd.

Rilla felt on the edge of hysteria and clutched at Jake's sleeve urgently. ''We must talk.''

''Sure! We'll leave in a few minutes. But we have to say our good-byes properly.''

It seemed to be accepted as quite understandable that the two of them would leave early. The newly engaged couple wished to be alone together, *naturellement!* Zelie, misty eyed with the romance of it all, kissed them warmly once more and began to shepherd them from the room, beckoning her husband to join them.

"What a pair of teasers!" Victoire exclaimed with a chuckle as he came up. "You were deceiving me. The title of my painting can be *La Belle Énigme* no longer. It shall be called instead *Portrait of Love*. And it will be my wedding gift to the happy couple."

Chapter Eight

"What the blazes did you think you were doing, letting Zelie Lamont get that lunatic idea in her head and then not denying it?" demanded Rilla furiously as they drove off from the Lamonts' house along the Promenade des Anglais. "Now you'll have to admit to everyone that the whole thing was just a stupid practical joke."

"Leave it until we're clear of the town," Jake said brusquely. Rilla held her tongue, forced to acknowledge that it was no place for a showdown, with fast-moving traffic all around them. In silent fury she managed to contain her impatience until they had climbed high above Nice and turned off the main highway.

"Well," she burst out at length. "I'm waiting for an explanation."

Jake drew in to the side of the narrow road and cut the engine and headlights. "Don't get in such a flap, Rilla. There's no harm done."

"No harm done!" she raged. "You've made a complete fool of me . . . and of yourself, come to that."

"Relax! The announcement of our engagement suits my purpose very nicely."

"Your purpose? And what bizarre purpose is that?"

Jake reached forward and pressed a button to let the driver's window down, and the coolness of the night air flowed in. Against the faint starlight Rilla could see his head and shoulders in silhouette, could see the glitter of his eyes.

"Naturally you'll accuse me of being arrogant and bigheaded," he drawled, "but the plain truth is that wherever Jake Carson goes, women throw themselves at him."

"Are you complaining?" she inquired sarcastically. "I was under the impression that you gloried in your Casanova role."

"The point I'm making is that I'm seen as a catch purely and simply because the name Jake Carson is internationally famous. Being pursued primarily for that reason gets to be a bore."

Trying to crush down a swift surge of jealousy, Rilla asked, "Why should you care, as long as the women are all so eager to jump into bed with you?"

"Because I prefer to do my own persuading," he clipped. "What man doesn't?"

"I wouldn't have thought that Princess Antoinette needed much in the way of persuading." It was out before Rilla could stop herself.

Jake laughed reprovingly. "Sheathe those claws, little pussycat." His tone changed, becoming serious. "My relationship with Antoinette started off nice and easy, with no strings on either side, but since I arrived back here she's been crowding me. I'm not suggesting that she's fallen in love with me—"

"Such modesty!"

Jake sighed. "But it's clear that Antoinette has decided that she'd like to marry again, and she sees me as good husband material. The fact that I'm a literary celebrity compensates for my inferior social status. And as for the financial aspect...the large income I make from my books would rob the gossip columnists of a chance to sneer about my marrying Princess Antoinette von Hohenzollern for her money."

"So why don't you go ahead and marry her, then?"

"Because I don't happen to want to. I'm not prepared to play lapdog to any woman, and that's what Antoinette would expect. You've seen the way she is with Ferdie. Besides, Antoinette isn't my type—not for a permanent relationship."

"What do you have against telling her that straight out?" Rilla demanded.

"It would be a bit premature, since the subject of marriage hasn't yet arisen."

"So why not wait until it does?"

"This seemed a better way. When Zelie jumped to conclusions tonight, I let it ride."

"At my expense," she pointed out bitterly. "But what's going to happen when you're forced to admit that you and I aren't really engaged at all?"

"I'll cross that bridge when I come to it."

"That means now—tonight," Rilla told him sharply. "Or at any rate first thing in the morning. I'm not letting this crazy lie continue."

"There's no need to be hasty," Jake argued. "It won't matter if we leave things as they are until you return to the United States."

"That's going to be tomorrow," Rilla stated flatly. "You've made it impossible for me to stay here any longer."

"But you can't leave tomorrow," Jake objected. "For one thing, Rilla, you're committed to sitting for Victoire Lamont."

"And that's just one more aspect of the ridiculous mess you've landed me in," she rushed on furiously.

"Victoire is planning to give us the portrait as a wedding gift. So that settles the whole thing. I just can't let him start it."

"But Victoire wanted to paint you the first moment he set eyes on you. That was before he heard anything about our engagement. So he'll still want to paint you, entirely for his own satisfaction."

Rilla bit her lip, remembering the virtual promise she had made to Zelie to indulge her husband's whim. Still, considering the circumstances, Zelie would surely understand and forgive her. "You'll just have to explain things as best you can to the Lamonts," she told Jake decidedly, "because I won't be staying."

"Not even if I ask you very nicely?"

"Oh, for heaven's sake...the joke's gone stale."

"But I'm serious, Rilla." Jake moved in his seat, half turning to her. "This pseudoengagement of ours.... Why don't we make it for real?"

"For—for real?" she stammered, shaken.

His voice quickened. "The more I think about it, the more I like the idea. You and I would make quite a nicely matched couple. It wouldn't do you any harm careerwise to be married to me. And as for myself, the existence of a wife would help me fend off the unwelcome attention of women fans. We can get along together just fine if we try, Rilla—today's outing proved that. And there's nothing incompatible about our physical relationship—we've proved that already, too. So why don't we follow through and actually tie the knot?"

"You've got to be joking!"

Jake reached out for her hand, linking his fingers through hers caressingly, causing little eddies of pleasurable excitement to ripple through her. "I tell you I'm serious, Rilla, totally serious. In fact, I can't see a single valid argument against the idea. You've made it clear that there's currently no special man in your life, and you've no family to raise any objection, so—"

"How can you talk about marriage in such a cold-blooded, calculating way?" she interrupted furiously. "Doesn't love have any place at all in your heart?"

"The heart, Rilla, is an exceedingly tough muscular organ whose sole function is to pump blood around the body. I prefer to be governed by my brain, which is a far more reliable guide."

"While I," she flashed back, "prefer a million times to be guided by my heart."

"Okay, so let me ask you a question. What does your heart tell you about me?"

Rilla was silent, feeling suddenly breathless. Before, it had seemed a bitter irony that she should have fallen in love with a man who didn't return her love. But the situation was doubly ironic now. What a cruel trick fate had played on her. She had only to utter one little word of assent to become Jake's wife; yet their marriage would be a hollow mockery....

Aware that Jake was still holding her hand, she snatched it away from him. "Please...let's drive on."

"But you haven't given me your answer yet, Rilla."

"Do I need to? It's totally out of the question."

"You may come to see things differently when you've gotten used to the idea," Jake suggested.

"I won't."

"At least sleep on it, Rilla. Give me your answer in the morning."

"I'm giving you my answer now."

"Then give it to me again in the morning."

"My answer will be exactly the same," she insisted.

"We'll see," he said quietly and started the car.

Never had a night seemed so long to Rilla. Much of it she spent sitting on the padded window seat, hoping that the cool fragrant air would help to clear her head and untangle the whirling confusion of emotion that was tearing her apart.

Her only sensible option was quite clear to her. First thing in the morning she would pack her bags and get to the airport for the soonest possible flight back to San Francisco. She would abandon all thought of writing the profile on Jake Carson, forget the dazzling opportunities it could lead to in her career, and scurry back to the safe cocoon of her comparatively undemanding job with the *Bay Area Arts Reporter*.

And she would be fated to remember Jake, yearn for him, every single day for the rest of her life. That couldn't be helped.

But sometimes during the long, seemingly endless hours of the night a tiny voice of temptation made itself heard above the clamor of her rational thoughts. Suppose...just for one moment suppose that she *did* agree to marry Jake, what then? She would be free to continue with her own career, he had made that clear, and her connection with a best-selling author would undoubtedly open doors for her. But it was a minimal consideration compared with the fact that she'd experience the happiness of being with the man she loved. Though Jake didn't love her in return, was that so vital? It was useless any longer to dream of one day finding the ideal marriage partner. Since she'd met Jake, she knew she could never attain complete fulfillment with any other man. So wasn't it sensible to settle for what she could get? Even the less-than-perfect marriage would still be infinitely better than many women were ever lucky enough to achieve. And perhaps—surely it was possible?—Jake might gradually grow to feel a small measure of love for her in return. . . .

No, it was crazy to think that way. The whole idea was utterly preposterous.

Dawn arrived at last, a delicate rosy flush in the eastern sky that quickly turned to golden splendor. Rilla splashed her face with cold water, donned jeans and a green cable knit sweater, and tied back her auburn hair with a black velvet ribbon. Then she descended the stairs quietly and let herself out into the dew-fresh glory of the morning.

The day before, Jake had been at work early. Although Rilla couldn't hear his typewriter—maybe because all the birds in the garden were singing fit to bust—she kept well away from the side of the villa where he had his study, taking a path that skirted two sides of the tennis court and led through an avenued walk of small orange trees. Strolling on without conscious aim, Rilla found that her footsteps had led her down to a small hexagonal belvedere, built on a natural outcrop of rock and protected by a decorative iron railing from which bougainvillaea hung in rosy festoons. With a morning haze still lingering in the still air, the vibrant Provençal colors were softly muted. She inhaled fragrance with every breath as butterflies and gauzy insects flitted among the clumps of purple thyme at her feet, gathering nectar.

Presently she heard footsteps on the path behind her. Spinning around, she saw Jake approaching.

"I spotted you heading in this direction," he said. "You're up early, Rilla. Couldn't you sleep?"

Rilla didn't answer that. She felt totally thrown by the unexpected encounter. She hadn't yet worked herself into a frame of mind to face Jake—if she ever would be ready!

"I'm sorry if I disturbed you from working," she murmured awkwardly.

"You didn't," Jake said. "I haven't been trying to work this morning. Somehow I'm not in the right mood."

"Oh!"

He came to stand beside her and leaned his elbows on the railing to look out at the view. His closeness was so disturbing that Rilla edged away a little. Then came the question she was waiting for and dreading.

"Well, Rilla... what's your answer this morning?"

"I—I gave it to you last night," she faltered.

"But you don't sound nearly as emphatic as you did last night." Jake paused, letting the emotional charge between them grow. Then he added with a coaxing smile, "Won't you reconsider, Rilla? You have to agree that my proposal makes good sense."

"Is good sense the proper basis for marriage?"

"All too many marriages fail for lack of it," he countered.

"But there has to be something else, too. A great deal more, in fact."

"Granted. There has to be mutual respect and liking, plus a strong physical attraction. Otherwise married life would be hell."

"But what I meant was—" Oh, what was the use of arguing the point, she thought wearily. "Jake, I want to call the airport right away and make a reservation on the first flight home."

Jake gave her a long look that held reproach. In the slanting sunlight the sculpted lines of his face stood out in sharp relief. "Are you really so uncaring about hurting the feelings of nice people like the Lamonts? Victoire has honored you, Rilla, in proposing to paint your portrait."

She hesitated. "I fully realize that, and I hate the thought of disappointing Victoire. Zelie, too. She meant well, and she can't be blamed for getting the wrong idea about us. That was entirely your fault, Jake. If there was a way of apologizing to the Lamonts, I'd do so, but—but I don't see how."

Noticing her indecision, Jake reached out to touch her arm in a persuasive gesture. At once Rilla leaped away as if she'd been stung. "Cut that out!" she said angrily.

There was a long, pulsing silence, then Jake said in a quiet voice, "And if I promised to keep my hands off you...if I never so much as laid a finger on you again, would that allow you to forget what it was like to be held in my arms? Don't fool yourself, Rilla."

"At least I'd be able to live with myself," she retorted.

"Much better to live with *me*. A marriage between us would have all the prerequisites for success. Friendship, mutual respect...and a satisfying physical relationship."

But not love, thought Rilla. Or rather, just a hopeless one-sided love. Yet maybe, the treacherous little inner voice of hers began to argue again, an unrequited love was better than no love at all?

Nonsense! Nonsense!

"It's not enough," she said vehemently. "You can't take such a coldly analytical view of marriage. You can't leave emotion out of it."

Jake's voice was scathing. "Like most women, Rilla, you dream of the great, all-consuming romance. But what is romance, when you come down to a basic definition? It's a state of highly charged physical excitement— just the same as you experienced with me that evening in Sausalito, and again on the day you arrived here."

"But it's much, much more," Rilla cried passionately. "It's— There's no way I can hope to explain. It's something that you'll never even begin to understand, with your attitude to sex as the be-all and end-all of everything."

"I've never claimed that sex is everything," Jake threw back. "It's only a part of any relationship... but a damn important ingredient. And you can't deny it, Rilla."

"Of course I don't deny it."

Jake nodded in satisfaction. "Right, then! So let's start over from the top." He used his fingers to tick off points. "One... we'd have a good physical relationship Rilla, you know that already. Two... we'd have friendship, because the potential is there between us for a strong, sustained closeness. Three... there'd be respect, that of two intelligent people for one another. And, last but not least, our marriage would be a matter of mutual convenience. So I'll ask you again, and I shall go on asking you until you see sense. Will you marry me?"

Rilla felt as if the fingers of some gigantic hand were gripping her heart and squeezing it tightly. She closed her eyes with the pain of it. Jake had moved closer, and the warmth of his virile body seemed to radiate across the narrow gap that separated them. She could feel his breath gently stirring her hair. She had an intense longing to reach out her arms to him, to have him gather her to him and hold her close. With her eyes tightly shut, the longing grew to a frantic, desperate need, but still she fought against it.

Jake's voice was throbbingly deep as he said once more, "Will you marry me, Rilla?"

"You—you're not being fair," she whispered.

"I think I am."

She should say no, she *had* to say no. From nowhere
a vision sprang into her mind of her breakup with Theo,
of the loneliness and misery she'd had to endure afterward. With Jake it would be ten times worse, she knew,
a hundred times worse. She would be parting with the
man she loved, never to set eyes on him again. A terrifying picture came to her of the years stretching ahead,
empty years from which even the excitement of building her career would have drained away. It wouldn't be
living, just existing...a life too dismal to contemplate.
And yet the alternative was unthinkable.

Unthinkable? So why did she have temptation creeping out from every corner of her mind? Her eyes
sprang open and she looked up at Jake's lean face, only
a few inches from her own. The strength of his gaze
seemed to mesmerize her, sapping her willpower, her
resistance.

"How can I marry you, Jake?" she said helplessly.

"Very easily. Just by saying yes."

"Please...please let me go." But Jake wasn't physically restraining her. Her plea to him was to cease con-
niving with her own desperate longing.

"No, Rilla, I won't let you go," he said remorselessly.

"But you must...."

He shook his head. "I shall keep on asking you to
marry me until you finally agree. If you run away, I
shall follow you."

"But why?" she asked, her breath catching on a sob.
"There must be a hundred other women you could
marry."

"I'm asking *you*. Will you marry me, Rilla?"

"I—I can't."

Jake's reaction was to move closer until she could no
longer focus on his face. Or was the blurring of her

vision caused by the prickly tears that filled her eyes? She could feel his sexual magnetism, smell the heady male odor of him, and she shivered under the imagined touch of those smooth-rough fingertips sensuously roaming her body....

"Will you marry me, Rilla?" he asked inexorably.

"No!" she said faintly.

"Will you marry me, Rilla?" His voice seemed to reverberate hollowly, as if in a great cavern. The world seemed to grow dark, and she felt as if everything were spinning around her. Her legs were suddenly boneless and she would have fallen but for Jake's strong hands supporting her, holding her by the shoulders. She was trembling in every limb.

"Will you marry me, Rilla?"

"Yes!" It emerged as a cry of despair, the only way to end the unbearable torment. "Yes," she sobbed again. "I will, Jake, I will."

For long, pulsing moments there was a breathless hush. It was as if Jake had been taken by surprise by her sudden capitulation. Then he said in a level voice, "So you've finally decided to be sensible."

Sensible? It was madness, sheer, unadulterated madness. Rilla knew—as far as she could comprehend anything in those moments of surging emotion—that she ought to be denying her fateful words. She ought to be insisting that she'd not really meant what she'd just said. But somehow her tongue was knotted, and no sound came from her lips. She could only stare at Jake, silently beseeching him to take her into his arms and put an end to her unbearable, aching need of him.

Incredibly, though, the hands on her shoulders dropped, and Jake turned away from her to look out at the view again.

"We must make plans, Rilla," he continued matter-of-factly. "There's no sense in wasting time. I suggest that a couple of weeks is all we need. Would that be okay with you?"

"You mean...get married in two weeks time? But that's out of the question."

"Give me one good reason why."

"Because...." Her mind reeled in consternation. "For one thing, I'll have to go back home to get things sorted out—my house and so on."

"You can do all that afterward. We'll go to San Francisco together."

Dear heaven...Jake was sweeping her along too fast. And yet, her decision had been made, so why should they delay? The thought that in only two short weeks she would be Jake's wife was deliriously intoxicating—and terrifying, too. She was afraid of herself, of the strength of her emotions, which even then were tearing her apart.

"I—I have clothes to buy, and—"

"No problem," he said crisply. "Don't be timid, Rilla. What's happened to the boldly determined young woman who came haring over here from California to pin me down to an interview?"

Rilla made no response. Her mind was spinning wildly and she felt hopelessly bewildered. Jake said softly, "So it's agreed, then? Two weeks from today." He turned back to face her and his voice became softer still. "I think we should seal it with a kiss, don't you?"

Robbed of breath by the thought, Rilla nodded her head slowly. Stepping forward, Jake encircled her with his arms and drew her close against his lean, muscular body as his lips came down to meet hers. But instead of melting against him as she longed to do, Rilla was so nervous that she kept herself rigidly still, not daring to betray the strength of her feelings.

Jake, unable to extract a response from her, drew away, shrugging, and his voice at once became brisk. "I promised to have you at Victoire's studio by ten o'clock. When he's through with you, I'll take you somewhere for lunch in Nice, and then we'll go shopping. There are various arrangements to be made, and the engagement ring to buy, apart from clothes you need. I'll tell Pierre we'll have breakfast right away. Then you can change, Rilla, and we'll get moving."

She said huskily, "What do you think I should wear for the sitting?"

"Talk to Victoire about that. This will only be a preliminary sketch, so it won't matter what you put on this morning."

"Will you—will you tell him about us?" she asked awkwardly. "I mean, that we've fixed on an actual day to get married?"

"Sure! I'll broadcast it to everyone. After all," he added with a twisted grin, "letting it be known that I'm no longer an available bachelor is the whole object of the exercise, isn't it?"

Victoire Lamont's studio was a large, sparsely furnished room on the top floor of his house on the Promenade des Anglais. Two huge skylights faced north to capture the best light for a painter, so although there was no direct sunshine, the white-walled room seemed to glow with a pearly radiance.

Zelie escorted both Rilla and Jake up there, but her husband immediately banished Jake.

"For the next two hours, *mon ami,* your fiancée is mine—to make of her what I will. So be off with you."

"Whatever you say," Jake agreed with a smile. "Incidentally, Rilla will not remain my fiancée for long. We're getting married two weeks from today."

Zelie exclaimed with delight, "Ah, but that is wonderful! I am overjoyed for you both. When you return to fetch Rilla, Jake, we will drink champagne to toast your health and happiness, eh Victoire?"

Her husband nodded absently. Already, it was clear, he had immersed himself in the artistic problems of transferring his vision of Rilla onto canvas. As the door closed behind Jake, Victoire began talking excitedly to his wife, almost as if Rilla were an inanimate object. The dress she had chosen, a pretty sprigged print with an almond-green background, he dismissed with a contemptuous wave of the hand. "It will not do! I see her in a classical role, as Venus awaiting her Adonis... *Ah oui,* the goddess of love and beauty. Fetch me something, Zelie *chérie,* something white and soft that will fall in beautiful folds."

Zelie departed and was back in a couple of minutes with a silk bedsheet. Rilla, having slipped out of her dress behind a Chinese screen, was instructed to sit on a low velvet stool while Zelie set about draping the silken fabric gracefully over Rilla's slender form, fastening it with a filigree gold brooch at her shoulder and a golden chain around her waist, to a rapid fire of exhortations from Victoire.

"*Ah oui, ah oui, c'est parfait!* Quite, quite perfect! Her head a little to the left, *chérie,* and her right arm so." He demonstrated. "There, that is enough, touch nothing more. You are a genius, my lovely wife!" He shot Rilla a sharp glance from beneath his bushy gray eyebrows. "Remain still, *s'il vous plaît*. Do not fidget."

Zelie left them alone then, and Victoire commenced working. Though he talked all the time, none of his remarks seemed really directed at Rilla. Rather, the artist chattered away to himself as he sketched rapidly in charcoal on his canvas.

With nothing demanded of her other than to sit still, Rilla allowed herself to dream of the future, wondering what it held for her. Nearly two hours later, when Zelie came bursting in with Jake right behind her, she was astonished to find how quickly the time had passed.

"That is quite enough for one day," Zelie instructed her protesting husband. "The poor girl must be quite exhausted."

"Very well," he agreed reluctantly. "*Merci beaucoup,* Rilla. You have been most patient."

Jake, she noted with pleasure, was viewing her with a look of glowing appreciation in his deep-set blue eyes. "You look ethereally beautiful," he murmured softly. "Like a piece of classical sculpture."

Flushing at this unexpected compliment, Rilla was glad to step behind the screen to change back into her dress. When she rejoined the others, Jake drew a small jeweler's box from his jacket pocket.

"I've not been wasting my time this morning," he told her. "Let's try this on for size."

"This" was a platinum ring, set with a huge emerald flanked by glittering diamonds. It fitted perfectly as Jake slid it on the third finger of her left hand. Rilla stared at the magnificent ring in awed delight, not daring to guess what it must have cost.

Zelie came bounding over to them. "Let me see! Ah, but how beautiful! And an emerald is so exactly right for your coloring, Rilla *ma chère*. You clever man, Jake. Now...kiss your fiancée and set the seal on your engagement."

Again Rilla felt herself trembling at the prospect, just as at the villa that morning. Yet, when Jake laid his hands on her shoulders and bent to touch his lips to hers, it was as if she were suddenly transformed to a block of ice. She saw Jake's mouth tighten in annoyance as he let her go and stepped back.

The butler entered the studio, bearing a bottle of champagne and four glinting crystal glasses on a silver tray. Victoire splashed out the bubbling golden liquid, and he and his wife raised their glasses in a toast.

"We drink to your lifelong happiness, *mes amis,*" he said. "May your union bring you all the joy and contentment that ours has brought to us."

Zelie took two quick sips, then said excitedly, "Jake and I have been busy making plans, Rilla. He told me that, alas, you have no parents, no relatives at all. So Victoire and I shall deputize for them. You are to be married here, and the wedding reception we will give you will be a memorable one, I promise you."

Rilla glanced quickly at Jake, but he was looking elsewhere, and she could see that he was still angry about her icy response to his kiss.

Chapter Nine

Daylight was fading when, after a long drive through the mountains, Jake and Rilla reached the frontier post between France and Switzerland. The Swiss officials were brisk, efficient, and courteous. In moments the big Citroën was waved past, and the honeymooners were on the last short lap of their journey to the lakeside city of Geneva.

Rilla sat beside her husband in a state of numb misery. Each day of the past two weeks had been hectic, with so much to do in preparation for her wedding. Apart from shopping for clothes with Jake, doing the rounds of fabulously expensive haute couture salons, she had written a number of letters to her friends back home in San Francisco. Jake Carson's marriage would be widely reported in the media, and she hated to think that anyone who knew her would first hear about it in a newscast. Also, she'd had to write to Bill Andersen to explain the situation and resign from her job on *BAAR*.

There had been a daily sitting for Victoire Lamont to be fitted in, too. The painter worked like one possessed, ignoring Rilla for the most part and muttering away to himself. He couldn't be persuaded to allow either Jake or herself to see how the portrait was progressing. "No, no, *mes amis,* I shall add the finishing touches while you are on your honeymoon. When you return, we shall have a ceremonial unveiling."

Aside from all that, Rilla had written her two-thousand word article for the *New York Globe,* which was to reveal to the world the secret of Jake's dual identity as an author. She felt reasonably confident that she'd acquitted herself well. Her profile of Jake wasn't a rave job—she deplored the machismo of his heroes and pointed to a couple of weaknesses in his literary style—but it was by no means the bitterly critical attack that her piece about Richard Kellerman for *BAAR* had been.

Before mailing the article she had offered it to Jake to read. He had refused, though, making a rueful face. "With less than three days to go before the wedding, I guess it wouldn't be such a good idea to find out what you really think of me."

"There's nothing in it that you could reasonably object to, Jake."

"I'm glad to hear it! Still, given the chance, I might feel tempted to suggest revisions that would present me in a more favorable light. You'd better let it go off as your own, unadulterated work."

It had been a strange interlude for Rilla. In public Jake behaved with all the warmth of an adoring fiancé. In private, though, he made no moves toward intimacy, contenting himself with a light kiss on her cheek to greet her in the morning and to say good night. Nevertheless, dismayingly, his slightest touch sent her rocketing to dizzy heights of longing. She felt ashamed of such intensity of feeling in view of the unromantic nature of their impending marriage. For pride's sake she steeled herself against betraying her true feelings, which made her tense and awkward whenever Jake

came near her. Even their conversation became painfully stilted.

Things would be quite different, Rilla kept promising herself, when the wedding was over and she and
Jake were on their honeymoon. She would be able to
relax then and respond to him spontaneously and naturally. Their relationship wouldn't be roses all the way—
she wasn't that much of a fool—but surely the very
strength of her love for Jake would smooth the path for
them. It might take time, but if she was patient, surely
she could hope eventually to win Jake's love in return.
And then...oh, then, their future together would be
far more wonderful than she'd ever bargained for when
she'd first agreed to marry him.

Those optimistic thoughts had buoyed her up throughout the inevitable hassle of the wedding preparations.
Though Rilla was inviting no one herself, Zelie had
compiled a guest list of hundreds, every single one of
whom, she insisted, *must* be asked. Everything had
gone without a single hitch—until just half an hour
before she and Jake were due to set off on their honeymoon. It was then that Rilla had accidentally eaves-
dropped on a conversation that completely shattered all
her hopes for the future.

The incident occurred when she'd chanced to find
herself alone and unobserved for a moment in the Lamonts' grand salon. Seizing the golden opportunity,
she had slipped behind one of the marble pillars for a
brief respite from the strain of holding a permanent
smile and murmuring polite responses to the shower
of congratulations and good wishes. While lingering
there, bracing herself to step out and face the throng
once more, Rilla heard a female voice coming from just
the other side of the pillar.

"Well, my friend," the woman was saying with a

soft chuckle, "you have undoubtedly cramped your style now. Never did I think to see the day when Jake Carson permitted himself to get hooked and landed."

Jake's answer came in an equally bantering tone. "But, Germaine *chérie,* I don't in any way regard myself as having been hooked and landed. Nor do I envisage a future in which I'll suffer any kind of deprivation."

At that point another couple joined them, and there was a general exchange of bright chitchat. Then Jake and the other man moved away together, and the two women were talking alone.

"It seems," drawled Germaine confidentially, "that Jake has not really changed his life—he still has every intention of sleeping around."

"Really?" There was an excited, amused gasp. "Do you mean he actually told you so?"

"Yes, just a second ago. He made no bones about it." Germaine laughed maliciously. "Rilla will have to reconcile herself to spending a couple of nights alone each week."

For a few moments Rilla's whole body was rigid with shock. Then humiliation and anger took over, and she felt the blood rush to her face. Her legs began to tremble and she leaned back against the cool marble pillar for support. It was there that Zelie found her a minute later.

"So this is where you've been hiding. My poor Rilla, I expect you're exhausted by all the excitement. But bear up. It won't be long now before you and Jake are alone together. And then two blissful weeks of honeymoon. How it takes me back. Victoire and I chose Switzerland also, you know. It is such a beautiful country. So *romantique!* Now, come along, *ma chère,* there are some charming fellow Americans I very particularly want you to meet."

Weakly Rilla allowed herself to be led away by the well-meaning Zelie and did her damnedest to act the role of happy bride. Dear heaven, what a bitter irony, she thought as she pasted on a smile again, for never in her whole life had she felt so wretched and despondent.

During the two weeks of their engagement Rilla had thrust to the edges of her mind Jake's explanation for wanting to marry her—for bullying her into it. But his words came flooding back to her. He had decided to take a wife for no better reason than to provide himself with a barrier against the predatory females who blatantly pursued Jake Carson, best-selling novelist. A barrier, specifically, against Princess von Hohenzollern. But how, Rilla was forced to wonder with a sick pang, did Jake interpret their arrangement? Did he view his marriage as nothing but a legal protection against other women's dreams of capturing him as a husband, without any thought of marital fidelity? Would he feel free to leap into bed with any woman who took his fancy, safe in the knowledge that they could expect nothing of him beyond a brief affair?

While struggling to make conversation with Zelie's friends Rilla caught sight of two faces from among the milling throng of guests—Jake and Antoinette, laughing and talking together. The princess suddenly seemed to become aware of Rilla's gaze and turned her head to look at her. The lovely, sensuous mouth was set in a cruel, spiteful line, and those jet-stone eyes bored into her with hatred. Then the moment was gone, and Antoinette was smiling up at Jake once again, her slender scarlet-nailed fingers resting possessively on the lapels of his pale gray wedding suit.

In Geneva the streets were wet from a recent shower. The sidewalks mirrored headlamps and advertising signs like splashes of color on an artist's palette. Their hotel was located right on the lakeside, a vast modern palace of stainless steel and glass. Jake handed the car over to a valet, and they entered through revolving doors into the grand lobby, which was festooned with luxuriant greenery. It took only a couple of minutes to check in, and they were escorted up to the bridal suite by a courteous assistant manager. He departed, bowing, and suddenly Rilla was alone with her newly wedded husband.

At once Jake came forward to embrace her, his lips curved in a smile, his blue eyes warm with admiration. But the moment he touched her, Rilla twisted away nervously.

"I—I must unpack and get changed," she murmured.

"Very well," Jake said with a little shrug. The smile gone from his face, he went on, "Do you want to go down and eat in the restaurant, or shall I call room service and have dinner sent up?"

If only things had been different, Rilla thought with a silent sob. How romantic it could have been to dine alone together in the bridal suite. "I—I'd prefer to go downstairs, if that's okay with you."

"Whatever you say." He strolled through to the adjoining sitting room while Rilla set about unpacking and putting away their things in the commodious closets and drawers. Then she changed out of her copper-colored suede traveling suit into a black velvet evening skirt and a romantic frilly blouse in pale yellow georgette. She swept up her auburn hair into a loose coil on the crown of her head and fixed it with tortoiseshell combs. She had just finished applying fresh makeup when Jake entered the room.

"I think I'll take a shower," he told her. "I won't be long."

When he had disappeared into the bathroom, Rilla stood at the foot of the king-size double bed and gazed around her unhappily. The bedroom was magnificently luxurious, plushly carpeted and furnished with silky brocades and velvets, all in muted tones of pink and gold. The sitting room, she found, was just as sumptuous, with deep soft armchairs and a long sofa covered in a rich shade of mulberry. French doors opened onto a spacious balcony. Rilla stepped outside into the balmy evening air that was fresh and sweet-scented after the recent rain, and stood with her hands resting on the curved balustrade. A crescent moon was rising above the dark waters of Lake Geneva, drawing a glittering finger of silver across the gently riffled surface. From somewhere far below drifted the sound of laughter.

"Rilla!" called Jake.

She turned and stepped back into the sitting room to see what he wanted, then stopped dead. He was standing in the doorway to the bedroom, stark naked, looking like a bronze statue in the muted lamplight. Seeing Rilla, he went on quite unconcernedly, "I can't find my shirts."

She was struck dumb, all the breath knocked out of her. When they had both been naked on the patio the night they'd made love, there had been only star glow and light that spilled from the house. Now the classical male perfection of Jake's physique was fully revealed to her: his broad, sculptured chest; his slim waist and hard, flat stomach; his lean hips and powerful thighs. The skin of his entire body, gleaming smoothly, was molded over hard muscle.

"Don't look so goggle-eyed," he said, sounding amused. "There's nothing you haven't seen before, and you'll have to get used to it. Now, where are those shirts of mine?"

Rilla's voice was choked and faint. "In the second . . .
No, I think it's the third drawer of the—"

"You'd better come and show me," Jake suggested.

To do so meant that she would have to pass close by
him, and Rilla steeled herself. Going through the doorway, she experienced such a force of magnetic power
emanating from Jake that it made her gasp for breath.
She longed to press herself against his strong, virile
body and run her hands over the bronze skin. Instead
she hurried past him and pulled open a drawer.

"Here," she said huskily. "They're all in here."

"Fine!" He strolled over unhurriedly and selected a
cream silk shirt. Rilla would have returned at once to
the sitting room, but Jake said crisply, "No need to run
away. How do you like the suite? You haven't expressed an opinion yet."

She sat down at the dressing table and pretended to
be fixing a stray tendril of hair. "It's—it's fabulous,"
she said nervously. "It must be costing the earth."

"Having the best usually does cost the earth. But it's
worth it."

Covertly Rilla watched him in the mirror as he pulled
on the pants of a charcoal-gray suit and tucked in his
shirt. Such casual intimacy between them seemed all
wrong, and yet . . . they were man and wife.

They dined in splendor beneath a pink-tinted mirrored ceiling and glittering crystal chandeliers. Huge
windows overlooked the lake, on whose dark waters
gleamed the lights of pleasure boats. The menu was
lavish and international, containing soufflés from
France, a dozen pastas from Italy, Dover sole from En-
gland, barbecued spareribs from the United States, as
well as Mexican, Creole, Spanish, Russian, and German dishes. There was even an exotic salmon concoc-
tion from Hawaii. Rilla chose a small Waldorf salad,

with broiled pork cutlets to follow. Jake opted for
Scotch broth, followed by a T-bone steak, and he
ordered a bottle of rosé from Portugal. The service
was excellent, and at the far end of the spacious restaurant a pianist played a selection of tuneful romantic
oldies.

After the meal they strolled for a while along the
lakeside Quai du Mont Blanc until Jake suggested returning to their suite. Leaving him in the sitting room,
Rilla went through to take a bath. She firmly closed the
bathroom door but didn't dare lock it against her husband. All the time she was in the tub she was fearful
that Jake might walk in, but mercifully he kept away.
When she left the bathroom, wearing a pure silk blue
nightgown under a softly flowing satin robe of a deep
peacock-blue shade, and having applied a touch of Parfum d'Or to her wrists, behind her ears, and in the cleft
between her breasts, she found Jake standing beside
the dressing table, jacketless. He paused in removing
his necktie and looked at her.

"Your beauty astonishes me each and every time I
see you," he murmured softly. Tossing down the tie,
he came to Rilla and enfolded her in his arms. She
shivered from shame at the intense desire his touch
was awakening within her. Though her body craved his
lovemaking, her mind and spirit fought against allowing Jake such a contemptibly easy conquest.

He began to run his fingertips slowly and erotically
down her spine, but somehow Rilla resisted the urge to
melt against him. As he pressed her closer to his firm-
muscled frame, needles of fire pricked through her,
and she stifled a gasp of arousal as his lips found hers in
a deeply passionate kiss.

Drawing away with a muttered exclamation of impatience, Jake pulled open her robe and pushed it back

over her shoulders. The two narrow shoulder ribbons
of her nightgown offered him no resistance, and the
sheer silk garment shimmered to the floor around her
ankles. For long pulsating seconds he gazed at her
naked body, his blue eyes alight with admiration, then
with a groan of desire he crushed her to him again. In a
daze Rilla felt herself being lifted in his strong arms
and carried to the bed, and then laid down upon the
feathered softness of the quilt. As Jake began to remove the rest of his clothes she drew the quilt up
around her to hide her nakedness. But her husband
would have none of it. With a soft laugh he dragged the
covering aside.

"Heaven knows that I've been patient these past two
weeks," he murmured huskily, as he stretched his
length beside her. "I've been driven nearly insane with
longing to possess your lovely body, Rilla, but for some
crazy reason you were withholding yourself. But we're
married now, sweetheart, and the time for holding back
is gone."

Yes, they were husband and wife. And so great was
Jake's arrogance, he imagined that however contemp-
tuously he treated her, however blatantly unfaithful he
might be, she would always respond to his advances
with a passion to match his own.

But that, at least, it was in her power to deny him.
Whatever the cost to herself, Jake was going to learn
that she was no meekly complaisant wife. She would
respond to her husband's passion only if he sincerely
intended to keep his part of their marriage bargain. She
had resigned herself to the painful fact that he wasn't in
love with her the way she was with him, but she had a
right to expect fidelity.

Rilla felt Jake's body quicken and shudder with the
urgency of his need as his lips met hers and crushed

them in a bruising kiss. He invaded her with his tongue, thrusting in and probing the innermost recesses of her mouth, while his hands caressed her breasts until the ferment of longing he had aroused threatened to erode her determination to resist him. In a sudden swift movement he abandoned her mouth and captured a tingling nipple between his lips. Rilla almost moaned aloud from the sheer rapture of it, while his hands added further delight by roaming the soft curves of her flesh, then sliding insistently between her tight-pressed thighs.

Swept along on a great tidal wave of longing, Rilla found her resolution slipping away. She was ready to abandon all resistance and welcome his lovemaking joyfully. She loved Jake with her whole heart and soul, and she wanted above everything to give him pleasure....

And then she heard an echo of her newly wedded husband's voice at the reception, telling an unseen female guest that he didn't regard himself as having been hooked and landed: *"Nor do I envisage a future in which I'll suffer any kind of deprivation."* Rilla suddenly grew tense, mind and body alike. For long painful moments Jake persisted in trying to arouse her to passion, but at length he gave up, rolling away from her with a muttered curse.

"What the devil's the matter with you, Rilla?" he demanded, his blue eyes glittering in frustrated fury. "If I didn't know better, I'd think that you were frigid."

"You wanted me as your wife," she stated in a voice of freezing hostility, "and now you've got me. What more do you expect?"

"I expect a little in the way of cooperation, damn you."

"Cooperation?" she echoed scornfully. "Do you imagine that putting a wedding ring on my finger has made me give up my rights?"

A pained look passed swiftly across his lean features. "I've the right to expect you to be straightforward with me, Rilla, and not play some devilish secret game. What's it all about, for God's sake? You act as if you hate me."

Hate him? Yes, in a way she did. Hatred and love could exist side by side, couldn't they? In a tight voice she said, "You haven't anything to reproach me for, Jake. I'm denying you nothing."

His body jolted violently as he exploded with rage. "You're denying me everything—everything that gives the relationship between a man and a woman any kind of meaning. Why, Rilla...I want to know why."

She kept silent, avoiding his eyes. To try and explain, to tell him what she'd overheard at their wedding reception would be to open up the floodgates of her wounded heart. Inevitably she would find herself betraying how much she loved him—and that was something her pride wouldn't permit. Raised on his elbows above her, Jake looked like a thwarted beast of the jungle deprived of its legitimate prey. Moreover he possessed the same stark beauty as a jungle beast, the mellow lamplight shining on his muscle-rippled skin. Rilla found herself trembling. She felt tears squeeze out from beneath her eyelids and roll down her cheeks to dampen the bedcovers.

Jake gave a low, bitter, scornful laugh that cut her like a whiplash. "You look scared to death—as well you might. You're playing with fire, fooling around with a man's passion like this. Murder has often been committed for less. But you're quite safe with me, you beautiful little tease. I don't take what isn't freely offered...even when the woman is my lawful wife."

With another muttered curse he rose from the bed. Gathering up his scattered clothes, he strode to the door leading through to the sitting room, a proud Adonis-like figure whose manhood had been affronted. Then he was gone, the door slamming shut behind him.

Rilla remained on the bed, frozen with misery. She heard sounds of Jake getting dressed in the adjoining room; then the outer door to the corridor was opened and slammed, and there was silence. Her husband had walked out on her on the first night of their honeymoon. Gradually she began to shiver until her whole body was shuddering painfully. Groping blindly, she dragged herself under the rumpled bedcovers, where she lay curled in a tight ball.

Where was Jake now? she agonized. Had he gone to find some other woman who would be more amenable and responsive than his new bride? Her shivering would not abate as the long minutes lengthened slowly into hours. It was somewhere in the lost time of deepest darkness that Rilla eventually found oblivion in sleep.

The brisk sound of splashing water was coming from the bathroom when Rilla wakened. She became alert in an instant. So Jake had finally returned. At what hour? she wondered bleakly. Somehow she had to face him.

The water was turned off, and a couple of minutes later Jake strolled out, rubbing his wet hair. He wore a thigh-length black terry cloth robe, loosely tied at the waist.

"So you're awake!" he clipped and asked derisively, "Did you have a good night?"

"Yes, thanks. Did you?"

His dark eyes gleamed at her sarcastic tone of voice, but he made no reply to her taunt. Instead, turning to get clean clothes from a drawer, he said lightly, "In a minute I'll ring for room service and order breakfast. Just orange juice, coffee, and toast for you, I assume?"

The short bathrobe was shrugged off and tossed aside. His obvious indifference to her gaze upon his nudity was like an affront to Rilla. She glanced away but found it strangely difficult to keep her eyes averted as Jake proceeded to get dressed.

"I don't want anything at all to eat," she told him, endeavoring to sound calm.

"No appetite?" His voice was muffled as he pulled a dark blue sweater over his head. "Strange, but I feel ravenous this morning. I'm going to order ham and eggs for myself."

Was that, Rilla wondered unhappily, the way things would be between them from then on? A battle of innuendo and nerve-straining spite? Her nightgown and robe still lay on the carpet in full view of Jake, so that he knew she was naked under the covers and would be unwilling to get out of bed until he'd left the room. Yet, for someone who was usually so quick and decisive in his movements, getting dressed seemed to take him forever.

Jake's mood was quite changed fifteen minutes later, when Rilla joined him next door in the sitting room, having showered and dressed in peach-colored pants and a matching silk blouse, with a tasseled leather belt hugging her slim waist. The waiter had just appeared with the breakfast cart, and she poured coffee for them both while Jake tackled his order of ham and eggs.

"I thought we'd spend today in Geneva itself," he said agreeably. "Other days we can go farther afield."

So their honeymoon was to continue. Rilla had half

expected Jake to announce that they'd be returning immediately to Villa Ambrosia. Presumably, though, he was remaining there merely as a face-saving exercise; he'd be reluctant to admit to his many friends on the Riviera that his marriage was already a dismal failure.

The hours they spent together looking around Geneva might have been blissful if she and Jake had been happy honeymooners. They strolled along the balustraded waterfront, and Rilla was fascinated by the gigantic waterspout that rose in a single jet to a height of four hundred feet, throwing a plume of white spray... the largest fountain in the world, so Jake told her. They lunched at a lakeside restaurant where reflections of the sunlit water shimmered dreamily across the ceiling. Jake had brought his camera and he took a number of pictures of Rilla. Once or twice he asked a bystander to snap the two of them together.

In the evening they dined at the hotel again, remaining at their table to watch the cabaret. Though the show was spectacular, Rilla found that after long hours spent in Geneva's bracing air, and a sleepless night, she couldn't prevent her eyelids from drooping. Jake, noticing it, suggested that she might like to skip the rest of the show and go up to bed.

"Yes, I think I would," she admitted. "It's been quite a tiring day. I've enjoyed it, though," she added with a nervous smile.

Surprisingly that was true. Despite the rift between them, she had found pleasure just being in Jake's company. Perhaps, she thought wistfully as they crossed the luxurious foyer to the elevators, it might be possible to make a fresh start. She couldn't ever hope to win her husband's love. That was an emotion Jake clearly lacked the ability to feel, she'd concluded. But at least if he could show her a little consideration and tenderness in his lovemaking, as he'd shown in his manner toward her during the day, she might be able to let herself respond to him.

However, to Rilla's utter astonishment, Jake didn't even go upstairs with her. In the elevator he gave her a light kiss on the cheek, then pressed the button for the fourteenth floor and stepped out again just as the doors were closing.

"Sleep well, my dear Rilla. I won't disturb you."

"But, Jake—" she stammered in protest.

It was too late. The doors had closed, and the mirrored cabin started its smooth ascent. Very well, then, Rilla thought with a defiant tilt of her head. If that's how he wants our marriage to be, that's the way he can have it. A business arrangement convenient for us both, kept on a polite, civilized basis. In future the most important thing in her life was going to be her career as a journalist. Her other career, as Jake Carson's wife, would be relegated to a secondary role.

The honeymoon days that followed kept to the same pattern as the first day, except that she and Jake traveled deeper into the beautiful Swiss countryside. They seemed to be spending their time together as friendly companions and, like a couple who were no more than just friends, they parted each night. Jake always slept on the long sofa in the sitting room when he eventually returned from his unexplained absences.

On the final evening, however, the pattern changed. Jake didn't say good night to her at the elevator but remained in the cabin with her as the doors closed. Surprised, Rilla thought that maybe he wanted to start packing; but they hadn't fixed an early departure for the next day, so there couldn't be any rush.

"There's a certain matter that needs to be rectified

before we leave Switzerland," he informed her in a matter-of-fact tone. "I don't propose to be made ridiculous—if only in my own estimation—by returning from the honeymoon with our marriage still unconsummated."

Rilla took a quick step back from him, her heart thudding wildly. "You—you're not suggesting—"

"I trust you've no objection, bearing in mind the fact that in the eyes of the law I'm your husband?"

"But—but you can't," she stammered. "It's so—cold-blooded, and—"

"I assure you," he drawled, "that there'll be nothing cold-blooded on my side, only on yours. Despite the fact that you've turned out to have ice in your veins, your body is still extremely enticing."

Cornered, her only weapon was contempt. "Have you failed to line up another woman for tonight, Jake, is that it? So you're turning to me as a last resort."

Rilla watched the ridged muscles of his jaw tighten, and she flinched inwardly, half afraid that in his molten anger Jake might strike her. Instead he turned and strode to the door of the sitting room. Glancing at his wristwatch, he grated, "I'll give you precisely ten minutes to get ready for bed, then I'll be back."

Despairingly, even knowing that it was dangerous to taunt him in his present mood, Rilla flung out, "I distinctly recollect you saying that you'd never take what wasn't freely offered...even from your wife."

Jake stopped abruptly, halfway through the door. His lean face was a cruel mask of fury as he turned to look back at her.

"You haven't become my wife yet, Rilla...not in the fullest sense of the word. So I intend, tonight, to break my rule and make you so. Afterward you may be sure that I shan't bother you again."

Left alone, Rilla wondered frantically what to do. Should she turn the key to lock Jake from the bedroom? But it was likely that he'd put his shoulder to the door and smash it open. In any case, she couldn't evade him forever. It was better, she decided with bitter resignation, to allow the consummation to happen, before yet more anger and hostility had built up between them.

With a feeling of numb misery she set about preparing for bed. She deliberately chose the least sexy of the nightgowns she'd brought with her, a simple soft blue lawn with a tiny white daisy design that had long sleeves and was high in the neck. She slid in between the silky sheets just as her husband reentered the bedroom.

Her eyes closed in embarrassment, Rilla was aware of him walking to stand beside the bed and gazing down at her for long silent moments. Then he wheeled and vanished into the bathroom, where there were splashing sounds of him taking a shower. The click of the bathroom door opening brought her to a state of tense, shivering apprehension. With her eyes tightly closed again she heard Jake's purposeful tread on the carpet, felt the covers thrown aside and the bed dip beneath his weight. When Jake touched her, his strong fingers curving warmly over her breast, Rilla jumped as if from some violent electric shock.

"What a demure nightgown," he murmured throatily. "I'd prefer to see you in something more revealing, Rilla. Still, it's unimportant, since it's coming off this instant."

Rilla made no attempt to assist him, but neither did she offer any resistance as Jake undid the neck ribbons and pulled the nightgown up and over her head. She didn't speak, and refused to meet his glance.

"There!" he said triumphantly, tossing it aside. "Now I can look at you, my beautiful wife. Will you believe me, Rilla, when I say that I've never seen a woman with such a magnificent body as yours? The interesting question is, are you going to remain marble cold tonight?"

Rilla didn't answer and stubbornly kept her face averted. She lay utterly still as Jake's hands began to roam over her, exploringly, caressingly. Then both his arms went about her, and she found herself drawn close against his naked body, made thrillingly aware of every muscled contour and the throbbing pressure of his male arousal. Yet, he was almost gentle then. His kiss, when his lips sought hers at last, was not the passionate assault she had known before; his tongue was sensuously soft, not a fiercely probing dart. He might almost, she thought despairingly, have been an adoring lover, filled with tenderness and devotion. His hands were on her breasts, cupping their rounded firmness and erotically stroking the tautening nipples with his thumbs. Sharp needles of desire pricked through her, and she longed to cling to him, yearned to reach up and tangle her fingers into his crisp fair hair. But by a fierce effort of will she fought off the impulse and remained very still, unresisting to her husband's demands yet utterly unresponsive.

"For God's sake," Jake growled from deep in his throat, "what in hell sort of woman are you?"

"What sort of man are you," she returned bitterly, "to force yourself on me like this?"

"You know what sort of man I am, Rilla." His voice was a serrated saw edge, ripping into her. "You knew when you agreed to marry me. You'd already had experience of what sort of man I am. So don't pretend it comes as a shock."

"Nothing you do could shock me now," she flung out in despair.

"I'm relieved to hear it."

Jake's irritated impatience turned suddenly to a savage kind of anger. Where he had been tender at first, his caresses were rougher, his kisses stronger in their passionate intensity. His hands slid down her back to knead the firm flesh of her buttocks, and finally, with a groan that seemed compounded of contempt, of rage, of desire driven beyond the point of control, he let his weight crush down on her and he took ultimate possession, invading her body with uncaring lust.

Incredibly, with all tenderness gone from him and only sheer passion remaining, Rilla found herself unable to hold back any longer. Against her will she felt her body responding, her hips arching to meet his thrust, moving rhythmically against him as his frenzy grew. A glorious excitement took hold of her, a mounting rapture that forced moans of delight from the deep well of her sensuality. Jake had ignited a flame within her that flared to searing heat. As their crescendoing fever exploded in a final paroxysm of ecstasy, she gave a joyous cry of exultation.

Satiated, they both lay still. Rilla unclenched her fingers, dimly aware that her nails had been raking his back in the intensity of her passion. Her own flesh felt bruised, and her eyes were damp with tears; tears for what might have been, tears for the hopelessness of the love she felt for her husband. If she had still been clinging to a flicker of hope that the act of sex between them might have meant something more for Jake than just the assuagement of desire, something beyond a token demonstration of their legal relationship, it died in an instant when he abruptly rolled away from her. Propped on his elbows, he stared down at her, his blue eyes glittering in the muted glow of the bedside lamp.

"Do you feel sullied, Rilla? Do you feel disgusted that the ice-maiden act of yours was swept away in those last few moments?" His voice was jagged with scorn and derision. "Now that you and I are man and wife beyond any dispute, I'll leave you in peace to try and erase the memory of those moments of wild abandonment." He rose from the bed, his naked body a gleaming perfection of muscled coordination as he went across to the closet and took out a green paisley silk robe. "We'll leave for home in the morning, right after breakfast."

Chapter Ten

Scarcely had the honeymooners arrived back at Villa Ambrosia when Zelie Lamont called. She was insistent that they should go at once to take possession of Victoire's portrait of Rilla that was to be their wedding gift.

Up in the large studio at the top of the house on the Promenade des Anglais, the four of them stood gathered around the finished and framed painting, which rested on an easel. As Victoire whisked off the covering white cloth with a dramatic gesture, Rilla gave a little cry of delight. She felt choked with emotion, overwhelmed to think that Victoire had perceived her as possessing such ethereal beauty. There could be no doubt that the portrait was a masterpiece. In every delicate brush stroke there was superb artistry, and the painting as a whole had a wonderfully subtle harmony, with a kind of Mona Lisa mystery about it. Against the muted greens and browns of an imaginary sylvan scene, the flesh tones and white silk drapery of the seated figure glowed with a softly luminous radiance. Truly it was a portrait of love.

Rilla and Jake expressed their gratitude and admiration in warmest terms, and Victoire accepted their congratulations with courteous modesty. But something seemed to be bothering him, and when Zelie and Jake were deep in conversation, he drew Rilla aside.

"This painting... Oh, I do not deny that it is good. Perhaps one of the best things I have ever done. But it is no longer an accurate portrayal of you, *ma chère*." He tugged his Vandyck and frowned in puzzlement. "You have changed, Rilla. What is wrong, may I inquire?"

Rilla summoned up a bright smile. "Nothing's wrong, Victoire. Why ever should you think there is?"

He took her elbow and led her to one of the long windows that looked northward, framing a magnificent view of the blue-hazed hills behind Nice. Somewhere up there was Villa Ambrosia... *her* home, as well as Jake's. But not for long! That very evening she would tell Jake that she'd decided to return to California... alone. He could explain her departure in any way he chose; she wouldn't say anything to contradict whatever story he told.

"Please, my dear Rilla, do not insult my artistic inner vision," said Victoire, regarding her with shrewd eyes. "The girl in my portrait exists no longer.... You cannot deceive me. If you wish not to speak of the cause of your unhappiness, very well, I will probe no further. But, remember, if you ever require someone with an older head than yours in whom to confide, I am here. And, of course, in Zelie you will always find a true friend, you are aware of that? But until such time as you wish to share your problems, I think it is better for Zelie to remain untroubled. Her heart is so full of joy for you both."

Rilla nodded in silent acknowledgment and blinked back threatening tears. It was useless, she knew, to try to conceal the situation from Victoire. She felt a bit ashamed that her breakup with Jake would inevitably bring distress to those two kindly people, who had been so very good to her, but there seemed no other way.

Rilla announced her decision to Jake over dinner, telling him that she intended to leave for the United States first thing the next morning.

"For heaven's sake, why?" he demanded with a black frown.

"Surely it's obvious, after—"

"After what?" he demanded belligerently.

She laid down her silver soup spoon. "Okay, if I have to spell it out... After last night's monstrous obscenity."

Jake's eyes narrowed to slits of anger, but when he spoke it was in a taunting drawl. "I won't quarrel with your description, Rilla, that's just about what it was. So you needn't fear a repeat performance."

"I should hope not," she retorted. "That's the whole point—our relationship is sterile and meaningless, Jake."

"I don't agree," he replied calmly. "As I recall, there were several other good reasons for us deciding to get married that had nothing whatever to do with the physical aspect."

"Yes," she said bitterly. "And one of them, I'll remind you, was the matter of respect—the mutual respect of two intelligent individuals. That's dead now!"

She expected Jake to hit back with one of his sarcastic comments. Instead, picking up his wineglass and twirling it in his long fingers, he said with quiet emphasis, "Sorry, Rilla, but I can't agree to your going away."

"You can't stop me."

"Is that a challenge?" His intent blue gaze seemed to burn through her.

"If I want to go, then I'll go," she insisted. "Or are you proposing to keep me here as a prisoner?"

"Don't tempt me," he clipped grimly. "Now, let's drop the subject."

Rilla glared at him mutinously, but inside she was quaking. When it came to the point, she would need all her courage to walk out on Jake. Her feelings about him were in perpetual conflict. He made her furiously angry, she despised him, and a lot of the time she really did hate him. But never at any moment could she stop loving him, too. His constant nearness, and especially the times when they inadvertently touched skin to skin, unnerved her completely. And yet she knew that to live apart from Jake would be even worse. His image would remain to torment her for the rest of her life with haunting fantasies of what might have been.

"What am I supposed to do here if I decide to stay?" she demanded at length. "You can't expect me to laze around the pool all day, as if life were just one long vacation."

"I don't expect you to. I thought you wanted to continue your career as a journalist. Heaven knows, here on the Riviera there are hundreds of opportunities for you. The whole coastal area is crawling with celebrities of one sort or another."

"You wouldn't make problems about me working, Jake?"

"Naturally not. I told you that, didn't I, when I first suggested our getting married. And aside from work on your own account, you could give me some assistance if you're so concerned about filling in your time."

"What sort of assistance?" she asked, her interest caught despite herself.

"For one thing, it would be a big help to have someone intelligent who could handle some of the research I need. And there's always the fan mail to be answered."

"In other words," she said chillingly, "you're looking for an unpaid secretary?"

"That's not what I meant. For all routine jobs I use the services of a secretarial agency wherever I happen to be at the time. Currently I'm using one in Nice. I'd expect more from you, Rilla, than I would from a secretary."

Their eyes met across the table, and it was she who looked away.

"So it's settled, then?" queried Jake.

"I—I guess so."

"Right! You can make a start in the morning. There's a guy I know who's very knowledgeable about the international drug racket. He was formerly a senior police officer in Marseilles, and he promised to supply me with relevant background data for the next Jake Carson book I'm planning."

"I'm to interview him? But how shall I know what to ask? Will you supply me with a list of questions?"

"I'll give you a rough idea of the plot and the sort of things I'll need to know. As a trained journalist, Rilla, you'll probably be more successful than I'd be myself at digging out the right sort of information. So I'll call Monsieur Delacroix first thing, and you can drive over to see him. Now that he's retired he lives in a small villa along the coast at Saint-Raphaël."

Despite herself, Rilla felt flattered by Jake's confidence in her ability. All the same, she couldn't help saying acidly, "Aren't you afraid of letting me out of your sight, Jake? I might decide not to come back."

"Is that what you're cooking up in the back of your mind?" His blue eyes were disturbingly penetrating, searching out the lie.

She shook her head weakly. "No... not really."

"Good!" Jake reached for a slice of melba toast.

"Don't let your soup get cold. It's artichoke flavored with garlic...one of Jeanne-Marie's specialties."

After dinner Jake went to his study to work, while Rilla wandered in the fragrant darkness of the garden, berating herself for being so weak as to let Jake talk her into staying on. Very faintly she could hear the insistent tap-tapping of his typewriter. He seemed, she thought sourly, to be caught up in a fever of work, as if intent on making up for the time wasted on their honeymoon.

Jake had arranged for the master bedroom in the villa to be completely refurbished while they were in Geneva. It looked magnificent in various subtle shades of blue, with the silk-covered walls accented in ivory and gold leaf, and some choice pieces of antique rosewood furniture. But that night Rilla occupied the king-size four poster marriage bed alone. She wondered what Pierre and Jeanne-Marie would make of the fact that Jake was still using his old bachelor room.

When at long last she dropped off into an uneasy sleep, it was riddled with the sort of tormenting dreams she'd experienced often during their honeymoon, in which Jake made tender, passionate love to her. Then, horrifyingly, at the very brink of a blissful climax, she realized that his partner was not her at all, but some other woman. That night, though, it was even more of a nightmare, for the woman in Jake's arms was Princess Antoinette, her gorgeous raven-black hair spread across the lace-edged pillows. Rilla awoke with a start, trembling in every limb.

During breakfast she and Jake talked about the assignment he'd given her. "I've jotted down a few specific questions I'd like answered," he explained. "But beyond that, I want you to get Delacroix reminiscing about his days in the drug squad. He'll prove to be a mine of information, you'll find. Take whichever of the cars you prefer.''

Rilla chose the convertible, reasoning that it was nearer in size to her own small Honda than the big Citroën. But the thrustful power of its engine was more than she'd bargained for, and she had to drive with extreme caution on the tortuously twisting coastal route, the Corniche d'Or, which was little more than a precarious ledge cut into the ruby-red cliffs. Below her the indigo sea broke in creamy white foam as it boiled over submerged offshore rocks. Emerald-green pine trees thrust up from every crevice, their resinous aroma deliciously scenting the air.

Monsieur Delacroix lived in a narrow-fronted old house on the Saint-Raphaël waterfront. He was a big man, though slightly stooped from age, with thin white hair and intelligent eyes, which were a silvery gray color. He led Rilla into his cramped living room and gestured her to a comfortable armchair set in a bay window, first removing from its high back a beautiful blue Persian cat that crouched purring contentedly in a shaft of sunlight.

''This is where I spend most of my days now,'' he told her, setting the cat on his knees as he took a chair himself. ''Always there is something of interest to watch here in this ancient harbor, and I like to dwell upon the historical past, too. Did you know that Napoleon landed at Saint-Raphaël after his flight from Egypt? And fifteen years later, poor Bonaparte embarked from this selfsame spot to his banishment on the isle of Elba.''

Rilla spent a fascinating couple of hours with Monsieur Delacroix and filled page after page of her shorthand notebook with his reminiscences from a lifetime of fighting the international drug trade. He was most pressing that she should stay and have lunch with him, and knowing that he had only recently lost his wife, she felt it would be a kindness to accept. Requesting her to set the table, he departed to the kitchen. During the next few minutes he dodged in and out, bearing a bowl of salad and a wicker basket with chunks of crusty bread, then finally he carried in a large oval platter from which enticing smells arose.

"This is cutlets of sea bass broiled with fennel," he told her as he served a generous portion. "Help yourself to salad, Madame Carson."

Rilla forked up a few flakes of the tender fish. "It's delicious, Monsieur Delacroix. Where did you learn to be such a good cook?"

"Of necessity, madame." He made a wry face. "My dear wife, God bless her soul, was a chronic invalid for many years before she passed away. She suffered, *pauvre petite,* but it was an honor for me to serve her in what little ways I could."

"It must have been hard for you, monsieur," Rilla murmured sympathetically.

His gray eyes misted over. "My Hortense was a re-markable woman. A wonderful companion. And you too, madame, are fortunate to have found yourself such a fine partner with whom to share your life, I think."

"Er...yes," she faltered.

"Cherish your fine husband, madame," he advised. "There are precious few men of his caliber in the modern world, alas."

It was midafternoon by the time Rilla arrived back at Villa Ambrosia. As she drew to a halt in the forecourt she found a handsome silver-gray Rolls-Royce parked there. Her fears as to its owner were immediately confirmed when she heard Princess Antoinette's artificial laughter tinkling from the direction of the patio. Rilla wanted to slip into the house and not show her face until the other woman was gone, but Jake must have heard the car arrive, for he called out to her to join them.

As Rilla walked through the arched gap in the cypress hedge, Jake rose to his feet and came to meet her. He had been sitting on one of the swings with Antoinette, who was wearing dark glasses and a daringly sexy sundress that left her magnificent tan thighs and shoulders bare and only just covered the tips of her breasts. Ferdinand had risen to his feet too, and he greeted Rilla even more charmingly than usual. His obvious admiration for her was a boost to the ego, in view of her strained relationship with Jake, but it struck her that the prince was a little embarrassed and ill at ease.

"Come and join us, Rilla darling," Jake said lightly, just as if the endearment were normal between them. "Antoinette and Ferdie dropped by to welcome us home. Wasn't it nice of them?"

"Very nice," Rilla said grittily, and immediately wished that she'd not made her jealousy so apparent. She saw Antoinette's quick smile of triumph.

"Jake has been telling us all about your honeymoon trip," the princess drawled in a silky voice, and her slight emphasis on the word *all* made Rilla flinch. Was Jake so totally insensitive that he'd tell Antoinette and her brother about the miserable failure of their marriage? She could scarcely bring herself to believe that he'd be so disloyal. And yet, it would explain the scarcely veiled look of satisfaction on Antoinette's face and also Ferdinand's embarrassment.

"Well, Rilla, how did you get on with Monsieur Delacroix?" Jake inquired.

She made an effort to pull herself together. "Oh,

very well, I think. He was most informative. I've taken lots of notes, which I'll type up for you this evening.''

Antoinette, who had removed her dark glasses and was languidly nibbling at the pointed end of one side piece, gave a soft laugh that held an undertone of derision. ''But, of course... with your qualifications in shorthand and typing and so on, you'll make a useful secretary for Jake.''

''I hope so,'' replied Rilla levelly, pretending to take the remark as a compliment. She strolled casually to the balustrade to look down at the view, her back turned to the others.

''What is wrong, *chérie*?'' asked Ferdinand solicitously, joining her a moment later. ''You do not have the appearance of radiant happiness that a new bride should.''

''Nothing is wrong,'' she said falteringly.

''But there is something,'' he persisted. ''You have quarreled with Jake, yes? Is it serious?''

Rilla bit her lip. She dared not admit to Ferdinand that things were less than perfect in her marriage; anything she said would undoubtedly be wormed out of him by his sister. Without question Antoinette still had designs on Jake, and she'd grasp at a rift between husband and wife as an opening for herself.

''I already told you, Ferdie, there's nothing wrong, nothing at all. I'm just a bit tired, that's what it is. I've had rather a busy day.''

''In my opinion,'' the prince went on, his handsome features creased in a critical frown, ''it was most inconsiderate of Jake to send his wife on such a mission. If he does not wish to do this research work for himself, then he should employ someone.''

''But I enjoyed going to see Monsieur Delacroix,'' Rilla insisted. ''It was extremely interesting.'' Maybe

Ferdinand only meant to be kind, but she wasn't prepared to have him criticize Jake and put her on the defensive. She said in a brisk, dismissive tone, "Let's forget about it, shall we?"

As she turned around to rejoin the others Ferdinand laid his fingers on her arm in a sympathetic gesture. "One thing, Rilla.... Never forget that I am your friend. If you should want me at any time...if you need help, anything at all, you have only to telephone, and I will come at once."

"It's very sweet of you, Ferdie," she said with a forced little laugh, "but I honestly can't imagine ever needing to take you up on that offer."

"I said if, *chérie*," he murmured. "Just remember, that is all I ask."

Ten minutes later, when the princess and her brother drove off in their Rolls-Royce, Jake demanded tersely, "What were all those significant looks from Ferdinand?"

"Significant looks?" Rilla tried to dismiss his challenge with a cool, amused shrug, but Jake gripped her arm and pulled her around to face him. His eyes were blazing.

"That's what I said. And I want an answer."

"Okay," she retorted, tilting her chin defiantly. "Since you're so interested, Ferdie was asking me if I was happily married to you."

"Considerate of him. And what did you tell Ferdie?"

"Don't worry, I didn't tell him the truth."

Jake's fingers tightened on her arm in a bruising grip. "So what is the truth?"

"As if you didn't know."

With an impatient exclamation Jake jerked her closer to him so that her hips were touching the hard muscles of his thighs and her breasts were crushed against the molded wall of his chest.

"How much longer does this nonsense have to continue?" he demanded harshly.

With dismay Rilla felt herself begin to tremble and she wished desperately that she had the strength of will to wrench away from him. She clenched her fists to fight against the longing to slide up her arms and encircle his neck. Somehow she injected the requisite coldness into her voice.

"I told you last night that I wanted to return to California at once, and it was you who vetoed the idea. So blame yourself if you don't like things the way they are."

For long angry moments Jake continued to hold her against his lean, hard body, and although Rilla wasn't looking at him, she could feel his angry gaze drilling into her. Then with an impatient curse he let her go abruptly.

"I'm going for a walk, to get a change of atmosphere. You can use my study for an hour or so, if you want to get that typing done."

Rilla watched his tall figure striding away from her, the sun glinting golden sparks in his fair hair, until he vanished around the side of the house. She felt strangely bereft, and all of a sudden immensely weary. It took great effort to make her way to Jake's study to begin transcribing her shorthand notes.

The ever-attentive Pierre brought Rilla some iced tea, together with a slice of chocolate cake. As he set down the silver tray on Jake's desk he gave her an odd, puzzled look. The situation must be inexplicable to him and Jeanne-Marie, she thought—a newly married couple just back from their honeymoon, not sharing a bed, and content to be separated for most of the day!

The iced tea seemed to act as a tonic and restored Rilla's motivation. An hour later she'd completed the job, a dozen neatly typed pages that she stapled together. She covered the typewriter and, before quitting Jake's study, she stood for a moment looking around, interested in what the room could tell her about her husband. It was the first time she'd been alone in the sanctum where Jake spent so much of his time.

It was almost the only room in the villa that didn't have a magnificent outlook. "I find that a view distracts me when I'm trying to work," he'd told her once. The walls were painted ivory and lined with gray filing cabinets and bookshelves, lending a very professional ambience. The desk looked a bit chaotic, but she presumed there was a kind of method behind the mess. Mrs. Bird, the maid at Casa del Sol, had mentioned that he was fanatical about not having his desk touched in any way, and Rilla had taken care while typing not to disturb anything—a fact she promptly pointed out to Jake when at that precise moment he came strolling into the room.

"I believe you." He grinned at her in an affable way, their recent clash seemingly forgotten. "Matter of fact, Rilla, you'd be doing me a favor if you cleared everything off that desk and got me organized. Sometimes I waste hours searching for a vital item of research that I've jotted down somewhere on a scrap of paper and let get buried."

"Really?" She was surprised that Jake should admit to any kind of failing. "I've thought of you as a very orderly sort of person," she commented. "Superefficient."

He laughed, his blue eyes mocking her. "That sounds suspiciously like praise. I was under the impression that you had a very low opinion of me."

"On the contrary, I rate you very highly...as a writer. You already know that." Rilla hesitated, running her fingers through her auburn waves. Then she asked, "Do you seriously want me to help you get organized, Jake?"

"Emphatically. There's so much you could do to help me." He picked up a sheet of work from the desk, and Rilla noticed that the original typing was scrawled all over with handwritten amendments and revisions covering almost every square inch of the paper. "The people at the French secretarial agency I use have trouble deciphering my scrawl, so that I often have to spend time cleaning up the pages myself. It would be fantastic if you could do that for me sometimes."

"I don't mind giving it a try." Rilla took the sheet from him and studied it interestedly. "I had no idea that you reworked your writing to this extent. Your books read so smoothly, it's as if they've come straight off the typewriter."

Jake made a wry face. "That's what being a novelist is all about, Rilla...not allowing the sweat and hard work to show. When you've retyped this draft, I shall start over again reshaping and rewriting it."

Rilla looked more closely at Jake's handwriting, which was firm and bold, with a strong cursive flow. The first time she'd seen it was when, as Richard Kellerman, he'd autographed her paperback copy of *Flowers of Chivalry*. But suddenly a new significance hit her.

"That bottle of Parfum d'Or that I found in the car after our visit to the *parfumerie*... It wasn't a gift from Monsieur Rigaillaud at all, was it?"

"Wasn't it?"

"No, it was from you, Jake! Seeing your handwriting again, I recognize it as the same as what was on the accompanying card." She shook her head apologetically. "I just can't understand why I didn't realize at the time that the perfume came from you."

Jake lifted his broad shoulders in a shrug. "Maybe it was lucky that you didn't."

"I don't get it."

"If you'd known the gift was from me, you probably wouldn't have accepted it. And I wanted you to, Rilla."

"But, why?"

"Why does a man usually give a woman perfume?" he parried meaningfully, letting his gaze rove over her slender curves.

Rilla felt hot color flooding to her cheeks, and a pulse in her throat began to throb. "You're quite right, Jake, I wouldn't have accepted the gift from you. It must have cost an enormous amount."

"And worth every single franc. It's a very mysterious thing, the way one particular perfume can be so very right for one particular woman. Parfum d'Or exactly expresses your personality, Rilla."

"In what way?" she couldn't resist asking.

Jake smiled, but there was a derisive look in his eyes as he studied her. "Fishing for compliments, my dear wife?"

"No...no, of course not." Chagrined, Rilla wished to heaven that she'd never raised the subject. "I suppose," she said sarcastically, "that a bottle of Parfum d'Or is your regular gift to women?"

"Why should you suppose that?"

"It's the sort of lavish show-off gift a man like you would think of. Most women would be impressed."

"But not you?" Jake's brows drew together in a harsh frown. "Whether or not it's been my habit to impress women by buying them expensive perfume isn't any of your business, Rilla. Nor," he added after a meaningful pause, "is it any of your business if I do so in future. I'd be robbing you of nothing you appear to value."

Rilla caught her breath in outrage. Did Jake really and truly imagine that he could go on having casual relationships with other women without causing her acute heartache? But then, she reminded herself with a pang of despair, Jake had no idea that she was in love with him. And he never would, she vowed.

Forcing a light frivolity into her tone of voice, she quipped, "No matter how many women you choose to give expensive perfume to, it's fine by me—just so long as you don't expect me to gift wrap it for you." She became brisk. "I'll go and change now. I'll make a start tomorrow on getting your desk sorted out. You can let me know when you won't be using the study, and I'll come in then."

"You can come in any time, as far as I'm concerned," Jake said. "There's a spare typewriter in one of the closets."

"But wouldn't my presence interfere with your concentration?"

The smile that lurked around his mouth faded away, and he drew a finger along one eyebrow in the little gesture that had become so dear and precious to her. "Oh, yes, Rilla," he said with soft intensity, "it most certainly would."

"Then I'd better keep out of the way," she riposted, unable to hold his gaze.

"But your absence," he said dryly, "would interfere even more with my concentration. Having you here, I'll at least be able to feast my eyes on you—even if I'm forbidden to touch."

Impelled by something beyond her control, Rilla found herself saying, "I really would like to feel that

I'm making myself useful to you, Jake. You only have
to tell me what you want done.''

"Don't worry, I'll keep you busy," he promised.
Then, as Rilla turned to the door, he added in a murmur,
"There's just one thing I must insist on, though."

"What's that?"

"During working hours, don't ever wear that perfume. Remember what I said at the *parfumerie*—that a
certain scent on a certain woman can rob a man of his
senses. That's what Parfum d'Or does on you, Rilla,
with devilish efficiency."

They stood looking at one another for long moments
of silence...a silence that grew to a throbbing intensity. Rilla felt herself drawn to him by powerful, invisi-
ble strands; she realized that in another instant she
would be unable to hold back from flinging herself into
Jake's arms. Then, suddenly, the unbearable tension
was snapped by the shrill ring of the telephone.

Jake answered it, listened a moment, then replied in
rapid French. When he replaced the phone, he said
with a shrug, "I'm afraid, Rilla, that I have to go out.
That was Antoinette, and it seems she left her purse
here. She said she remembers tucking it between the
cushions of the swing. I promised to drive down with it
right away."

"I see!" Rilla was gripped by a cold sense of dismay,
followed swiftly by anger. "Will you be long, Jake?"

"If I'm not back, don't wait dinner for me," he told
her in a flat tone, already at the door. "See you, Rilla."

Alone, she sank down despondently into a leather
armchair and put her two hands to her flushed cheeks.
She didn't for a single instant believe that Antoinette
had left her purse there by accident. For pity's sake,
couldn't Jake see through such an obvious ploy? A
ploy designed by the wretched woman, Rilla had no

doubt, to demonstrate that she still had power to make him come when she beckoned.

But, maybe Jake was fully aware of Antoinette's little deceit. Maybe he was only too glad to be provided with a ready-made excuse to pay the princess an evening visit.

It looked, Rilla decided, furiously gulping down a sob, as if Jake wouldn't be back in time for dinner... looked as if he wouldn't be back until very late. If at all that night!

Chapter Eleven

It hardly seemed worth the bother of changing her clothes to eat dinner alone, Rilla thought despondently, but while she was in her bedroom freshening up she heard the sound of a car. Thinking that it must be Jake returning after all, she hastily chose from the closet a silky russet-colored dress with a softly flaring skirt and slipped it on, thrusting her feet into flat ballerina pumps. After fastening on earrings and a chunky beaten-gold necklace, she was checking the effect in the mirror when she heard a tap at the door.

"Jake?" she queried.

"No, madame." It was Pierre's voice. "Prince Ferdinand has called."

With a downsurge of disappointment Rilla crossed to the door and opened it. "What does Prince Ferdinand want, Pierre?"

"It seems, madame, that when he and his sister called this afternoon, the princess inadvertently left her purse here. Regrettably, though, I cannot find it anywhere, and as Monsieur Carson is not at home, I thought that possibly you might be able to assist."

Rilla stared at him in astonishment. "But Princess Antoinette phoned about her purse a little while ago, and Monsieur Carson is taking it to her. That's why he went out."

Pierre looked equally astonished. "I will explain the position to His Highness, madame."

"No, wait..." Rilla thought quickly. "Prince Ferdinand might think it impolite if I don't see him myself. Ask him to wait a moment, please, and I'll be right down."

It looked as if she had misjudged the situation, Rilla told herself as she quickly flicked a comb through her hair and applied fresh lip gloss. Perhaps the princess hadn't deliberately inveigled Jake to her home, after all. Still, it didn't make her feel any more kindly toward Antoinette for having thoroughly ruined the evening by her forgetfulness.

A couple of minutes later when Rilla descended the stairs, she found Ferdinand in the living room, studying a brilliantly colored abstract painting that hung on one wall. He made, as always, an elegant figure... tall and slim in a dark suit that was a perfect fit. Hearing her footsteps, the prince spun around and his soft brown eyes lit up with warm appreciation.

"*C'est parfait!* Never have I seen you, Rilla, when you didn't look beautiful." He crossed to her swiftly, raised her hand to his lips, and held it there for moments longer than the salutation required. "But I fear that I am causing a nuisance of myself. I came expressly to collect my sister's purse, yet Pierre informs me that Jake is at this very moment on his way to take the purse to Antoinette."

Flushing slightly, Rilla withdrew her hand. "Yes, that's right, Ferdie. I really can't understand how the mix-up has arisen. Antoinette herself phoned Jake about it, and he promised to drive down to Saint-Jean-

Cap-Ferrat with the purse. Didn't she know that you were intending to call here to collect it?"

He spread his hands in a gesture of resignation. "But this is so like my sister; she is always impetuous. She said to me this evening, 'Ferdie, I have forgotten my purse and I am quite lost without it, so you must drive to Villa Ambrosia and fetch it.' And then she made this different arrangement with Jake on the telephone and omitted to inform me."

The whole thing was so stupid, Rilla thought crossly. After a brief hesitation she felt obliged to say, "Anyway, Ferdie, since you're here, perhaps you'd like a drink?"

"*Mais certainement,* that would be delightful. For the company," he added with a gallant, heel-clicking little bow, "more than for the refreshment."

"What would you care for? Whiskey, sherry, vodka? Or perhaps a glass of wine."

"Wine, if you please."

Rilla rang for Pierre and asked him to bring a bottle of chilled Chablis. Two minutes later she and the prince were seated on the patio in chairs that faced toward the panoramic view, their glasses of wine frosting in the warm evening air. Ferdinand proved to be good company. They talked about Geneva, which he knew well, and he questioned her about California.

"For many years I have longed to see San Francisco," he confessed. "Some people say it is the most beautiful city in the whole world."

"I won't quarrel with that," Rilla said with a laugh. "You should take a trip there one day, Ferdie."

"Alas, I think this is most unlikely. Antoinette says that she has no desire to travel to the United States."

Rilla began to relax and enjoy herself. She felt that

she could identify with Ferdinand to some extent, both of them fated to live under the domination of a much stronger character. Ferdinand was bound to his sister from economic necessity, lacking the initiative to go out and make his own way in the world, while she was chained to Jake by her one-sided love for him, lacking the courage to make a clean break, even though their marriage was a proven failure.

Daylight faded to a glorious lilac dusk, and all the lovely scents of the garden mingled and drifted on the warm air. Pierre emerged from the house, coughed discreetly, and inquired about dinner. It seemed only natural for Rilla to ask Ferdinand if he'd like to stay and eat with her. "That is, if you've no other arrangements for this evening."

The prince awarded her one of his most dazzling smiles. "No other arrangement, *chérie,* could compete with this. I accept your invitation with the greatest of pleasure."

"You'd better set the table for three, Pierre," she instructed, "just in case Monsieur Carson gets back before we've finished."

They drank the rest of the Chablis with the meal, which was tender pieces of veal cooked in a tangy lemon cream sauce. For dessert there was a butterscotch flan smothered with flakes of toasted almond. When Pierre brought the coffee, Ferdinand inquired with an apologetic little grin if they might not take it out to the patio, since it was such a lovely night.

"Good idea," Rilla agreed. "I should have thought of it myself."

Ferdinand insisted on carrying the tray. He set it down on a low table, which he placed before one of the swing hammocks.

"How very agreeable this is!" he said as he took a

seat beside her. "An excellent meal, with excellent wine, and the company of an exquisitely beautiful woman. What more perfect way of spending an evening could any man hope for?"

Rilla heaved a wistful sigh. The evening would indeed have been perfection...in the company of the right man. If only it were Jake sitting beside her on the swing, Jake who was paying her such extravagant compliments.

Then, because she thought her sigh might have been too revealing, she said quickly, lightly, "I'm so glad you dropped by, Ferdie...even though it was on a fruitless errand."

"But I would travel many, many kilometers for the sake of a mere half hour in your company, Rilla. It was good fortune indeed for me that Antoinette made such a muddle of things."

Silence fell between them. A light breeze stirred the leaves of the nearby lemon tree, making a faint rustling sound and releasing a waft of its tangy fragrance. She could hear the cicadas, and now and then the song of a night bird.

Ferdinand's voice was very low when he spoke again. "I am sorry if I upset you this afternoon, Rilla, by speaking of your unhappiness. It was just that it grieves me to see you looking so distressed, and I long to be of some assistance."

"But—but I am *not* unhappy," she protested.

He sighed. "You are so loyal—as I would expect a woman of your fine nature to be. It is cruelly unfair that your wonderful qualities should be wasted on someone who is as undeserving of you as Jake Carson."

"Please," she begged, "you mustn't talk like that, Ferdie. It—it's not right."

"You hurry so quickly to his defense," he said sadly. "A man who can leave his beautiful new bride at home in order to spend the evening in the company of another woman!''

"But Jake only went out to return your sister's purse," Rilla reminded him. All the same, she thought bitterly, there could be no possible justification for the way Jake had treated her. Which was precisely what Ferdinand went on to point out, with incontrovertible logic.

"You know very well, my dear Rilla, that Jake could just as easily have sent Pierre with my sister's purse. Alternatively he could have suggested that you accompany him, taking you afterward to dine somewhere in Nice—perhaps at a romantic candlelit bistro on the waterfront down by the old harbor, with a balalaika player strumming in the background. But, alas, your husband has no sensitivity, no romance in his soul. He fails to appreciate what a woman wants and needs from a man.''

"You don't understand, Ferdie," she stammered desperately. "American men—well, it's an accepted fact that they're never as demonstrative as men from your part of the world.''

"Then American men are fools!" he declared. "They deserve nothing if they refuse to treat women the way they should be treated.''

"But I love Jake," Rilla insisted, surprising herself by her vehemence. "I love Jake with everything that's in me.''

"I know you do! And this is what makes it so tragic— that the wonderful, intensely felt love that you have in your heart to bestow upon a man should have fallen on such sterile ground." Ferdinand laid his hand over Rilla's where it rested on the cushioned seat and emitted a deep sigh. "If only things could have been different, my dearest one, and you had not rushed into this disastrous marriage. You cannot deny that it has brought you great unhappiness—that you are utterly wretched and miserable. Do not try to conceal it from me, *chérie,* when I so long to offer you my help in any way possible—when I so long to give you comfort and solace."

"Oh, Ferdie," she faltered, his sympathy finally breaking through her armor of pride. "What am I to do? What am I to do?"

There was a brief pause, then Ferdinand murmured softly, "It is the fondest wish of my heart to help you, dearest Rilla. I torture myself with thoughts of how happy we would both be now if we had come to know one another sooner. Oh, if only I could have realized my feelings for you before it was too late."

Startled by his intensity, Rilla drew back from him. "But, Ferdie, you mustn't say such things."

"Why should I not? Is it a crime to express one's undying adoration?"

"To a woman who's just got married, yes."

"You call this relationship you have with Jake a proper marriage?"

"Marriage is marriage." With a shudder Rilla thrust away the memory of Jake insisting on an act of consummation to establish the viability of their union.

"Nevertheless I love you," Ferdinand said huskily, "and I insist on my right to say so. I want only to serve you, Rilla. If it is to be my fate to stand on the sidelines and observe you wrecking your life in this hollow mockery of a marriage, then—God forbid!—so be it. But I shall be here, Rilla...always. You will have only to give me one small sign, and I'll come to you, to support and sustain you...to love you as a woman has a right to be loved."

Faced with such expressions of devotion, Rilla gave up the battle and dropped her defenses, letting the tears spill from her eyes and trickle down her cheeks. When she felt Ferdinand's arm slide about her shoulders, she turned to him blindly, sobbing out her unhappiness against his chest, clutching his sleeve with convulsive fingers.

"Oh, Ferdie, I've made such a terrible mistake. I love Jake, but he doesn't love me."

"I know, my darling one, I know. Cry all you want, I understand."

Lost in a welter of tears and emotion, Rilla didn't hear the sound of a car approaching down the driveway, or the slither of tires as it came to a stop. She was oblivious of brisk footsteps on the flagstone patio. Her first awareness was of a rough hand on her shoulder, dragging her forcibly back from Ferdinand's embrace.

"What the devil's going on?" Jake demanded furiously.

Ferdinand scrambled swiftly to his feet. Though quite tall, he looked almost puny beside Jake's towering frame. He sounded scared—and with good cause—but he confronted Jake as if driven on by a force stronger than himself.

"How can you pretend to be surprised, my friend? Having abandoned your beautiful wife to her own devices while you visit with—I will not mince my words— a former lover, why should you expect her to have higher moral standards than yourself? Rilla is a warm and sensitive woman—*n'est-ce pas?*—with a warm and sensitive woman's needs and desires."

"But, Jake, it wasn't like that," Rilla protested, appalled at the implication. "I—I was just—"

"I saw what you were doing, so save your breath," Jake snapped at her. He took a threatening step toward Ferdinand, who cowered back. "As for this philandering playboy, I've a good mind to punch him silly."

"No!" Rilla rose to her feet, her legs feeling weak. "It—it wasn't Ferdie's fault, Jake. He knew that I was unhappy and he was trying to—to—"

"It's only too evident what he was trying to do," Jake flung at her bitterly. "And I've no doubt that he'd have succeeded if I hadn't arrived on the scene." He turned back to Ferdinand. "You're not worth soiling my hands on. Just get yourself off my property right now, and stay away from my wife in future. Do you hear me?"

It looked for a moment as if Ferdinand were going to stay around and argue, and Rilla feared there'd be violence. But then, with a shrug, he turned to walk away.

"Perhaps, *ma chère*," he called over his shoulder, "I should not, after all, have allowed you to persuade me to stay this evening. But I forgive you the embarrassing scene you have caused me. You were clearly not expecting your husband to return so early."

"But—but it wasn't like that," she protested again. "Listen to me, Jake...."

He ignored her, though, and in the light spilling from the villa's windows Rilla saw her husband's lean jaw thrust out aggressively. "Get going!" he ordered Ferdinand in a clipped voice. "I won't tell you again."

Ferdinand hesitated no longer. Almost at a run, he headed across the patio and through the arched gap in the hedge. Jake and Rilla waited, neither of them speaking, until they heard his car burst into life and drive off.

When Jake spoke at last, his voice grated harshly on the warm calm air. "Go to bed, Rilla!"

"But—but you have to try and understand..." she said pleadingly.

"I understand all right," he said. "Do as I say. Go to bed."

"Please listen," she begged. "You've got it all wrong, Jake. Just give me a chance to explain."

"Do you seriously imagine," he raged, his blue eyes glittering, "that I'm prepared to hold a debate with you right here and now, when only moments ago you were on that swing in the arms of another man? What would your defense be, Rilla? That I needn't worry, because you weren't intending to make love with him?"

"Of course I wasn't."

"Can you be so positive?" he flung at her viciously. "With a passionate nature like yours, it doesn't take much for a man to get you going."

"You—you're being horribly unfair."

"We'll leave it till morning to argue about what's fair," he gritted. "Also to discuss what's to be done next. Meantime, get to bed."

Rilla still hung back, filled with a desperate need to make Jake understand the truth. It was the quiet menace in his voice when he spoke again that finally convinced her. "I said get to bed, Rilla, and this is the last time I'm going to tell you."

What was the use? she thought bleakly. In any case, perhaps it was better to have the final showdown with Jake in the morning. She felt too bewildered by the devastating speed of events to make any rational decisions.

Walking the few yards to the sliding glass doors was like walking a tightrope from which the slightest false step would bring disaster. She felt Jake's gaze drilling in between her shoulder blades, but she refused to glance around. Upstairs, without switching on any lights, she sat on the edge of the bed and looked out at the serenely beautiful night sky, a spangled splendor of stars. Her eyes burned painfully and her cheeks were crusted with dried tears. Despite the warmth of the evening a feeling of cold desolation had taken hold of her, and she found that she was shivering.

Aeons later—minutes or hours, she had no idea— she heard Jake's convertible start up and drive away. So he was leaving her again... going back to Antoinette? It was the ultimate contempt, a deliberate demonstration that he cared nothing at all for her feelings.

The following day she would leave him, she was quite determined on that. Meanwhile, she had to get some rest to cope with what lay ahead. Still without putting on a light, she slipped out of her clothes and climbed wearily in between the cool smoothness of the sheets.

Surprisingly Rilla slept. But not for long. She awoke to the deep hush of night. She could sense, from a strange feeling of emptiness in the villa, that Jake had still not returned.

She found that in her sleep the decision to leave him had crystallized. She was impatient to get away. If she left it until morning, she would have to face Jake and announce her intention. It would be better, much better, to present him with a fait accompli.

But how to organize her escape, that was the problem. Returning home to the United States was her only practicable step, and that involved making a plane reservation. There was a phone beside the bed, but no directory, so Rilla drew on her peacock-blue robe and made her way downstairs to the living room, switching on a shaded lamp on the antique bureau where the phone stood. As she was about to find the number of Nice airport she hesitated. That would be Jake's first thought, too, and he'd probably be in a mood to go after her. He would view his wife's desertion so soon after their wedding as a mortal blow to his male pride.

Switching her plan of action, Rilla picked up the phone and got through to the international operator. Within no time she'd made a reservation on the noon flight from Geneva to New York.

Returning to her bedroom, she began packing her bags. By and large she took only what she'd brought with her from California, leaving all her glamorous trousseau items in drawers and closets. Finally, when she was all ready, she sat down to write a note for Jake to find when he returned. "I'm leaving...it's the only sensible course. You're free to fix things any way you like—divorce, annulment, whatever. I won't oppose you or make any sort of claim for alimony. I just want out. I'm borrowing the Citroën and I'll let you know in due course where you can pick it up."

Rilla sealed the letter in an envelope addressed to Jake and propped it on the bedside table for Jeanne-Marie to find and take to him in the morning. Then, with a last sad glance around, she crept out of the villa and made her way to the garage. She wished she could have driven the smaller car, but Jake had taken that. She slid in behind the wheel, started the engine, and in moments she was steering out of the driveway and onto the twisting narrow road to Chabroux. Her confidence that she could handle the big Citroën began to grow with each zigzag bend she negotiated.

Once on the wide Route Nationale she speeded up, the car's headlamps striking through thin skeins of mist on the mountain highway. Dawn was breaking, and the eastern sky was flushed with a delicate apricot hue. She was well past Digne, well on the way to Grenoble, when a glance at the gauge showed her that she was getting low on gas. She pulled in at the next filling station, where there was also an all-night café, so she took the chance to grab coffee and a sandwich.

It was then, in the shabby rest area for truck drivers, that Rilla had her first moments of quiet thought since waking. Her mind began to spin with doubts, regrets, but it was too late for second thought. She managed to swallow down the coffee, scalding hot and reviving, but most of the sandwich she left untouched.

In the hours that followed, Rilla existed in a daze: at Geneva airport, where she parked the car and mailed the ticket to Jake; during the bumpy flight across the Atlantic and the touchdown at Kennedy in a blustery rainstorm; and during the wait that seemed interminable for another flight headed west, following the sun until darkness finally overtook them. Still, she arrived at San Francisco International Airport before midnight local time. It seemed strange that she had gone so far, achieved and destroyed so much, all within the space of twenty-four hours as measured by the clock.

Exhausted, Rilla rode home in a cab. The little house on Russian Hill was silent and smelled of dust. She felt too tired to bother with anything that night and went straight upstairs. Peeling off her clothes, she fell into bed. The muted sounds of her native city, a city that never slept, surrounded her, lulled her, soothed her jagged nerves. Slowly she drifted into the unconsciousness of sleep.

She was wakened harshly by a loud burring sound in her ear. Bright sunlight pouring in through a gap in the window blinds dazzled her eyes. She glanced around, bemused, getting herself together. The noise was coming from the phone on her bedside table. She looked at it in a sort of terror. Could it be Jake, already on her trail?

She couldn't lie low forever. Life, whatever it held for her then, had to be lived. She picked up the phone, announcing clearly in her long-accustomed way, "Rilla Yorke."

"Sorry," said a hasty voice. "Wrong number."

As Rilla replaced the phone she thought ruefully that already, in her mind, she was Rilla Yorke again. Rilla Carson was dead—or had never truly existed.

She went through her morning routine like some kind of zombie. Black coffee and crackers was all that she could manage, noting that she would need to go grocery shopping later. She made her bed, finished unpacking, then dropped in on her next-door neighbor to announce her return.

"Well, look who's here! What have you come back for, Rilla, so soon? I guess you're planning to sell the house, huh? Is your husband with you? I'm dying to meet him."

Rilla's heart sank. Vinny Schofield was one of the people to whom she'd scribbled a brief note with the news of her impending marriage to Jake, and there had been a delighted, congratulatory reply waiting on their return from Geneva. She just couldn't begin to explain the whole sorry situation, so she said hastily, "It's a long story, Vinny, and I'm in a great rush. I only looked in to say hello so you'd know it was me if you saw signs of life next door. Thanks for looking after my plants, they seem in great shape."

Vinny, harassed wife and mother, gave a long, envious sigh. "What a fantastic time you must be having, Rilla, traveling around, mixing with the jet set all the time. That Jake Carson must be quite some guy to be married to." She laughed. "My Brad's okay, but say what you like, there's not much glamour in real estate."

Rilla managed a wan grin. "You have a great life, Vinny, and you know it."

"Oh, sure! I just love cleaning house, fixing meals, and doing laundry day after day. Like some people have fun banging their heads on the wall."

"Listen, I've really got to go. See you."

If only she knew, Rilla thought as she walked downtown toward the *BAAR* office, how envious I feel of her ordinary uncomplicated life with a cheerful, loving husband and four boisterous kids whose high spirits seemed to fill every corner of their commodious Victorian house. Vinny Schofield had it made.

It was going to be hell facing Bill Andersen and the others, but it was preferable to all the hassle of trailing around looking for a new job elsewhere. She wanted only to get back to her old, familiar routine and thrust the disastrous interlude to the back of her mind. A vain hope, of course, but she had to try.

Reaching Sutter Street, she walked two blocks and turned in at the narrow entry beside the fast food café, walking up the dark stairs. In the third floor hall she hesitated a moment at the outer glass door, rubbing her moist palms together as she gathered her courage. Then she drew back her shoulders and walked straight through into the editor's den.

"Rilla, what the—" He was staring at her in astonishment.

"Have you filled my job, Bill?"

"Not yet, but—"

"Then I want it back," she told him. "Just that. No questions... not for the present, anyhow."

Lumbering to his feet, Bill Andersen came around the desk and gazed anxiously into her green-gold eyes, then he nodded. "Okay, you've got yourself a deal. Get out there and dust off your desk. What you tell the others is your own business." As Rilla turned away he caught her hand. "But if I can help, just ask."

"I will, Bill. Thanks."

Hank and Steve were both out, and the only occupant of the general office was one of the part-time typists. Bill, bless him, found her an undemanding assignment interviewing a folksinger from way back when, who lived in a memento-cluttered room above a bargain bazaar in Chinatown. He turned out to be a delightful old man who was happy to unwind his store of reminiscences without much prompting from Rilla. When she arrived back at the office, Hank and Steve reacted to her warily, like men faced with a trigger-happy gunman. Obviously they'd been warned by Bill to go easy on her. Steve couldn't avoid casting pained looks at her from time to time, but he said nothing out of line.

By the end of the afternoon Rilla felt burned out and just wanted to crawl home and hide. Bill insisted on driving her, pretending that he had to go and see a man down at Fisherman's Wharf.

"You okay, Rilla?" he asked her in the car.

"I'm fine, Bill."

He cast her a quick look. "Okay you might be, fine you aren't! Have you eaten today?"

"I had a sandwich for lunch," she lied. "And I'll drop by at the deli on the corner for something."

"You do that." Bill drove the extra half block to the deli and waited to see her go inside. Rilla bought a loaf of sourdough bread, butter, and a slice of turkey pâté. Bill was right, she had to eat or she wouldn't be able to keep going.

At home she made coffee and listlessly chewed a few mouthfuls of the food. It lay leaden in her stomach. She switched on the radio, switched it off, and did the same with the television. She stood at the window, watching a reflection of sunset colors that filtered through the feathery leaves of an overhanging pepper tree. Finally jet lag caught up with her, and she dragged herself off to bed early while it was still light.

Someone was ringing her doorbell. A heavy fist thumped the front door. It was quite dark then. Puzzled, and a little apprehensive, Rilla sat up and reached for her fleecy plum-colored robe. She turned on lights, then crept nervously down the narrow staircase. The doorbell pealed again.

"Who is it?" she asked huskily.

"Me, Jake. Open the door, Rilla."

She swallowed a lump in her throat. "What—what do you want, Jake?"

"Let me in," he said curtly. "Unless you prefer to have the entire neighborhood awakened."

"Just a minute." She paused, irresolute, her heart thumping against her rib cage. The hall mirror reflected her tousled hair and bleary eyes. *Oh, what the hell,* she thought. *Let him see the real me.* She quickly raked her fingers through her hair to give it some semblance of order, then unbolted and drew the latch. As Jake stepped inside she took a quick, cowering step backward. He slammed the door shut behind him, and they stood looking at one another in the hallway for long moments that seemed frozen in time. Rilla watched the interplay of emotions on his face but couldn't read them. There was a look of wariness in his intelligent blue eyes.

"Rilla, you crazy loon," he burst out at length. "What did you imagine you were doing, running away from me like that?"

She made herself tall, trying to subdue the trembling that had seized her whole body. "You left me no alternative."

"But you're a fighter, Rilla, not a quitter."

"I don't call it quitting to get out from under when the situation is hopeless. Our marriage was doomed from the outset, Jake. I was a crazy loon for ever agreeing to such a harebrained notion in the first place."

"Won't you give it another try?" he asked softly.

Rilla realized bewilderedly that the intimidating force of Jake's presence was suddenly gone. Standing there before her, he looked diffident, vulnerable. She felt an urge to close the gap between them, to fold her arms around him and comfort him, but she firmly resisted the temptation. Where Jake was concerned, her feelings were useless as a guide, and she couldn't risk making yet another mistake.

"There'd be no point in trying again," she said in a cool voice. "Our views on what a marriage should be are diametrically opposed, so how could we possibly make a go of it?"

"You believe in the power of love, Rilla, don't you?"

"Of course I do, you know I do. Mutual love is the only possible basis for a happy marriage."

"But love," he said slowly, "can grow. Doesn't being together, living together, provide a fertile soil for love to flourish in? Even when there's love on just one side, isn't that a promising beginning?"

"Love on one side?" she echoed, not understanding what he was getting at.

Jake ran a finger along his eyebrow in that little gesture that always tugged at her heartstrings. "I'm not surprised that you find it hard to accept," he said with a self-deprecating smile. "I was surprised myself when I finally realized."

"Realized what, Jake?"

His vivid blue eyes seemed to glow with a radiant warmth, and his voice was like a soft caress. "That I love you, Rilla." She heard her own gasp of incredulous disbelief as Jake went on urgently. "It's true, you've got to believe me. I love you, my darling, and I can't bear the thought of losing you. Please...can't you somehow find it in you to forgive me for the rotten way I've treated you? Can't we start fresh?"

"You—you love me?" Rilla whispered the magical words, then her fragile confidence wilted, and a chilling doubt struck through to her heart. "Jake...don't play games with me," she said harshly. "It isn't fair."

He flinched visibly, as if she'd struck him. "My darling, I'm being totally honest. I love you. I love you more than I ever believed it possible for a man to love a woman. Imbecile that I was, I always scorned falling in love as romantic garbage. Arrogantly I tried to insist that sexual attraction was the only thing that counted between a man and a woman. It's no wonder that you turned away from me in disgust. I feel so ashamed now when I recall what I said to you about the vital ingredients for success in a marriage—friendship, mutual respect, and a good physical relationship. I left out love completely, but that's the only thing that really matters, isn't it? Because when there's love, everything else will automatically grow." Jake paused, shaking his head bewilderedly. "What I don't understand is why you ever agreed to marry me, Rilla, when I was such an insensitive bastard."

She smiled through a mist of tears. "Because I loved you, Jake, that's why I agreed."

With a shuddering sigh of thankfulness Jake reached out and drew her close against him. Rilla shut her eyes, overwhelmed by a flood of emotion. She felt intoxicated by his nearness, the sensual heat of his hard body, the rapid thudding of his pulses, the exciting rasp of his chin against the softness of her brow.

"Thank God," he breathed, "that we've found one another before it's too late."

Rilla clung to her last few shreds of common sense and said shakily, "How can I believe that what we call love means the same to both of us, Jake? You broke my heart during those nights in Geneva that you spent with other women."

She felt a shock wave pass through his body, and he drew back a little, looking down at her with earnest pleading in his eyes. "I never did that, my darling... you've got to believe me. Going to another woman never even crossed my mind."

"Then what--"

"I could have gone out and got drunk, I guess. But alcohol has never appealed to me as a means of escape. What I did those nights was walk—walk and walk around the city until I eventually returned to the hotel in the small hours, bone tired. The doorman must have thought I was the strangest occupant of the bridal suite he'd ever encountered."

Desperately Rilla tried to sort out her tangled emotions. She still felt a bit dazed from being jolted out of sleep, and part of her mind was questioning if it could actually be happening. Was Jake really and truly there in San Francisco, insisting that he loved her? They hadn't moved from the small hallway, which seemed silly. With an inviting gesture of her hand she moved into the living room, and Jake followed her.

"Darling Rilla," he said softly, moving forward to take her into his arms again. But she raised a hand to stop him.

"No, Jake, please..." She longed to believe in him utterly, to accept his protestations of love and agree to start fresh as he wanted. Yet, wasn't it madness to let him convince her so easily with smooth words?

Wouldn't she only be exposing herself to extra heart-ache? "There's something we've got to get straight-ened out first."

"What's that?"

"It's about Antoinette. Where does she—"

"Antoinette belongs to my past," he cut in, "before I met you, darling. It isn't fair to hold her against me."

"You're sure she doesn't belong to your present, too?"

Jake shook his head emphatically. "She'd like to, I admit, and she tried damn hard to make it so. But there's been nothing between me and Antoinette since before I left France to come to California last year."

"Yet she only had to whistle and you were off like a shot," Rilla reminded him in a challenging tone.

"With her purse, you mean? That was a ploy, Rilla, and I walked right into it. When Antoinette telephoned that night, asking me in her usual coaxing way to drive down to Cap-Ferrat with her purse, I damn near re-fused. I didn't see why our whole evening should be ruined. She could just as easily have sent Ferdinand to pick it up instead. But then I thought, why not go? I noticed earlier, when you returned from Saint-Raphaël and found Antoinette there, that you were a bit jealous of her. And I figured that it wouldn't do any harm to give that jealousy an extra stir. That way, I thought, you might start to appreciate me when I re-turned home again. I wasn't planning to stay longer than just to have a drink, but even before I tried to leave, Antoinette astonished me by more or less kick-ing me out. She muttered something untypical about it not being fair to keep me from my new bride, and that she'd hate to feel that she was responsible for any trouble between us."

Rilla gasped as understanding crashed down on her

sickeningly. "So Ferdie came to the villa with the deliberate intention of—of getting me into a compromising situation?"

Jake nodded somberly. "Ferdinand is totally under his sister's thumb, because Antoinette controls the cash. So he does what he's told to do, like it or not! His instructions that night were to create an intimate scene, which I was to arrive home and discover. Antoinette was shrewd enough to guess that things were less than perfect between us, and she reckoned that she had a chance to break us up completely."

"Oh, Jake, she very nearly succeeded. You were in a horrible rage when you found us together."

His mouth tightened, deepening the cleft of his chin. "I've never felt so mad in all my life as when I saw you in Ferdinand's arms. But after I sent you off to bed, I went out to mull things over in my mind. When I'd cooled off a bit, I started to add two and two together and I realized that there was something very phoney about the whole setup that evening. It penetrated my skull suddenly that my coming back and finding you in Ferdinand's arms was precisely what had been *meant* to happen. That little scene had been carefully planned with meticulous timing, right from the start—from the moment when Antoinette deliberately left behind her purse, tucked well down between the swing cushions so that it wouldn't be noticed too soon."

Rilla yearned to go into Jake's waiting arms and relax against the warmth of his body, but she steeled herself to resist temptation.

"Jake," she began stumblingly, "about our honeymoon..."

"We'll have another honeymoon, darling," he promised. "And this time—"

"No," she interrupted, "this has got to be said. I

have to know exactly where we stand, Jake. At our wedding reception I happened to overhear you talking to some woman called Germaine. I heard you tell her that despite getting married, you weren't going to suffer any kind of deprivation. Which explains," she added with a bitter edge to her voice, "why I was so cold and unresponsive when you tried to make love to me that night."

"Oh, my darling." His tone was soft and tender, and a little bit reproachful. "For heaven's sake, you didn't seriously believe that I planned to fool around with other women? That wasn't what I meant at all. I was merely saying to Germaine, who'd made some idiotic remark about marriage cramping my style, that in you, Rilla, I'd have everything I could ever wish for in a woman. And that's a hundred percent true! Ever since the moment I walked up from my swim that morning at Sausalito and found you sitting on the veranda, you've obsessed me completely. No other woman has ever filled my thoughts, night and day, the way you have. You seemed to me the loveliest, most desirable woman I'd ever set eyes on."

Rilla felt a warm, incredulous joy flooding through her, quenching the flames of her doubts. "So that's the reason you worked out such a complex scheme to lure me to France... dangling before me the dazzling opportunity you guessed I couldn't resist, of writing a piece for the *New York Globe*?"

"Right. Like a fool I imagined that we could have a brief, exciting affair, which would enable me to get you out of my system. But I also genuinely admired your frankness and resourcefulness as a journalist, Rilla. I believed that you were the right person to handle the story about Jake Carson and Richard Kellerman being one and the same."

"And then you saw another way of making use of me, didn't you?" she said on a last faint flicker of resistance. There was something she'd always been curious about, and she voiced it. "Did you fix it in advance with Zelie about jumping to the conclusion that we were engaged?"

Jake shook his head, and there was an unabashed sparkle in his eyes as his glance met hers. "When the idea of marrying you suddenly hit me that evening, I just sowed the seed and left the rest to Zelie's romantic nature."

Rilla emitted a long soulful sigh. "And all because you thought it would suit you to have a wife, to stop women like Antoinette from pressuring you."

The corners of his mouth twitched. "That was my crazy line of logic. I was in love with you, but I couldn't admit it to myself, so I concocted a theory that we could have a workable marriage that was based on friendship and respect—plus the fantastic physical relationship I knew we could achieve."

It was unforgivable, Rilla decided, and promptly forgave him. Smiling herself, she postponed the lovely moment of utter capitulation. "When did you first realize that you loved me, Jake?"

"Was it yesterday, a week ago, a month?" He made a small uncertain gesture, as if trying to conjure the answer out of the air. "Maybe since before we met. Because I believe now, my darling, that you and I were destined for each other. I somehow felt that instinctively from the first instant I saw you. Yet I fought against the knowledge...fought against accepting that I'd genuinely fallen in love with you. I tried desperately to make myself believe that it was just the uncomplicated sexual need that I'd felt for other women in the past, only stronger. But now, at long last, I've come to my senses and I realize what you mean to me. I know now that if I was to lose you, life just wouldn't be worth living. Oh, my darling Rilla, how can I ever tell you how much I love you?''

They kissed then, and it was very, very sweet, the flame of desire kindling slowly, as if they both wanted to savor to the fullest every beautiful, precious second. Rilla parted her lips eagerly before Jake's warm, probing tongue, clasping her hands about his neck as he caressed the soft curves of her body. After long spellbound moments, Jake drew back. He glanced around him as if for the first time noticing his surroundings.

"Upstairs?" he queried meaningfully.

"Yes, but—"

"No buts," he said firmly, scooping her up into his arms.

"I was only going to suggest," she explained, with her cheek against his shoulder, "that you might want some food first."

Jake dropped a kiss on her brow. "There's only one thing I'm starving for at this moment, darling. And for that I can hardly wait long enough to carry you to the nearest bed."

Jake carried her carefully, edging sideways up the narrow staircase. The door to her room was ajar, the light spilling out, signaling the way. Jake laid her down on the rumpled bed, paused long enough to strip off his clothes, then dropped down beside her and clasped her to him fiercely.

"Oh, Rilla, darling Rilla, when I found that you'd left me, I was terrified out of my mind. You'll never know."

The white telephone at the bedside swam into her line of vision, and she asked, "Was it you who phoned me this morning? Or rather, yesterday to you."

"Sure, that was me. I felt triumphant when you answered and I knew where you were. I wanted to shout over the phone that I loved you. But I was scared I'd start you running again, so I muffled my voice and said wrong number. Then I got over here just as fast as I could."

"Darling Jake," she murmured and tilted her face to meet his lips with her own in a long kiss.

Lying wrapped in his arms, she could feel the tide of tension ebbing from his lean body as they caressed one another. When his eyelids fluttered and closed, she gazed tenderly at his beloved face. Every line, every plane and angle, betrayed total weariness. Perhaps she should insist on him eating, but she knew that Jake could face food no more than she. Lovingly she placed her cheek against his and reached up to tangle her fingers into his wheat-colored hair.

"Go to sleep, my darling," she whispered softly. "We're together now, that's what matters. I'll still be here when you wake."

At first Jake resisted, his hands roaming her body in sheer joy. But slowly he fell under the soothing influence of her quiet voice and slipped into a sleep of utter exhaustion. Turning off the light, Rilla gently pulled the blanket up and tucked it around him, then lay there rejoicing in his warmth and closeness. She did not think ahead. That present blissful moment was enough for her.

Morning sunlight streaming through the slatted blinds was dappling their faces when they woke. Jake blinked and drew her nearer, smiling. "So it wasn't all a dream?"

"I'm real, Jake, you don't have to worry."

"Yesterday," he said huskily, "I faced having nothing. Now I have everything I could ever want...and more. I love you, Rilla darling.''

"I love you too, Jake. I love you so much.''

With impatient hands he pulled away Rilla's nightgown and slid his hands over her warm flesh. As he kissed her the roughness of his unshaven chin rasped against her cheek, and she reveled in it. The full length of his hard-muscled body was pressed to hers, the throbbing of his surging arousal making her breathless with anticipation. When finally Jake made love with her, Rilla gasped with joy, delighting in his superb virile strength. Never in her wildest dreams had she imagined that passion could be so gloriously unrestrained, yet at the same time so infinitely tender and caring. Their lovemaking seemed to last forever, jewel-bright moments of ecstasy in an endlessly mounting succession, until in a final rapturous crescendo they both cried out exultantly into the golden brightness of the morning and then lay still.

"My beautiful wife!" Jake murmured throatily, his lips against the silken strands of her hair.

"My wonderful lover!" she whispered into the warm curve of his neck.

After an age of drowsy, floating contentment, she roused herself. "Breakfast?"

"Brunch," he corrected, his fingers trailing across the soft velvet of her flesh. "A very late brunch."

"But I have a job to go to," she protested with a smothered laugh. "I'm back with *BAAR*."

"To hell with that," he said adamantly. "Today I come first."

"Today and every day, Jake. You'll always come first with me."

Chapter Twelve

"Give me one good reason why not, Rilla," said Martin Whitehead as he snapped and then buttered a crisp breadstick. "It's right up your alley."

Mrs. Rilla Carson, presiding at her dinner table in the luxurious Fifth Avenue co-op apartment, regarded Martin and her husband with a troubled look in her green-gold eyes. Twelve floors below, the rumble of New York's traffic was scarcely discernible on that warm October evening.

"Because..." she began, and wasn't sure how to continue.

"Because nothing," Jake insisted. "Martin's right, darling. This is an assignment that's tailor-made for you. Imagine, a whole series of feature articles for the *Globe* on celebrated writers who've made their home on the French Riviera. There are at least twenty I can think of... American, British, German. Even the odd Russian. What better excuse could we have, if we need an excuse, for spending the winter months in Provence?"

"I wish you'd find an excuse for sending me there, Martin," chipped in Jo-Ann, his petite, darkly vivacious wife. "The farthest south we'll manage to get is Christmas at my parents' place in Washington."

Rilla smiled awkwardly. Evading the three pairs of puzzled eyes, she glanced up at the Victoire Lamont portrait that graced the wall above the fine carved pinewood fireplace of the lofty room. Her own eyes gazed back at her with that serene half smile... truly a portrait of love. Rilla let out her breath in a sigh. Jake still owned Villa Ambrosia, and naturally he expected that they'd spend part of their time there, just as they were intending to spend a couple of months each year at the small Queen Anne house in San Francisco, which Jake declared he'd loved on first sight. "Maybe not quite on first sight," he'd amended afterward. "That night I only had eyes for you, darling. I was blind to everything else."

While Rilla served the lemon chiffon pie, Martin kept up the pressure. "That profile of Jake you did for me caused quite a stir," he reminded her.

"Well, it could hardly have missed," Rilla countered. "That was a big story... Jake Carson being Richard Kellerman, too. And on top of that, it was written by his newly acquired wife."

"There are plenty more headline stories for a top journalist," Jake said easily. He rolled the wine around in his glass, and it glinted ruby lights. "Rilla and I will go to Provence this winter, Martin, and she'll turn in those profiles like the pro she is. You have my personal guarantee."

"Great," said Martin. "Let's drink to it."

Three glasses were promptly raised. Only Rilla's remained on the table, and Jake shot her a questioning look. A curious sort of panic had seized her. It was as if she were being rushed headlong into a decision that she dreaded making. But she didn't want to spoil the happy atmosphere of that evening's dinner party so, curving nervous fingers around the smooth coolness of her wineglass, she finally raised it to her lips. However, she didn't actually drink. It was her insurance against being irrevocably committed.

She was aware, though, that Jake's shrewd eyes had missed nothing. As the four friends chatted and laughed his glance returned to her constantly.

"What beats me," Martin joked, "is why you didn't propose to Rilla when you two first met in San Francisco. Why all that devious plotting to get her to follow you to France—even dragging me in on the act?"

"I wanted to see what she was made of," Jake stated.

"I reckon you knew already."

"I reckon I did at that. But we're all allowed one crazy mistake now and then, aren't we?"

"Hey, you guys," Rilla broke in. "I do happen to be here, you know. Hasn't it crossed your chauvinistic minds that if I'd been asked in San Francisco, I just might not have accepted?"

Jake laughed. "I guess you wouldn't have accepted, the mood you were in then. So maybe there was logic behind my craziness."

"Seems to me," Jo-Ann observed, "that you were taking one hell of a chance, fella, of losing this woman."

"I could always have come back for her," Jake replied with a confident grin.

"Would you have done?" challenged Jo-Ann interestedly. "What if Rilla hadn't turned up in Provence? What if she'd said no to Martin's offer of doing that Jake Carson profile?"

Jake's eyes met Rilla's across the table, and in that fleeting instant it was as if only the two of them were in the room. "Seems to me, Jo-Ann," he said slowly, "that you're being altogether too iffy. It happened the way it happened. Maybe it had to. Maybe it wouldn't have worked out for us any other way."

Rilla felt a delicious shiver ripple through her at the notion that their coming together had been the careful scheming of fate. But their future...was that predestined, too? The return to Provence that winter and what might happen there.... She had an irrational fear that refused to be quenched.

"What's this all about, darling?" asked Jake later when their guests had departed. "You always seem to shy away from any mention of Provence."

"Do I?" Rilla began collecting glasses together, but Jake stopped her, taking her hands in his and looking down at her with concern.

"You know you do, Rilla. And I want to know why."

She kept her eyes averted, afraid to meet his questioning gaze. "I love it here in New York," she parried. "I just don't see why we need to go rushing off to France."

"A New York winter might change your mind, my sweet."

"There's always San Francisco, then. Which reminds me, you still owe my old professor from Berkeley that Richard Kellerman lecture."

"I'll get around to it. But let's stick to the point." Jake's glance sharpened and he gave Rilla the sort of look she was accustomed to, a look that seemed to go clear through to her soul. "What are you scared of, darling?"

"Scared? That's a stupid thing to say."

"Then we'll go to France, okay? Next month?"

She gave a defeated shrug. "I guess so, if that's what you want."

"I want you to want it, too."

"You want the moon, Jake."

"I already have the moon," he returned, his blue eyes intent and serious. "I wish you thought you had, too, darling."

"Oh, but I have, I have!" It emerged as an apologetic wail, and Jake's arms folded around her, giving her the belovedly familiar sense of his comfort and protection. "I know I'm being idiotic, and selfish, too. Only—it's just because everything *has* been so perfect for us these past few months. I want it to go on and on like that forever."

"And why should going to Provence prevent that?"

Rilla sighed, pressing her face into the curve of his shoulder. "Happiness...it's such a fragile thing. I guess it's a sort of superstition I feel, that if you go back to your old haunts—"

"I'll go back to my old ways? No chance! There's only one princess for me, darling Rilla, and that's you." He lifted her chin with one finger and gave her a smile that was tender and teasing. "If you want to know how much I love you, just stick around for the rest of my life."

She gazed up at him mistily. "I wouldn't run away again, you know. I'd stay and fight."

"I'm relieved to hear it," he said with satisfaction. "I think this is the right moment to give you a piece of news I read only yesterday. Princess Antoinette von Hohenzollern, apparently, has landed a prominent Italian banker and will be living in Rome from now on. With the faithful Ferdie tagging along, naturally."

It felt to Rilla as if the sun had come out and melted sharp crystals of ice in her veins. "Oh, Jake...I don't think I could have faced up to meeting her again."

"So you won't need to. I seriously doubt that we'll be invited to the wedding."

"I could always offer to cover it for the *Globe*." She giggled, all of a sudden feeling wildly lighthearted.

Jake shook his head with a reproving grin. "There are laws against libel, darling. Come to think of it, you were lucky not to have a writ slapped on you by a guy named Richard Kellerman."

"Did you consider doing that, Jake?"

He pondered, his fingertip tracing the delicate curve of her cheek. "I thought about a number of things I'd dearly have liked to do to the author of that infamous article. But suing her for libel wasn't one of them."

"What things?" Rilla queried, and her voice had suddenly become husky.

"Haven't I demonstrated what things often enough?"

"I'm a shockingly slow learner." She sighed.

"How lucky, then, that I'm an extremely patient teacher. It's time, I think, for another lesson."

Their arms entwined, they switched off lights behind them as they crossed the hall to the spacious master bedroom that was romantically furnished in a scheme of green and gold, with beautiful silken damask drapes and bed hangings. As so often before, they undressed one another, teasing out the delicious moments with long sensuous kisses.

"You're so beautiful," he murmured, letting his hands run lingeringly over the gentle swell of her hips.

"And you," she said dreamily, "you're perfect, Jake."

"Richard Kellerman was one crazy guy," he commented, "getting you so mad."

Rilla pressed herself close to the lean hardness of the body she knew so intimately. "Don't you dare say a single word against Richard. He's the man I fell in love with."

"In Sausalito?" Jake queried, willingly replaying a familiar scene. "Right back then?"

"Right back then."

"Me, too! If only we'd both realized."

"You were so psyched up about not letting Richard Kellerman trade on Jake Carson's name," she said reminiscently.

"Such was the nature of my insecurity." He laughed. "When the *History of California* gets published next spring, it'll probably sell twice as many copies, all due to your exposé of my double life."

"You won't mind?"

Jake laughed again. "Whatever people's motivation for buying the book, it'll do them nothing but good to read it. So why should I mind?" He nuzzled his nose into her sweet-scented hair. "I'm getting bored with this subject, darling."

"So what shall we talk about?"

"We don't have to talk at all."

Rilla looked up at him with wide-eyed innocence. "Whatever can you mean?"

"I'm about to show you."

Jake stooped to gather her up, but she dodged his arms and darted away. He caught her in two quick strides, and together they tumbled, laughing, onto the soft wide bed.

"I love you, darling," he murmured huskily as they broke apart from a long drowning kiss.

"Oh, Jake and I love you. So very much!"

On such a night as that, the thought drifted into Rilla's mind after their loving had reached a new crest of bliss, the intensity of their passion exceeding anything that had gone before.... On just such a Tristan and Isolde night as that...she wanted their first child to be conceived. Perhaps they would be blessed in Provence, when the mimosa was blooming and stirrings of new life were everywhere. She had no doubts anymore, no vague fears of impending disaster. Jake's love for her was steadfast, their marriage rock sure.

Jake buried his face in the soft fragrant valley between Rilla's breasts. "Parfum d'Or!" he murmured in a muffled voice. "Worn by you, sweet darling Rilla, it's the most powerful aphrodisiac ever invented."

"Then, cost what it may," she said on a gurgle of laughter, "the instant we reach Provence I shall order a whole gallon. I mean, as an insurance in case Monsieur Rigaillaud ever decides to stop making Scent of Gold."

"Will just one gallon be enough?" Jake teased. "We've got a whole lifetime of loving ahead of us."